PRAISE FOR *IT WAKES IN ME*

"Once again, Kathleen O'Neal Gear has brought alive, with extraordinary vividness and realism, the lives of the first Americans in her splendid novel, *It Wakes in Me*. I read this dramatic and haunting novel in one sitting. Gear is more effective than any time machine in transporting the reader back to the vast, beautiful, and unspoiled world of prehistoric North America."
—Douglas Preston,
New York Times bestselling author of *Tyrannosaur Canyon*

"This dramatic and involving story will transport readers to another time, where women were the power players in society. The historical detail and vivid descriptions make this a fascinating and compelling read." —*Romantic Times BookReviews*

"A multilayered, complex plot with lushly evocative prose and darkly erotic passages." —*Booklist*

"Vivid . . . Gear provides plenty of intrigue . . . and spices things up now and then with steamy, erotic passages."
—*Kirkus Reviews*

PRAISE FOR *IT SLEEPS IN ME*

"Jean Auel meets Nora Roberts in this exciting new series."
—Douglas Preston,
New York Times bestselling author of *Tyrannosaur Canyon*

"Readers will appreciate the strong female characters and the powerful role women play in the intriguing Black Falcon Nation." —Juliet Marillier,
bestselling author of The Sevenwaters Trilogy

**By Kathleen O'Neal Gear and W. Michael Gear
from Tom Doherty Associates**

THE ANASAZI MYSTERY SERIES

The Visitant

The Summoning God

Bone Walker

THE FIRST NORTH AMERICANS
SERIES

People of the Wolf

People of the Fire

People of the Earth

People of the River

People of the Sea

People of the Lakes

People of the Lightning

People of the Silence

People of the Mist

People of the Masks

People of the Owl

People of the Raven

People of the Moon

People of the Nightland

People of the Weeping Eye*

BY KATHLEEN O'NEAL GEAR

Thin Moon and Cold Mist

Sand in the Wind

This Widowed Land

It Sleeps in Me

It Wakes in Me

It Dreams in Me*

BY W. MICHAEL GEAR

Long Ride Home

Big Horn Legacy

The Morning River

Coyote Summer

The Athena Factor

OTHER TITLES BY
KATHLEEN O'NEAL GEAR
AND W. MICHAEL GEAR

Dark Inheritance

Raising Abel

To Cast A Pearl*

*Forthcoming
www.Gear-Gear.com

IT WAKES IN ME

KATHLEEN O'NEAL GEAR

TOR®

A TOM DOHERTY ASSOCIATES BOOK
NEW YORK

This is a work of fiction. All of the characters, organizations, and events portrayed in this novel are either products of the author's imagination or are used fictitiously.

IT WAKES IN ME

Map and chapter ornaments by Ellisa Mitchell

A Tor Book
Published by Tom Doherty Associates, LLC
175 Fifth Avenue
New York, NY 10010

www.tor.com

Tor® is a registered trademark of Tom Doherty Associates, LLC.

ISBN-13: 978-0-765-35026-8
ISBN-10: 0-765-35026-2

First Edition: July 2006
First Mass Market Edition: March 2007

Printed in the United States of America

0 9 8 7 6 5 4 3 2 1

Sandhill Crane People

Lily People

Persimmon Lake

Oak Leaf Village

Blackbird Town

BLACK FALCON NATION

Minnow Village

Eagle Flute Village

Loon People

Palmetto River

NORTH

Alike Mitchell 2014

A SHIMMERING DUST OF RADIANCE, FAINT VOICES, A floating sensation . . . but that's all.

I can't feel my heart beating. My lungs don't seem to be moving air.

Where is my body?

For a time, I allow myself to ride the waves of light while I search for my hands, my legs . . . my face.

Nothing.

I am gone. The world has vanished, and along with it, everyone and everything I have ever loved.

An ugly, high-pitched voice whispers, "You killed my father. . . . I hate you. . . . Mother hates you. . . . You deserve to die. . . ."

Grief shivers the brilliance, and it turns white-hot, blinding. Who is that? I don't recognize the voice.

I must *be dreaming.*

The dazzling ocean washes around and through me, but it has no warmth, no feel on my skin.

Maybe I am dead.

Is this what it feels like when the reflection-soul, the soul that travels to the afterlife, slips out with the last breath and hangs in the air around the body?

Somewhere deep inside me, a silent scream rises.

How did I die?

Was I sick? Was Blackbird Town attacked?

I remember being afraid that we were going to be attacked, that war was about to break out.

But with whom?

Words again. Very soft. The deep voice comforts me. It . . . it sounds like Flint. But that can't be. I have a vague memory that he, too, is dead. Blessed gods, maybe he's come to lead me along the treacherous trail that leads to the afterlife.

According to the tradition of the Black Falcon People, each person has three souls: the eye-soul stays with the body forever, but at death the shadow-soul and the reflection-soul slip out together. All the evil leaches into the shadow-soul, leaving the reflection-soul pure and clean, fit to live among the Blessed Ancestors in the Land of the Dead. Usually the evil shadow-soul dissipates into the air, but on rare occasions it sneaks into a passerby and uses the body of the living person to commit hideous crimes.

. . . Perhaps I am dead and this is my eye-soul?

Is this all I am now? A nothingness that dwells in rotting bones forever?

Anger flickers.

Why didn't anyone tell me it would be like this— this strange disembodied floating sensation?

What am I supposed to do now?

Old Priest Teal once told me that at death the reflection-soul has to make a decision. It can either go directly to the Land of the Dead, or spend ten days speaking with loved ones, saying the last things that need to be said.

Perhaps that's where I am? Suspended between decisions? Blessed gods, I hope so.

As if in answer, the radiance shifts, twisting into a shining path that seems to lead upward.

I climb, or think I do.

The path becomes clearer, crystallizing into a vast spiraling blanket of stars.

. . . The voices are louder.

Confusion fills me, rapidly followed by fear.

If Flint has come to lead me to the afterlife, I know I can fight the monsters that inhabit the dark underworld forests, but what if my reflection-soul is entering the living world again?

Perhaps this is my last chance to tell people how much I love them.

It takes every bit of my strength, but I manage to open my eyes for a single heartbeat.

. . . Log roof beams . . . flame shadows on the walls . . .

As the hazy council chamber comes into focus, terror floods my veins.

He stands three paces away, with his long black cape swaying around him like midnight wings. His face is darkness.

From somewhere far away, I hear a great voice like raging water whisper, "Seven. She has killed seven people, and Chief Blue Bow's murder may start the worst war the Black Falcon Nation has ever known. We must do something. . . ."

VEILS OF RAIN SWEPT THE DARK FOREST, DRENCH-ing War Chief Feather Dancer where he stood guard outside the front entrance to the Matron's House. He drew his buckskin cape more tightly around his shoulders. A tall, muscular man, he could feel the scars on his face pull tight when he frowned out at Blackbird Town.

The enormous earthen mounds of the rulers, each five to six times the height of a man, rose from the forest like unnatural hills. Atop them, the massive log buildings were dark. Quiet. The only light came from the door curtain to his left. Inside, he could hear Matron Wink, Priest Teal, and the loathsome outsider named Flint talking. He couldn't make out their words, but he heard the strain in their voices.

"What's Flint talking you into now, Matron?" he

murmured to himself. "The destruction of the entire Black Falcon Nation?"

Feather Dancer's stomach muscles clenched. He longed for nothing more than to get his hands around Flint's lying throat.

For fourteen winters Flint had been married to High Chieftess Sora. When he'd divorced her three winters ago and gone home to his own people in Oak Leaf Village, it had broken the chieftess' heart, but she'd remarried and was getting on with her life. Then, ten days ago, Flint had secretly returned to Blackbird Town, with his best friend War Chief Skinner, and thrown the entire nation into an uproar. War Chief Skinner had been murdered and Chieftess Sora accused of the crime. At this very moment, the Chieftess lay on a litter inside the Matron's House drifting in and out of fevered dreams brought on by the Spirit Plant Flint had forced her to drink to keep her asleep while the Matron decided what to do.

Feather Dancer expelled a gruff sigh. Flint had talked everyone, including Matron Wink, into believing that the chieftess was a murderer.

As he stood there gazing into the rain, his shadow-soul drifted, remembering everything that had happened in the past three hands of time. . . .

He and the Matron's son, Long Fin, had been dispatched around midnight to meet an enemy war party, led by Chief Blue Bow of the Loon Nation. The old chief had supposedly come to discuss a Trade: he was holding eleven men, women, and children from Oak Leaf Village hostage. He would release them if Chieftess Sora and Matron Wink would agree to send warriors south to steal a beautiful green stone called jade from the southern barbarians. Around two hands of time past midnight, they'd seen the war party approaching through the forest.

Blue Bow had bravely marched out in front, followed by his war chief, Grown Bear, and twenty warriors. Blue Bow was a bald, frail old man, but he wore his massive copper breastplate as though it weighed no more than a milkweed seed.

Feather Dancer had called, "I recognize you, Chief Blue Bow. You are welcome in the Black Falcon Nation. Matron Wink asked us to escort you safely into Blackbird Town. Do not be alarmed when our warriors come out of the trees. They are here to protect you." He'd lifted his hand, and men filtered through the dark oak trunks to surround the Loon party.

Blue Bow's old eyes had narrowed. "To protect us from whom, War Chief? If your matron welcomes us—"

Long Fin had called, "Do all the Loon clans agree on political decisions, Chief?"

Blue Bow's grizzled brows had lowered. "No. They do not. Which clans oppose my presence in the Black Falcon Nation? I would know so that I might prepare myself for their treachery."

Long Fin had answered, "No one has openly opposed your visit, but my mother is cautious. She truly wishes to keep you from harm."

"I appreciate that." Blue Bow had turned to his war chief and added, "Grown Bear, I wish to speak with Long Fin alone. Please follow twenty paces behind us."

"But my chief!" Grown Bear had objected. "That is too risky. They may be plotting—"

"I will take that chance. Do as I say."

Grown Bear had murmured something unpleasant and backed away.

Blue Bow came forward and looked up at Feather Dancer with starlit eyes. "Let me walk out front with Long Fin for a time, War Chief."

"As you wish."

He'd heard Blue Bow ask Long Fin, "Is it true that Chieftess Sora has offered her life to Matron Sea Grass to compensate her for the loss of her son, War Chief Skinner?"

"It is."

Blue Bow had shaken his head. "It saddens me to hear of it. These sorts of things make political negotiations much more difficult."

"I'm sure the chieftess will put her own personal concerns aside during her time with you."

"Yes, I'm sure she'll try, but when one's life is at stake it's impossible to concentrate fully on difficult negotiations, don't you agree?"

"I am just the matron's son. Trade agreements are not my expertise. I do not even understand why this green stone is so important to possess."

Feather Dancer had squinted at the lie. Over the past hand of time, Long Fin had talked of little else.

He wanted the stone badly. What was the youth up to? Had he worked this out with Matron Wink?

Obviously confused, Blue Bow had asked, "What green stone?"

Long Fin frowned. "The jade." When Blue Bow's expression didn't change, Long Fin clarified, "The jade brooch you sent to Chieftess Sora."

The warriors following twenty paces behind had muttered among themselves, probably exchanging insults, as enemy warriors did. Someone chuckled, and another man growled a response.

Blue Bow's sunken face contorted. "I didn't send her any brooch. What are you talking about?"

"You sent your war chief to Chieftess Sora with a brooch—"

"It was her broken promise that forced me to send Grown Bear to your chieftess. There was no brooch."

Clearly taken aback, Long Fin had said, "Explain."

A twig had cracked behind Feather Dancer, and he'd heard the soft hiss of a lance cutting the air.

"Get down!" Feather Dancer had shoved Long Fin aside.

Blue Bow staggered, gasped, *"No, dear gods!"* and toppled to the ground.

Warriors had raced forward to surround them. Copper-studded war clubs glinted like torches as they waved in the starlight.

Feather Dancer had dropped to his knees to examine Blue Bow, and hot blood spurted over his chest. Blue Bow writhed on the ground, clutching his throat, trying to clamp the artery shut.

"How bad is it?" Blue Bow screamed.

The chunkey lance had lodged below his left ear, neatly slicing the big vein in his throat. They couldn't pull the lance out or it would make things worse. The chief's life had drained away onto the forest floor with stunning rapidity. Through gritted teeth Grown Bear repeated, "Who did this?"

Long Fin had gestured to their warriors. "Follow me. We must find the chief's killer!"

His men instantly obeyed, lunging into the trees behind Long Fin, their war clubs up and ready.

Grown Bear had shouted to his party, "Go with them! See that the killer is brought to me unharmed. I must question him!"

Several terrible heartbeats later Long Fin cried, *"Quickly! Someone help me!"*

A cacophony of voices had erupted as warriors raced to his location from every part of the forest.

Feather Dancer leaped over Blue Bow and ran. Through the weave of tree trunks, he saw Long Fin kneeling near a body that lay at the edge of a starlit meadow.

"Who is it?" Feather Dancer called. "Do you recognize him?"

Long Fin answered, "It's Far Eye!"

Feather Dancer and at least ten warriors converged on the scene at the same time. He had to shoulder through the crowd to get to the body.

Far Eye, Matron Wink's nephew, lay on his back staring up at the night sky.

A pool of blood spread around his crushed skull. It had looked black and shiny in the starlight.

Feather Dancer and Long Fin had immediately run back to notify the matron, and she'd ordered Feather Dancer to get the chieftess out of bed.

But she hadn't been in bed, or even in Blackbird Town. Fearing for her life, Feather Dancer had taken a war party out to search the forest. Two hands of time later, she'd come in from the forest, covered with blood, and claimed she could remember nothing. Flint had convinced Matron Wink that the chieftess had murdered both Blue Bow and Far Eye. Matron Wink, desperate and frightened, had immediately set up a Healing Circle for their chieftess.

. . . Feather Dancer was jerked from his memories by a faint glimmer. Out on the lake.

He sucked in a breath, and his hand dropped to the war club tied to his belt as he scanned the shimmering expanse of Persimmon Lake. Was this it? Had the Loon People rallied their forces and come to take revenge for the murder of their chief? Surely the Loon Nation could not have gathered enough warriors this quickly?

He squinted at the commoners' houses that lined the shore. The bones on the roofs gleamed. No one allowed the bones of the animals they'd caught in traps or snares to touch the ground. It was disrespectful. Instead, they placed the bones on their roofs, where the souls of the animals could keep watch for their new bodies. If animals were killed

correctly, with reverence, death was only a temporary thing. Within a few days, Skyholder, the Creator, would send a new body, identical to the old one,
and the soul would rise up from the bones and resume its life.

The flash came again, this time longer, and he
knew it was not a warrior's signal.

The owl fluttered, then soared down across the
water, hunting. Its wings shone in the diffused light
of Sister Moon that penetrated the Cloud People.

Feather Dancer sank back against the log wall and
let out the breath he'd unwittingly been holding.

After a night of cries and running feet, the townspeople had finally settled into their blankets, leaving
an odd stillness in possession of the world. Every
sound, every glimmer that might be a raised weapon,
caught his attention.

"Sleep, you fools," he whispered. "I thank the
gods you have no idea what's going on. I wish I
didn't."

As though to mock him, Priest Teal's hoarse old
voice seeped from the leather door curtain: "Flint
tells me you have chosen Long Lance to Heal her.
What if he refuses?"

"We must offer him so much that he cannot re-
fuse," Matron Wink answered.

"Wealth is of little concern to an old man, Matron.
He will be far more worried about the consequences
if he fails."

"What do you mean?"

Teal's voice rasped: "Well, he knows he must succeed. She is the high chieftess of the Black Falcon Nation. That means he has to use every Spirit Plant and technique he knows to try to Heal her. Do you understand?"

Matron Wink hesitated for several long heartbeats before she said in anguish, "Yes, I understand."

Feather Dancer clamped his jaw. So . . . the matron had chosen the legendary witch Long Lance as the chieftess' next Healer.

Footsteps suddenly padded down the hallway inside, and Feather Dancer straightened. He knew the sound of the matron's steps as well as his own.

As the wind gusted, yellow light spread across the mound top, strengthening the shadows of the trees that lay like dead arms across the wet ground.

Matron Wink pulled the curtain aside, stepped out, and anxiously smoothed her hands up and down her purple sleeves. The seed-beads that covered her bodice shimmered. Was she shaking? She'd piled her graying black hair on top of her head and secured it with a polished shell comb. It, too, glimmered.

Quietly, she ordered, "Come inside, War Chief."

"Yes, Matron."

Feather Dancer followed her down the torch-lit hall and into the council chamber. Twenty paces across, the room's only adornments were the twelve sacred masks on the walls and the four log benches that framed the fire hearth. The masks represented the divine beings that watched over the Black Falcon People. The empty eye sockets, long fur fringes, and gaping beaks sent a prickle up his spine. They seemed to be watching him with a predator's intensity.

He stopped five paces from the fire, and Matron Wink walked back to stand between Priest Teal and Flint.

Teal whispered something he couldn't hear. The little bald elder resembled a walking skeleton. His white-filmed eyes might have been frozen lakes.

"No," Matron Wink whispered.

Feather Dancer wished she would just make the decision, give him his orders, and allow him to go back to his duties. Blackbird Town was in danger. She didn't need him here. He needed to check on the guards he'd posted and make certain they were still alive.

"We can't wait until morning," Matron Wink said, barely audible. "Flint must leave now. There's no time to waste."

Neither Flint nor Priest Teal responded. They both just stared at her. Flint, a tall handsome man, had a perfectly chiseled face and large black eyes. His cape was a splash of darkness in the firelight.

It set Feather Dancer's teeth on edge.

The Black Falcon People loved colors, the brighter the better. The fact that Flint chose garments that blended with the shadows made Feather Dancer distrust him even more. It was as though the man deliberately sought to set himself apart from the rest of the people—just as witches did.

To stifle his raging emotions, Feather Dancer

turned to study the beautiful woman lying on the litter beside the fire. Long black hair haloed Chieftess Sora's pale face. Her blankets, the color of bloodred earth, had been woven from the finest buffalo wool and dyed with dog-tail weed. Her fingers jerked, grasping at something no one else could see. Feather Dancer feared that her shadow-soul—the soul that walked in dreams—was traveling through a terrifying land.

Priest Teal had tried to Heal her, but she'd kept denying the murders, and Teal had been forced to declare the Healing Circle a failure. Apparently no one, except perhaps Feather Dancer, believed her when she said she was innocent.

Chieftess Sora made a soft pained sound. Tears leaked from her eyes and dropped onto her red blankets like perfect dewdrops.

Matron Wink said, "She probably heard us talking about Long Lance."

Flint swiftly walked across the floor and knelt at the chieftess' side. His cape draped around him in sculpted raven folds. As he gently brushed the tears from her cheeks, he said, "Don't cry, Sora. He won't fail. I won't let him."

Matron Wink pressed her fingers to her lips as though to keep her own cries locked in her throat. In a shaking voice, she whispered, "Dear gods, I've betrayed her. I've betrayed her."

The chieftess' mouth opened in what might have been a silent cry; then she laughed.

Perhaps it was the resemblance to a sob, or the rage that lived inside the laughter, but the room went deathly quiet.

"No," Flint answered. "You're trying to save her life—and the thing she cherishes most, her people."

Feather Dancer shifted irritably. Dawn was not far away. If Matron Wink wanted Flint to take the chieftess to Long Lance, then he *did* need to go, quickly. The trip was risky at best, and Flint had already lost the cover of darkness.

"War Chief?"

"Yes, Matron," Feather Dancer squared his shoulders, glad that he was finally going to be dismissed.

"I want you to accompany Flint. Do whatever he says. Do you understand?"

"But, Matron . . ." Feather Dancer felt like he'd been bludgeoned. "We may be attacked at any moment. You need me here in Blackbird Town! You can't send me away on a Healing mission when the lives of our people are in danger."

She marched across the floor and gave him a hard look. "You're the only one I can trust to make certain Chieftess Sora lives through this. Besides . . . there's more going on here than your ears are hearing."

"What do you mean?"

She turned away to grimace at Flint. "I can't answer that, not yet."

"Did you receive new information?"

"Yes. Just moments ago."

Feather Dancer blinked. No one had entered through the front entrance of the Matron's House.

Had a messenger passed by the guard he'd posted at the rear entrance?

"Who brought you this information?"

"Flint. Flint told me."

Feather Dancer glared. "The man is a scoundrel. Why do you believe him?"

"Because I can't afford to disbelieve him! If he's right, I must do something."

Did she mean they were about to be attacked? Perhaps by the Loon People? "Do something? To stop what?"

She turned toward the chieftess and squinted as though it pained her to see her lifelong friend looking utterly helpless. "I pray she will understand. In the end."

In a clipped voice, he said, "She may, Matron, but I certainly do not."

Matron Wink ran a hand through her graying hair as though to ease a building headache. "I want you to obey Flint as you would me. Is that clear?"

He stepped closer to her and, just above a whisper, pressed, "Matron, if I am to protect our chieftess, I must know what I might be facing out there. Please tell me this new information."

She seemed to be considering it. Her lips pressed into a thin bloodless line. "I can't risk it. Just do as Flint says. He knows far more about this than I do."

Feather Dancer's gaze shot to Flint, and the man had the audacity to smile at him. His white teeth gleamed in the firelight.

Matron Wink would never give control of her war

chief to anyone unless the situation was grave and a transfer of power absolutely necessary.

Feather Dancer asked, "Where is the Loon People's war chief, Grown Bear?"

Grown Bear had stayed for the Healing Circle at the Matron's request.

Flint rose to his feet, and his bushy black brows plunged down over his straight nose. "Gone. He left right after the Healing Circle failed. Grown Bear said that if he hurried, he could catch his warriors on the trail home. Why do you ask?"

"I don't trust him. He believes Chieftess Sora killed his chief, Blue Bow. Grown Bear is in a difficult position. If he returns home without having taken some kind of revenge, his people will cut him apart and feed him to their dogs. Matron, I recommend you have a war party accompany us until we reach the northern lands of this Healer, Priest Long Lance."

"No." She shook her head. "As you've pointed out, we are in danger. We need our warriors here. You'll have to protect yourselves."

Though it angered him that she would throw him into a boiling pot with a man he would just as soon stab as look at, in her position he would probably do the same. Chieftess Sora was precious to the Black Falcon People, but her single life was nothing compared to the hundreds who might die if Blackbird Town was attacked. They would need every man and woman who could wield a bow.

"Matron?" Priest Teal propped his walking stick and gingerly started across the floor.

She hurried to meet him halfway. "Sit down, Teal, before you collapse. Over the past few days you've worked so hard to Heal her that you've barely slept."

His head trembled. "I will rest once our chieftess is away. One last time"—he paused to give the matron a piercing look through his white-filmed eyes— "are you certain that Long Lance is the person you wish to Heal her?"

"Yes, I—I think so."

Teal stared at her, apparently waiting, perhaps hoping she would change her mind. When she didn't, he turned to Flint and said, "Don't give the chieftess any more of the sleeping potion until tomorrow night."

"But what if she wakes during the day?" Flint asked. "If she starts screaming—"

"Tie her up and gag her if necessary, but *do not* give her the potion more than once a day or you will poison her and she will never wake up. I know you think you are a Healer, Flint, but trust me, you are a novice at best. *Listen to me.*"

Flint's expression hardened, but he tilted his head in reluctant agreement.

Feather Dancer felt as if a huge hand were squeezing his chest. He narrowed his eyes at Flint. *All of this is your fault.*

"Feather Dancer?" Matron Wink said. "Before you leave, I want you to come to my chamber. You may be questioned along the way. I must give you her ceremonial celt to verify her identity."

A celt was a ceremonial chert war club, only carried by rulers. "Of course, Matron."

Matron Wink pointed her finger like a stiletto at Flint's heart. "Now you and I must talk."

Flint followed her across the chamber, far enough away that it would be difficult for Teal or Feather Dancer to overhear their conversation.

Nonetheless, Feather Dancer strained to hear every word.

With the softness of an assassin's footfall, she said, "Only you and I know . . . details . . . we are taking grave . . . if Sora dies, we will never . . . do you . . ."

Flint's black eyes sparkled when he looked down at her. "I understand perfectly, Wink. Did you send . . . messenger . . . Strongheart?"

"Yes, I've taken care . . ."

A gust of wind flapped the door curtain and drowned out their voices.

The iron-gray flash of dawn briefly streaked the floor; then it was gone, replaced by the warm gleam of the fire. The clouds must have broken.

Feather Dancer's hands clenched to fists at his sides. Flint had mentioned Strongheart, the chief priest in Eagle Flute Village. Blue Bow's village. Were they truly taking Chieftess Sora to Long Lance in the far north? His roiling gut told him Flint was engaged in a desperate game that had little to do with Chieftess Sora, but he couldn't prove it.

The matron said, "There is one more thing I want to say to you, Flint."

He straightened as though expecting something unpleasant. She had not always been kind to him. During the time Flint and Sora had been married, Wink had frequently threatened Flint's life. Once, when Feather Dancer had seen fifteen winters, Flint had reportedly hurt Sora and Wink had chased him out of Blackbird Town swinging a war ax. "What is it, Wink?"

"For the sake of the gods, you *must* keep her safe." Tears made her voice shake.

It took five heartbeats before Flint replied, "If your war chief follows my orders, she will be safe. If not, her death will be his fault."

Feather Dancer propped his hands on his hips. "My matron has ordered me to obey you. Therefore I will. I don't like it. I don't like you. But so long as breath lives in my body I will obey my matron."

A faint smile turned Flint's lips, and behind those dark eyes Feather Dancer saw something akin to triumph. "Good. Then gather your things and let's be on our way before it's too late. We must hurry."

3

In the dream, I lock my legs around him and hold him tightly. "I just want to feel you inside me. This may be the last time we . . ." Tears constrict my throat. I start moving.

"Blessed gods," Skinner whispers, matching my rhythm. "You cannot know how I need this. It keeps me here. Here with you. Just as it keeps your reflection-soul home. Tell me what to do. I'll do anything you want."

I sit up with him still inside me and move in frantic fits, bringing him close, then stopping, just petting him, before I slowly begin again. A low moan sounds in his throat. He doesn't have to do anything except give me the freedom to please him. When my own body flushes on the verge of ecstasy, he rasps, "Harder, Sora. Hurry."

I move faster. As the fiery wave builds, he grips my hips and violently shoves me down on his manhood.

He moans, "Oh, gods! I love you so much."

His hands move up my arms and clench around my throat. When I start gasping for air, it is as though white-hot fire explodes inside me. My entire body bucks and quivers. He wraps his arms around me and rolls us both over so that he is on top. His long hair falls around me like a dark curtain.

Abruptly, he lifts his head and chokes out, "Who . . . who's there? Sora? Do you see him?"

"Who?"

"Him."

I try to rise to look, but he shoves me down and his fingers tighten around my throat again. "Quickly, before he comes, tell me how you did it." He glares at me with huge feral eyes, more animal than human. "How did you do it!"

"Do what?" I beg and tear at his hands. "What are you talking about?"

"How did you kill her? Did you slip something into her food? Did you hire someone to do it?"

I strike him with my fists, fighting to shove him away. "Stop it!"

He shakes me so violently I think my neck might snap. "How did you get that close to her camp without someone seeing you? Witchery? Did you fly in on raven wings?"

The edges of my vision go gray. Just before I lose consciousness two gleaming eyes blaze to life inside me and I . . .

Skinner rolls off me and shouts, "No, don't! You don't understand! Talk to Wink. She'll tell you . . . Wait!"

Then he roars.

And keeps roaring.

Like a man fighting for his life.

. . . *The cry of a night bird jolts me, and the dream dissolves into darkness.*

I suck in a deep breath and slowly realize that the mossy fragrance of Persimmon Lake is gone, replaced by the sandy odor of the inland trails leading northward. Where am I?

I flex my fingers and touch blankets.

Below them, I trace poles.

I'm being carried on a pole litter.

This is real.

Blessed gods, I'm alive.

I'm waking up.

"How many times must I tell you? She is sick! We are taking her to the one man in the world who might be able to Heal her. Why can't you understand that?"

I would know Flint's deep voice anywhere. We were married for fourteen winters. When he left me, my world ended. I loved him desperately. I remember running after him, begging him to come home, to . . .

"I can't understand it because I don't believe Chieftess Sora needs to be Healed. She didn't kill any of those people. You did! Or you and your allies did."

That's my war chief, Feather Dancer. . . . His words are tiny sharp bolts of light behind my eyes.

"Why would I do that?"

"Because you are plotting to bring about her downfall so you can put someone else in her place. If Matron Wink hadn't ordered me to be here, I wouldn't be."

Wink ordered Feather Dancer to accompany Flint? Where are they taking me? And where is "here"?

"You really dislike me, don't you?" *Flint asks, and I can hear the smile in his voice. He's enjoying Feather Dancer's hostility.*

"If I could just slip a stiletto between your ribs, I'd like you much better."

"And who do I have in mind to replace Sora?"

Feather Dancer shifts; his damp leather sandals squeak. "I'm not sure, but I suspect you're plotting to install Long Fin."

"Ah, I see," *Flint says with exaggerated interest.* "Then if I'm trying to replace Sora with Wink's son, I must be plotting with Wink, is that right? Matron Wink and I want to overthrow Sora?"

Feather Dancer does not answer. He can't. If he says yes and is wrong his traitorous accusation might result in his own death.

Somewhere out in the forest the night bird cries again. The shriek carries on the wind, rising and falling until it fades to silence.

I fill my lungs just to feel the air move. How far are we from Blackbird Town? How long have we been on this journey?

More importantly, am I ill?

*I search through the shining jumble that has be-
come my memory. Images flash; mouths move without words. I remember Wink's face appearing out of
the darkness, suspended above me like a war club.
Wink is my oldest and most trusted friend. We are
from the same clan, the Shadow Rock Clan. While
she rose to the position of matron of the Black Falcon Nation, I became the high chieftess. If Wink ordered my war chief and former husband to take me
to a man who can Heal me, I must be sick.*

What's wrong with me?

*My fingers snake down over my hips. I am bundled
in blankets. Wink must have wrapped me up for the
journey. I know because on many occasions she has
personally cared for me when I've been sick or injured. The way the blankets are layered and tucked
around my body is her work. She made certain I
would be warm. Love for her fills me, and for the first
time I can take a full breath.*

*Somewhere close by a fire crackles. If I concen-
trate, I can hear tree branches rustling in the cool
night breeze.*

Feather Dancer's voice again, angry: "Know this,
Flint. If she mysteriously dies on this trip, you will
be next."

*I manage to tug up my eyelids and see them sitting
in a halo of firelight five paces away, facing each
other across the blaze like mortal enemies. Both men
are tall, muscular, but where Feather Dancer's heavily scarred face proves he has fought valiantly in*

*many battles, Flint's smooth features convey some-
thing far different. No matter where he goes,
women's eyes follow him, and he knows this. Long
black hair hangs down over his buckskin shirt, fram-
ing his large black eyes, straight nose, and full lips.
Lips that seem to be suppressing mirth, but the
amusement does not reach his angry eyes.*

Flint responds, "Just do as I say, Feather Dancer,
and Sora will be safe. If you do not, the Black Falcon Nation will blame *you* for her death, not me."

*Feather Dancer's scars contort. He throws the last
dregs of his tea into the fire and stamps away into
the darkness.*

*Flint chuckles softly. For a time, he stares at the
windblown flames, listening until he seems certain
Feather Dancer is gone.*

Then he asks, "Did you hear all of that, Sora?"

*How did he know I was awake? Did I move? He
must be watching me very closely.*

". . . part."

*I'm not certain I've actually spoken, but he re-
sponds immediately by walking over and kneeling at
my side. The firelight flutters across his handsome
face like transparent orange butterflies.* "But you
heard enough to know that we're taking you to a
Healer, didn't you?"

"Yes."

*He gently pulls the blankets up around my throat
and bends to kiss me.* "You're going to be all right. I
give you my oath."

His lips are soft. I started wanting this man when

*I'd seen fourteen winters, and I've never stopped—
despite the fact that I am now married to another.
My husband, Rockfish, is a great Trader. He . . .*

"Stop thinking about him, Sora."

"What?"

"Your husband. You were thinking about your
husband. Your brows drew together like they always
do when you're feeling guilty."

*Flint knows me better than I know myself. In a cu-
rious way, our souls are linked. I concentrate on
what I want to ask him.*

"Are you . . . plotting against me?"

*His hand moves down my blankets to my breast,
and he squeezes gently.* "Where were you a half-
moon ago when White Fawn was killed? We were
supposed to wed. Did you kill her, like you did all
the others? Your father, your sister, your mother. Far
Eye and Blue Bow? And many more, I suspect."

*The list of names stuns me. Especially Blue Bow.
He is a chief from the Loon Nation; he's holding
eleven of Flint's kinsmen hostage in Eagle Flute Village. It's a battle over territory. The gathering
grounds have belonged to the Black Falcon Nation
for generations, but the Loon People now claim
them. When the small party from Oak Leaf Village
went out to gather fresh spring tubers, Blue Bow
captured them. I'll work it out; I just need more time.
I . . .*

"Answer me, Sora. Did you kill White Fawn?"

". . . Who?"

"You are such a good liar, my sweet murderess."

Flint stretches out on the ground beside me and tenderly brushes away the hair that has tangled with my eyelashes. I am so weak, I cannot even find the strength to resist.

"Your reflection-soul is loose, Sora. We're taking you to a Healer who may be able to fix it in your body. If not . . ." He makes a sound like a war club striking a skull. "Wink will have no choice."

Insanity is caused when a person's reflection-soul is jarred loose and gets lost in the forest. Only very powerful Healers can find it and bring it back to the body. If the soul can't be found, it is the clan's responsibility to ensure the sick person will never harm anyone else.

My reflection-soul is loose?

How did this happen? Was I struck in the head?

This stirs a feeling of horror inside me, as though something has happened recently that I should remember. There was a shadow-soul . . . loose. . . . It had stolen a living body. . . .

"My memory," *I whisper.* "What's wrong?"

Flint props himself on his elbow and smiles down at me. "What are you trying to recall?"

"There was a . . . a shadow-soul . . . living inside someone. . . ."

Flint slips his hand beneath my blankets and slides it up my thigh. "We're giving you a sleeping potion. Your thoughts will be confused for a time. But a few days after we stop the potion, it will all come back."

"A few days? Is that how long it will . . . take . . ."

My thoughts dissolve like ice in bright sunlight. I can't recall what I wished to ask him. Images appear and melt behind my eyes: running, running through dark trees, screams in the distance, shouts . . . a shining copper breastplate . . . warriors calling insults . . . Far Eye's muted laughter.

"Is that how long it will take us to get there?" Flint suggests.

"Yes."

His hand moves to the warmth between my legs. As his fingers sensually press the fabric of my dress against my opening, he whispers, "I love you, Sora. You know that, don't you? You know I'm trying to help you."

I have known him all of my adult life. I can tell from the dire way he's looking at me that he's telling the truth. "Yes. I know that."

He presses the fabric deeper, and I feel his fingers moving inside me.

"Then trust me. Trust me as you have never trusted me, and I'll make certain you are safe."

Feather Dancer walks back into the firelight, sees Flint stretched out beside me, and hoarsely calls, "What are you doing? Get away from her!"

Flint removes his hand and turns. His black eyes are sheathed in the fire's glow like orange moons. "She's awake. We need to give her more of the sleeping potion. It's in that small pot beside the fire. Bring it to me."

Feather Dancer is clearly irked by the order, but

he obeys: picks up the pot and carries it to Flint. As Flint pulls out the wooden cork, a bitter odor rises.

He says, "You hold her mouth open and I'll give her the potion."

Feather Dancer shakes his head. "I'll give her the potion while you hold her mouth open."

"I've studied Spirit Plants with the greatest Healers in the Black Falcon Nation, Feather Dancer. I'm better at judging how much is safe. Now do as I asked and hold her mouth open."

It happens swiftly. Feather Dancer's strong hands pull my jaws apart, and Flint pours the acrid brew down my throat.

I can't fight both of them.

I swallow.

As their faces fade, my thoughts fly apart like hundreds of shattered rainbows. The brilliant shards flash and tumble all around me, and I hear Flint's voice saying over and over again . . .

My   sweet   murderess . . . murderess . . . my sweet . . .

4

THE LAST REMNANTS OF MOTHER SUN'S GLORY shot through the tall pines like amethyst spears and fell across the path Feather Dancer and Flint traveled. Feather Dancer concentrated on the beauty, hoping it would relieve the pain in his hands. Since long before dawn, he'd been trotting along behind Flint, carrying the rear litter poles. They had to make it as far as they could today. If they passed the northern shore of Jasper Lake before they camped, they would enter Oak Leaf Village around noon tomorrow, resupply, and be on their way to the far north, where Priest Long Lance lived.

Feather Dancer would feel better once they were beyond the easy reach of Flint's relatives. Every move the man made, every gesture and facial expression, told Feather Dancer he was more than he seemed. From the instant they'd left Blackbird Town, Feather Dancer's suspicions had been smoldering. Flint never took the main trails. He selected smaller, less-traveled routes, as though he were avoiding someone or something.

In the distance, an alligator bellowed.

Feather Dancer's pace slowed. The last thing they needed was to come upon an alligator in the darkness.

The creature's hoarse voice carried on the evening breeze, along with the thunderous cracking of deadfall caused by a whipping tail.

Another alligator roared.

"Two males fighting," Feather Dancer said.

"Don't worry," Flint called over his shoulder. "I know a trail that veers around their pond. Those two old men won't have a chance at us."

Feather Dancer followed Flint into a dense cluster of palmettos. Fronds racked his leggings as he jogged past.

A short time later, Flint said, "Here it is," and turned onto a deer trail. "This will take a little longer, but we need to make camp soon anyway."

"No, we don't. We can travel for another two hands of time," Feather Dancer answered. "We should keep going until it gets too dark to see the trail."

"I decide when and where to camp, War Chief. I planned to make it to the southern shore of Jasper Lake tonight. That's just ahead, and that's where we're going to camp."

"But that's ridiculous. The longer we are on the

trail, the more poison we must give the chieftess to keep her asleep. For her sake, we *must* run as long and as hard as we can every day."

"No," Flint said coldly. "The only thing you must do is what I tell you to. We will make camp where I say."

By the time he saw Jasper Lake come into view, Sister Moon's gleam coated the surface, turning the dark water into a broad twinkling expanse of light and casting silver reflections upon the ancient oaks that lined the trail.

"We're going to camp right over there." Flint used his chin to point. "I've used it many times."

Feather Dancer saw the sandy spit surrounded on three sides by moonlit water, and his belly muscles knotted.

Flint stopped at the edge of the water, and they lowered the chieftess' litter to the sand. While Flint stretched his taut back muscles, Feather Dancer surveyed the location. Charcoal from old fires dotted the spit. People must camp here often, but that fact did not alleviate his concerns.

"This is not a good spot," he said. "We must move."

Flint groaned and flapped his arms, which made his black cape billow. "Feather Dancer, it's surrounded on three sides by water. It's far more defensible than an open place where we could be attacked from four sides."

"The advantage to an open place is you can run in four directions. Here, they can come at us from the land, force us into the water, and almost certainly capture or kill us." He reached down to grip the litter poles. His fingers cramped. "Come on. Let's move."

"No," Flint said. "I have camped here many times. I know it's safe! Besides, I'm dead tired and starving. Aren't you?"

Feather Dancer's stomach had been eating a hole in his backbone, but he said, "I can starve for a time longer to ensure the safety of my chieftess. Grab your end of the litter. It won't take long to find a better place."

Cursing under his breath, Flint lifted the litter, and Feather Dancer led the way out of the spit. They walked along the lakeshore for a good hand of time, until he spied an old sand dune that overlooked the lake. "We'll camp there." He pointed with his chin.

"You actually think that tiny hump is better than my spit?"

"It will be once I'm through with it."

They trudged up the sandy slope and rested the litter on the very top. Chieftess Sora rolled to her side as though close to waking. Her long hair spilled over the litter poles.

The powerful scents of rotting vegetation filled the air. Feather Dancer removed his waist pack and gratefully dropped it to the sand, then placed his bow and quiver beside it. He still had his war ax and stiletto tied to his belt.

Flint said, "If you'll go scavenge for dry firewood, I'll tend to Sora's needs."

"You look for dry firewood. I have more pressing concerns."

Flint propped his hands on his hips and in exasperation, shouted, "Have you forgotten that Matron Wink ordered you to obey me as you would her?"

"She also ordered me to make certain Chieftess Sora lives through this. Whenever your orders appear to endanger my chieftess I may choose to disobey you."

"Wonderful." Flint ran a hand through his long black hair. "That ought to get us all killed."

"There is no 'us,' you fool. There is only me and my chieftess. You are one of *them*."

Feather Dancer caught the hot glare Flint gave him as he strode down the dune and headed for a copse of dead trees.

Sometime in the past the trees had burned. Their blackened arms reached skyward as though pleading with the Star People for salvation. Feather Dancer untied the war ax from his belt and began chopping down the smaller trees. They were dry and old. It didn't require much effort. What took time was dragging them back to camp. About twice his height in length, they were awkward. He could only haul two or three at a time.

As he dragged the last saplings to the top of the dune, Flint looked up from the small fire he'd built. Two pots hung from tripods over the flames. He said, "I used your pouch of dried fish to make a stew. It'll be hot soon."

"My pouch? You searched through my pack?"

Feather Dancer dropped the saplings with dramatic thuds.

"What did you expect me to do? You didn't leave your fish out in the open for me. I had to find it. I used the last of my venison jerky this morning."

Feather Dancer glowered. He had a number of things in his pack that he had not wished Flint to steal. Especially, the ceremonial celt that Matron Wink had given him. It was Chieftess Sora's symbol of office and would unquestionably mark her as a woman of high status—in case someone questioned her identity. But it was also extremely valuable. Flint was exactly the sort of person who would steal it and sell it to the highest bidder.

Flint stood up and gestured to the pile of saplings. "While we wait for the stew, why don't you let me help you? I assume we're building a makeshift fort."

Feather Dancer let out a disgruntled breath, but answered, "We are. Let's lay out the logs in a square and overlap the ends until they're waist-high."

A short time later, they were surrounded by a wall that would deflect most arrows and spears.

"Can we eat now?" Flint asked. "I'm about to faint."

"We should feed the chieftess first. She hasn't had anything since—"

"She's not the one who's been hauling around a heavy litter all day. Sit down. I'll feed her as soon as we finish."

Feather Dancer crouched before the fire, but he felt guilty about obeying. In the cool wind that blew off the lake, Chieftess Sora's hair fluttered across her face like a dark silken web. She looked both beautiful and vulnerable. He tugged his gaze away. A strong, brave woman, she would not wish anyone to see her like this. Half the world feared her. The other half worshipped her. According to the traditions of her people, she was divine, descended directly from Black Falcon himself. He felt certain she would rather die than be in this current situation.

Flint said, "Here. Eat," and handed him a wooden bowl of stew in which stood a horn spoon.

Feather Dancer took it. Spiced with dried palm berries, the fish stew had a sweet flavor that satisfied his ravenous hunger.

Flint filled his own bowl and sank down on the opposite side of the fire. Orange light wavered over his handsome face, and Feather Dancer could see the exhaustion in his eyes.

Around a bite of food, Flint said, "Tomorrow night we should enter the lands of the Sandhill Crane People. I pray Wink got a message to their matron telling her we would just be passing through. I don't want to have to fight—"

"You? Fight?" Feather Dancer grunted disbelievingly.

Flint's eyes narrowed. "I knew neither of us would enjoy it, but I'm endeavoring to make conversation."

"Well, don't. I don't care to hear anything you have to say." He scooped another bite of stew and ate it while his gaze scanned the dark lake and trees.

"We have to talk, Feather Dancer. We'll be on the

trail for moons. Besides, I'd like to get to know you better. You've been war chief of Blackbird Town for what? Two winters?"

"Yes."

"Sora appointed you right after she murdered her mother, Chieftess Yellow Cypress, didn't she?"

"Chieftess Sora appointed me right after her mother died in an *accidental* fall."

"Accidental? Do you really believe that?"

Feather Dancer didn't look at him. He concentrated on emptying his stew bowl. He vividly remembered how heartbroken Sora had been, but she'd taken quick, decisive action to repair the damage done by her elderly mother's last bad decisions. They'd been on the verge of going to war over a silly insult from the Red Owl People. Before the war party could leave, Chieftess Yellow Cypress had fallen to her death. Sora had accepted the position as chieftess and immediately reconvened the Council of Elders. She'd convinced them that an insult wasn't worth losing the lives of their young men and women; then she'd suggested something everyone found shocking. She'd told the elders that her mother's war chief, White Pelican, had grown old and much too fond of warfare. She wished to replace him with Feather Dancer. After days of arguing, the council had finally agreed. White Pelican was outraged, of course. It had taken Feather Dancer several moons to smooth over—

"Where has your soul drifted to?" Flint asked.

Feather Dancer chewed and swallowed before answering, "You wouldn't remember it. You were gone by then."

Flint's bushy black brows pulled together. "Then you'll have to tell me about it. What happened?"

"Nothing."

Flint grimaced. "Oh, tell me. What else do we have to do?"

Feather Dancer looked up from his bowl. "I could accuse you again of plotting the downfall of the chieftess."

"I'd just deny it. What's the point?"

Feather Dancer reached for his pack, drew out his ceramic cup, and dipped it into the tea pot hanging from the tripod to his right. Fragrant flower-scented steam curled from the cup. He smelled it and took a sip. "You have everyone of importance in Blackbird Town believing my chieftess is a murderer. I just don't understand why. How does it benefit you?"

Through a taut exhalation, Flint replied, "She's been killing people since she was seven winters old, Feather Dancer. It has to stop. I spent half my life trying to learn enough about Spirit Plants to Heal her. I was apparently too dim-witted . . . or just not Powerful enough to do it. We must get her to someone who can Heal her before Wink has no choice but to end Sora's life to protect the people of Blackbird Town."

"Chieftess Sora killed no one. How did you convince both the matron and Priest Teal that she was guilty?"

Flint took a drink of tea and rested his cup on his

drawn-up knee. "It doesn't matter, does it? No matter what I tell you, you won't believe me."

Feather Dancer shoveled more stew into his mouth, chewed, and swallowed. "Are we really taking her to Priest Long Lance? He's very old, isn't he?"

"Yes. Too old, maybe. I'm not sure he's strong enough to handle her. She is a Powerful personality." Flint stared into his bowl, but his gaze was far away, perhaps roaming the past.

"Then why did you choose Long Lance?"

"I didn't choose him. Matron Wink did."

Feather Dancer frowned, and he could feel the scars that wormed across his forehead pull tight. "Did she have any other choice?"

Flint chewed his last bite of stew before continuing, "Yes. She did. Teal and I both told her we believed Sora's only hope was Priest Strongheart. He is the greatest Healer in our country. I think he may even be more Powerful than Long Lance. He's certainly younger. He's seen only twenty-three winters."

Wind Woman whimpered as she meandered through the dead trees, and Feather Dancer thought he heard a twig crack. A sandal carelessly placed in the darkness? He turned slowly and examined the blackened trunks.

He said, "Strongheart was an idiotic suggestion. The man is a high priest of the Loon Nation. After he receives word that Chieftess Sora murdered Blue Bow, Strongheart is far more likely to harm her than to Heal her."

Flint shook his head. "I don't think so. From what

I've heard, he's a good man. Strange, but good. I think he would do his best to Heal her."

Feather Dancer ate three more bites of stew before he said, "Last winter a Trader told me that Strongheart was a madman. He said Strongheart had called down one of the meteorite people to crush a village elder he didn't like. They found a grand total of six pieces of the poor man."

"Then he's exactly the priest that Sora needs. He may actually be Powerful enough to find her lost soul and fix it in her body."

The chieftess must have heard her name; she murmured and rolled to her back.

"Sora?" Flint set his bowl down and walked over. "Are you all right?"

She dreamily smiled up at him, as though happy to see him.

Feather Dancer's gut roiled.

In a bare whisper, she said, "Thirsty."

Flint knelt and kissed her lips. "I'll get you a cup of tea."

As he rose, he briefly glanced out at the blackened grove, then walked to his pack, pulled out a cup, and filled it for the chieftess.

While Flint carried it back, Feather Dancer, again, studied the grove. The wind had picked up, blowing veils of sand across the shore. In Sister Moon's light, the grains twinkled as they tumbled through the air.

"Here, Sora," Flint said, and Feather Dancer turned to see him lift the chieftess' shoulders and tip the cup to her lips. She drank greedily. Streamers poured down her throat.

Feather Dancer called, "Would you like me to fill a stew bowl for her? She must be very—" His head snapped around.

Two cracks in rapid succession.

"What's the matter?" Flint asked.

"I heard . . ."

"What?"

Softly, he replied, "Something's out there."

"You probably heard those raccoons," Flint said, and gestured with his chin.

Feather Dancer pulled his gaze away from the trees and looked up the shoreline to where three raccoons waddled through the driftwood at the edge of the water. Moonlight reflected from their long tails.

"You're just jumpy, Feather Dancer. You should try to relax or you'll—"

"You're surrounded!" someone shouted from the dark grove. "Throw out your weapons!"

In one fluid motion, Feather Dancer pulled his war ax from his belt and spun in the direction of the voice. Black shapes trotted from the grove and rushed toward them. As an arrow cracked and bounced off the log in front of Feather Dancer, he dove, grabbed his bow and quiver, and rolled behind the wall.

The shore came alive with war cries. Through the slits between the logs, he saw warriors sprinting toward them, shooting as they ran. Their ululating shrieks made his blood turn to ice.

"Flint!" he ordered. "Protect the chieftess! I'll hold them off for as long as I—"

The blow made a hollow thunk, and lights flashed before Feather Dancer's eyes. As he toppled to the sand, his weapons slipped from his fingers. He lay still, listening to the whooping voices. There had to be fifteen or twenty of them. If he could just play opossum long enough, maybe . . .

Flint bent over him with a war club in his fist. "You'll understand in a few days. I swear it," he whispered, then lifted his club and waved it at the enemy warriors coming up the shore.

"He's unconscious!" Flint shouted. "Lower your bows!"

"Are you sure?" a man cried. "Check him again. He's a crafty one."

Flint stabbed a toe into Feather Dancer's ribs. When he didn't move, Flint cupped a hand to his mouth and called, "He's meek as a clubbed fish, Grown Bear. Now tell me where you've been? We've been here for two hands of time!"

Grown Bear. Blue Bow's war chief.

Rage spun white-hot through Feather Dancer's waning senses.

Grown Bear shouted back, "You told us you'd be camped on the spit, my friend. We surrounded it and waited for you. By the time we figured out you'd already been there and left, it was pitch black. We just saw your fire a short time ago! Did you bring her?"

"Of course I did. I keep my promises. Now make sure you keep yours. You promised me sanctuary."

Grown Bear laughed as he climbed over the log wall and embraced Flint like an ally of many battles. Feather Dancer struggled to keep his slitted eyes focused; a gray haze was rapidly crowding out the world.

In a voice too low for his warriors to hear, Grown Bear hissed, "My warriors know only that you agreed to help us capture Chief Blue Bow's murderer. Say nothing else. Do you understand?"

All pretenses to friendship gone, Flint coldly responded, "Oh, yes, I do."

5

SORA JERKED AWAKE WITH HER HEART POUNDING.

She'd heard footsteps. She was sure of it.

"Flint? . . . Feather Dancer?"

She blinked at the unfamiliar house. Round, and four body lengths across, it was a domelike structure. The builder had set poles into the ground, then bent them over and tied them together at the top. Thatched grass and palmetto fronds created the walls and roof. A fire burned in a shallow hearth in the middle of the floor. Beside it, two drying racks covered with thin strips of venison were soaking up the sycamore smoke that curled from the flames.

Sora inhaled a deep breath. The air was sweet with the scents of long-dried herbs and boiling clams. A low bench, for sitting or sleeping, curved around the walls. Baskets and pots crowded beneath it. She could see inside a few of the pots, which contained corn, hickory nuts, dried palm berries, and acorns.

"Gods," she whispered. "Where am I?"

She craned her neck to peer at the rawhide shield hanging on the wall to her left. It was painted with the image of Spearfinger, the man-killer. The Loon People had many stories about the ancient witch. It was said that she could take any shape she wanted. She could appear as your dearest friend or dead lover, but the painting showed her as a hunchbacked old woman with dirty white hair straggling around her wrinkled face. When the Loon clans went out in the autumn to set their ritual fires so that they might collect the chestnuts that had fallen on the ground, they were always wary, for Spearfinger, also known as "the Liver Eater," was never far away. If anyone grew sick, the Loon elders were certain Spearfinger had used her awl-like finger to skewer his liver for her supper.

"Feather Dancer?" she called again.

A pot sat in the ashes at the edge of the fire. By the standards of her people, it was crude pottery. It hadn't been incised or painted. Instead, dried corn cobs had been pressed into the wet clay to create the decoration.

As the smell of boiling clams grew stronger, her empty stomach knotted. But when she struggled to sit up, her vision faded, as though she might faint. She eased back down to the blankets.

"Blessed Black Falcon," she whispered. "I'm as weak as a newborn pup."

Fabric rustled behind her.

Sora tried to turn around, but didn't have the strength. "Who's there?"

A man responded, "They tell me you are a murderer. Is it true?"

She twisted, but still couldn't see him. "Who are you? Where am I?"

Light steps.

"I'm a priest. You're in my house. It's the only place you are safe. Unfortunately I'm not certain how long I can keep you here." His voice was deep and soft.

Frightened, she asked, "What village is this? I'm in the Loon Nation, aren't I?"

He didn't answer. Instead, he said, "Your people have asked me to Heal you. Do you know that?"

Sora swallowed down a dust-dry throat. "Am I ill?"

He seemed to appear out of nothingness standing in the firelight in front of her. Tall and muscular, he wore a painted deerhide cloak decorated with bright yellow starbursts. Beneath the cape, his heavily tattooed chest blazed with strange azure, red, and black designs.

She studied his tattoos admiringly. The intricate geometric images made it appear that a dozen red and blue swallow wings had been sewn together into a necklace and draped around his throat. More wings appeared to flutter down his chest to his woven palm frond loincloth. Beneath it, bands of connected red-and-black human eyes ringed his long muscular legs. She saw none of the jewelry that would have marked him as a member of the elite clans: no pounded copper, or rare shells, no exquisitely woven fabrics. He was a priest? He looked like little more than a well-treated slave. He had seen perhaps twenty-two or twenty-three winters. Short black hair clung to his head. It had been recently cut, as though in mourning, and he had a round flat face with a hooked nose. But his eyes . . . his eyes bulged slightly from their sockets. She couldn't stop looking at them. The color of polished walnut, all the despair in the world seemed to be concentrated there.

"You carry a wound inside," she said with a tired sigh.

He stared at her. "Your count is off."

"What?"

"Your count. You said *a* wound."

Sora rolled to her side to see him more clearly. "Don't try to impress me. You're too young to have seen many of life's horrors."

He crouched beside her. "Is it true?"

Sora frowned at him for several instants before it occurred to her that he had returned to his first question. "No, I am not a murderer."

"You don't remember any of the killings?"

"I didn't kill anyone."

He seemed to be examining her more closely. "Why do you think they say you are a murderer?"

"Who is 'they'?"

"Your people."

"*Which* people?"

"Your old friend, Matron Wink, for one."

Sora felt like she'd just been stabbed in the heart; her entire body ached. He had to be lying. Wink would never betray her.

Though she had a vague memory that she'd heard Wink say . . . what?

"And your former husband, Flint, for another."

"Whoever says I am a murderer is trying to destroy me. To bring about my downfall."

He seemed to be studying her long hair, as though taking note of every twig and blade of grass. "What about your war chief, Feather Dancer?"

"He *never* would have told you I was a murderer."

The priest reached out to touch her blankets and rolled the exquisite fabric between his fingers. The Loon People had nothing like it; he must find the weave extraordinarily soft. "No. He didn't."

"Where is Feather Dancer? I would like to speak with him."

"Do you trust him?"

She hesitated before saying, "I don't trust anyone."

"Do you trust yourself?"

She exhaled hard in irritation. "Yes. I'm the one person in the entire world that I do trust. Now answer some questions for me. I—"

"But I've been told that as recently as a few days ago you doubted your own sanity. Did they lie to me about that, as well?"

Fragments of memories drifted through her souls. She *did* remember being worried that her reflection-soul might be out wandering the forest. Was that just a few days ago? Why had she been worried about that? Faces swam before her. Teal. Priest Teal told her that her reflection-soul was loose.

"I have dreams of . . . r-running," she stammered, "of being lost in the forest. I've had them since I was a child. I wrestle with myself over this, but I don't think my soul is loose."

"You wrestle with yourself?"

"Yes, it's only natural. Don't you wrestle with yourself when you can't make a clear decision?"

His smile warmed. "The person who said we wrestle with ourselves obviously didn't understand the number of 'wrestlers' inside us. Which 'wrestler' is the one you trust?"

"You're speaking nonsense. Stop it. Do you wish people to think you're an imbecile?"

He rose to his feet. "I am an imbecile. All priests are. There's no sense trying to hide it."

She frowned at him. How curious that he would agree with her. Most priests, if he was a priest, considered themselves quite superior to the average person. "You truly are a priest?"

"Until someone manages to assassinate me, yes."

"Only very Powerful priests are worth assassinating. Are you worth that much?"

He bowed his head and smiled. "Apparently, since there were seven attempts on my life this past winter."

"What's your name?"

As silent as a hawk's shadow, he leaned forward to stare straight into her eyes. "My name is Strongheart."

Fear tickled the back of her throat. "You—you are Blue Bow's high priest."

"I was, yes."

"Was?"

"Yes. He's dead." He cocked his head and studied her for what seemed a long time. "They say you killed him. In fact, Matron Wink assures me that you've killed at least seven people, including one of your dearest friends, War Chief Skinner from Oak Leaf Village. She sent a runner to ask me if I would be willing to Heal you. She said many had tried and failed. When you arrived, I thought you'd come because I'd said yes."

"But . . . that's not why I came?"

He reached down to brush away the sand that coated her cheek. His hand was large and gentle, the fingertips calloused. "I didn't find out until after I'd ordered you brought to my chamber that Grown Bear had taken you captive because you murdered our chief, Blue Bow. Whether or not I will be able to keep my promise to your matron is now uncertain."

Fear turned her breathing shallow. "Then I'm here for punishment."

"Perhaps."

If the situation were reversed and Feather Dancer had just delivered Wink's murderer to her, Sora would not care what excuses the murderer gave. Her people would demand that the murderer be killed, and no matter what her personal feelings, she would obey the will of her people.

In a shaky voice, she asked, "Am I to be killed to-day or tomorrow?"

"The new chief, Blue Bow's son, Horned Owl, will call a village council meeting tomorrow to decide."

"When?"

"Dawn."

She had maybe twelve hands of time to decide what she would say to defend herself, and the Spirit Plant Flint had been giving her still lived in her veins. Clear thought was impossible.

She massaged her forehead. "Tell me about Horned Owl. How old is he?"

"He has seen fourteen winters."

"Barely a man, then. What's he like?"

Strongheart clamped his jaw, as though trying to decide what to tell her. "He's brash. I pray that ascending to the chieftainship will force him to grow up."

"When you say 'brash,' do you mean he's reckless? Cruel? Perhaps, stupid?"

"Of those choices, I think 'cruel' best describes him."

The sensation of danger filtered through her numb bones, and she again asked, "Where is my war chief? I would like to speak with him."

"He's being held under heavy guard in the Captives' House, where I'm sure you will be taken shortly."

"I can't stay here?"

"I don't think Chief Horned Owl will allow it."

"And my former husband? Where is he?"

Strongheart's expression tensed. He propped his hands on his hips, and as his cape resettled about him, the fragrance of cypress bark rose. He must store his clothing in a cypress box. "At this very moment, Horned Owl is feasting Flint and showering him with wealth. By betraying you, he has assured himself a place of honor among our people. He is a hero. Already our most beautiful maidens are parading before him, hoping to be selected as his new wives."

A log exploded in the fire, and the sudden burst of light fluttered the air like a hundred luminous scarves.

"Flint betrayed me?"

"Yes, in exchange for a great deal of wealth and a promise of sanctuary."

He walked across the floor and dipped a cup into the boiling pot. As he carried it back to her, he said, "They'll be coming soon. You must eat. I don't know when they will feed you again—or if they'll feed you again."

Flint's voice seeped up from a locked chamber deep inside her: *Trust me. Trust me as you have never trusted me, and I'll make certain you are safe.*

"I don't believe Flint betrayed me."

Strongheart gave her a sad smile, as though he pitied her. "And you called me a fool."

6

HER HAND TREMBLED WHEN SHE LIFTED THE FIRST spoonful of clams to her mouth. She fought to steady it, but she was surprisingly weak. As she gobbled the stew, broth spilled onto her blankets. How many days had it been since she'd left Blackbird Town? She had no idea. Gods, had she ever felt this lonely and frightened? She longed for the magnificent peaked-roof houses, beautifully incised copper breastplates, and elaborate jewelry that distinguished the elite rulers of the Black Falcon Nation. The Loon People had different ways, different gods.

Most of all, I miss Wink.

A gaping hole had opened inside her and sucked out her heart, leaving a thunderous emptiness. She and Wink had been friends for twenty-five winters, since the day Sora's father died.

"Where is your shadow-soul roaming?" Strong-heart asked.

She chewed another bite of clams and looked up at him. He paced at the foot of her blankets with his arms folded beneath his cape. His round face, hooked nose, and shorn black hair had picked up the orange gleam of the fire.

"I was thinking about my friend, Wink."

"Were you remembering something from the past?"

"Yes. The day my father died."

"Ah." He smoothed a hand over his chin. "You had seen seven winters, hadn't you? What happened?"

She ate two more bites before she decided whether or not she would tell him. "My mother, Chieftess Yellow Cypress, went mad. That's no secret. People for five moons' walk in every direction knew about it."

"Yes, one of our elders told me that she ran through Blackbird Town screaming."

"Mostly she ran up and down the halls of the Chieftess' House, but on occasion she went outside."

Sora recalled the terrified looks people had given her when she finally was allowed to leave her mother's house. She hadn't understood at the time. Later, she realized that many of the townspeople feared her father's shadow-soul had slipped inside her and driven away her reflection-soul. Shadow-souls desperate to stay alive moved from body to body.

"Did Matron Wink help you?" Strongheart's

voice came softly, as though he did not want to disturb her remembrances.

"Yes." She looked down, and her reflection-soul gazed up at her from the stew broth, its dark eyes sad. Long black hair framed her oval face, but she appeared pale and vulnerable. "I remember that first day with perfect clarity. I was lying on my sleeping bench with hides pressed over my ears, trying to block Mother's shrieks, when Wink came in. She was four winters older than I was: eleven. She curled against my back and stroked my hair. I don't—"

"Where was your older sister, Walks-among-the-Stars?"

Sora shrugged. "I don't know. We had different interests. She was almost a woman. I was still a child."

"She died three winters later, didn't she?"

"Yes. In a canoe accident. I was with her. I made it to shore. She didn't." A chill went through her, and her shadow-soul flashed backward in time until she found herself staring up through green, almost opaque water at her sister's body floating above her—eyes wide open, arms and legs sprawled. Blood flowed out from her sister's mouth and left a dark cloud in the water. *Cold. I'm so cold.*

"I interrupted you," Strongheart said. "Please go on. You were saying that Wink came in and comforted you after your father's death."

She closed her eyes and forced herself to breathe. "I don't think we spoke much, but Wink was there every time Mother burst in and started ranting at me. While I shivered, Wink screamed back, trying to protect me."

When she opened her eyes, Strongheart was peering at her with a strange expression—not sympathy, more like anxious curiosity. "You must have loved her for that."

"The love for Wink that was born in my heart that day will never go away, no matter what Wink does, or fails to do."

"Then it must be difficult for you to know that she sent you here."

Angrily, she answered, "No one, *no one*, will ever convince me that Wink betrayed me! If she sent me here it's because she truly believes I need to be Healed and you can do it."

Dear gods, I've betrayed her. . . .

Sora shook her head. Despite what she thought she remembered Wink saying, it simply was not in Wink to do something like that.

Though . . . she was brilliant at political intrigue and deception.

Sora's pulse increased, pounding in her ears. Blessed gods, is that what was really going on? She was caught up in some elaborate plan that Wink had spawned to . . . accomplish what?

"Priest Strongheart?" a man called from outside. "May we enter?"

Strongheart stared at the door curtain, and his jaw clenched. He whispered, "Hurry. Finish your clams. I'll occupy them for as long as I can."

Sora gobbled down the last few bites while she watched Strongheart slowly walk to the door, pull the leather curtain aside, and drape it back over a peg on the door frame. Two men stood outside, their tall bodies silhouetted against the lavender gleam of sunset. Warriors. They both carried clubs in their fists and wore painted deerskin loincloths.

Strongheart said, "Whose orders do you carry?"

"The Council of Elders requests that you bring the prisoner out so that our people might see their chief's murderer."

Strongheart looked back at Sora.

She set her bowl aside and unsteadily got to her feet. When she looked down at her dress, she blinked. It did not belong to her. It was one of Wink's best dresses. *She dressed me for the journey.* Pearls covered the bodice of the finely woven sky blue dress.

Sora made an effort to smooth her hair and the wrinkles from her sleeves; then she drew herself up and said, "I did not murder your chief, but I will face your people."

She squared her shoulders and walked forward. The warriors backed away to allow her to exit. Just before she ducked out, Strongheart touched her shoulder, stopping her.

In a bare whisper, he said, "Our people are forbidden to speak with new prisoners, but that does not mean they will obey. No matter what they ask, tell them only that you do not recall the murder. My people have great sympathy for those whose souls are wandering the forest lost and alone. They have no sympathy for the arrogant."

She swallowed hard. "I understand."

As she ducked beneath the curtain, the crowd eddied and a din of hushed voices filled the air. Wide eyes fastened on her. Both men and women wore their hair long and had pointed fingernails that could clearly be used as weapons. Perhaps fifty people had gathered to see her, but she recognized no one of any status. They were all commoners, wearing rough colorless garments and ordinary shell bracelets, necklaces, and carved wooden earpins. Interestingly, only a few people had tattoos, and they were of simple design. Nothing like the intricate geometric wonders that covered Strongheart's body.

If tattoos are a sign of rank, where are all of the elite? The rulers? As a common act of courtesy they ought to be here to first lay eyes upon a foreign chieftess.

A man in the rear of the crowd, said, "Blessed Spirits, she's more beautiful than the Traders claimed!"

A woman responded, "Yes, but look at her eyes. Her reflection-soul is not there. You can tell it's out wandering!"

People shoved each other to get a better look at her eyes. As they hissed behind their hands and pointed at her, Sora tried to take in as much of her surroundings as she could.

In the distance, a larger crowd had gathered around a low mound. Each person held a bowl in his or her hands. Sora couldn't see what was in the bowls, but the mound, ten body lengths across, was made of sand and stood six hands tall. On top of the mound, seven people stood around the corpse of a young girl. Heavily tattooed and wearing shining copper necklaces, they were old and gray-headed, probably elders. One of the women braced her walking stick, then stepped forward to sprinkle powdered red ochre over the dead body. Her quavery old voice carried on the wind, but the crowd around Sora was too noisy; she couldn't understand any of the words.

"Who died?" Sora asked Strongheart.

"Elder Littlefield's niece. That is her family burial mound."

"What happened to the girl?"

"A Night-goer cast a spell upon her. She suffered from the Rainbow Black."

Sora searched her memory, struggling to recall everything she could about Loon People witches. She knew they were called "Night-goers," but she'd never heard of the Rainbow Black.

"What is this illness? I don't know it."

"It is a dizziness where the victim sees rainbows, then falls down and jerks all over." He pulled his gaze from the burial and studied her for several intense moments. "I have heard that you suffer from the Rainbow Black."

She couldn't find the words to speak.

"Your former husband told me," he explained.

From the age of seven winters, an Evil Spirit had tormented Sora. As the world went black, two gleaming eyes burned to life inside her. It came like a glittering blue torrent spilling out of the night, and the next thing she knew she woke with a mouthful of blood feeling exhausted. She remembered nothing of what happened after the eyes sprang to life. During her tenth winter she'd named the creature the Midnight Fox. Her mother had told her that when the Fox came Sora fell to the ground and her jaws snapped together like a foaming-mouthed dog's. Throughout her childhood, her mother had sent her to one Healer after another. She'd eaten so many Spirit Plants that even the smell of them now sickened her. As she'd grown up, the Fox seemed to come less often, but she still felt him watching her, always there, right behind her eyes, ready to leap for her throat when she least suspected it.

"Couldn't you cure her?" She gestured to the burial mound. "You are, after all, the most Powerful priest in this region."

He smiled sadly. "There are many Night-goers who are far more Powerful than I am."

"Then what makes you think you can cure me?"

His smile faded. "I'm not sure I can. First I must determine why your reflection-soul won't stay home, what it's afraid of."

"Afraid of?"

"Yes. There's something in your body that keeps driving it away. My task, if my people allow it, will be to find out what it is, and how it got inside you."

The Fox . . .

"Can't you give me a potion, some Spirit Plant, to make me remember?"

The mournful look he gave her told the answer was no.

And she realized that since she'd seen seven winters, she'd been begging people for a potion to fix her life. First, she'd begged her mother. Then she'd begged Flint. Yet no potion, no plant, no plea to the gods had been able to kill the monster that nested inside her. She had come to believe that she and the Fox were intertwined like ancient lovers whose limbs had grown together over the eons. If one of them died, she was certain the other would, too.

Elder Littlefield wept loudly as she wrapped the body of her niece in a bright cloth; then all seven elders gripped the blanket and helped to lower the girl into the grave. After the mourners walked away from the mound, the people who'd been standing below came forward to empty their bowls of sand into the hole, covering the girl.

Sora took the opportunity to more closely examine Eagle Flute Village. It consisted of around thirty domelike houses spaced five body lengths apart, and arranged in a rough square that ran forty body lengths per side. Only two houses stood in the middle of the square: the Priest's House and what she guessed was the Chief's House. The village population appeared to be about three hundred, perhaps three hundred and fifty—small in comparison to her own Blackbird Town, where over one thousand people lived. A ring of magnolias encircled the village, and a short distance away she saw a vast marsh filled with reeds and fluttering birds. All around the marsh, fields of corn, beans, and squash glistened an unearthly green.

"There is our new chief," Strongheart said, and pointed.

She craned her neck to see the young man over the heads of the crowd as he stepped out of the largest house in the village. Almost twice the size of Strongheart's house, the chief's residence stood four body lengths tall and eight across. Horned Owl wore only a leather skirt and held . . . *her ceremonial celt!*

Her mouth fell open, and Strongheart said, "Yes, I know that belonged to you."

"Where did Horned Owl get it?"

"Flint gave it to him."

Angry confusion filled her.

Tattoos covered Horned Owl's skin, spiraling across his face like tightly coiled serpents, then winding around his arms, chest, and legs. He had a supercilious air about him. As he waved to call up his guards, the movement seemed exaggerated, almost comical. Four men stepped forward to surround him.

She started to ask a question, but her voice faded when the Loon war chief, Grown Bear, stepped out behind the new chief, followed by Flint.

A mixture of anger and longing filled her. Tall and muscular, Flint had seen thirty-two winters, but his long hair was still black, his handsome face with its chiseled features unmarked by the wrinkles of most men his age. A crude but attractive cape adorned his broad shoulders—clearly a gift from the Loon People. Made from woven hanging moss and decorated with circlets of abalone shell, it shimmered wildly in the pewter gleam that streamed through the magnolias.

Five very beautiful young women exited and stood behind Flint. They smiled shyly, as though proud to be near him.

As she had once been.

"Are those the young women being offered to Flint?"

Strongheart nodded. "Yes. I suspect he will accept all five as his wives. It will increase his prestige in our lands."

Chief Horned Owl turned, saw Sora standing outside Strongheart's lodge, and his eyes narrowed. He stalked across the village toward her. Flint said something to his future wives, who nodded. As he rushed to follow Horned Owl, the women sat down in a circle and began whispering excitedly. Grown Bear brought up the rear, accompanied by the four guards the young chief had motioned to earlier.

Strongheart whispered, "I've told him you are sick, not evil. That you have no memory of the murder. Do not make me out a liar, or we will both regret it."

"I *don't* remember it. Because I didn't do it."

She squared her shoulders as the crowd parted, leaving a pathway for the young chief, who tramped down it like an executioner with orders to carry out.

About her height, he had dark brown eyes and a sharply pointed narrow nose. He stopped before her, and the crowd went as quiet as the hush before a hurricane. They seemed to be waiting to see if he would strike her dead.

"Did you murder my father?" he demanded to know in a high, boy's voice.

Sora stared straight at him. "Truly, I don't know. I remember almost nothing from that night."

Flint shouldered through the crowd and stood behind Horned Owl. After fourteen winters of marriage, she knew his every gesture, every expression. Beneath that serene exterior, his guts were knotted up. He gave Strongheart a desperate glance.

Strongheart said, "Matron Wink's messenger told me that she is very ill, my chief. She needs our help. If our people will allow me to—"

"Silence!" the youth ordered. "I haven't even decided if she will live through the night, let alone if I will allow the Loon People's greatest Healer to cure her! Why should I? She killed my father!"

Strongheart bowed his head and softly answered, "Our people are wise and kind, my chief. I think they will be generous."

Sora gave Strongheart an askance look. How cleverly he'd reminded the new chief that the decision was not his, but his people's.

It seemed to humble Horned Owl. He turned back to Sora and lowered his chin. "Ordinarily the Loon People do not kill those who are ill; instead we work very hard to cure them. Death is only considered if the sick person cannot be cured and continues to harm others. We—"

"Then our peoples have similar beliefs, Chief Horned Owl. We gather the sick person in our arms—"

In the shrill voice of an angry child, he shouted, "Do not ever interrupt me again or I will send your pretty head back to Matron Wink in a net fishing bag!"

Sora just stared. Was he that politically inept?

Horned Owl continued, "Your former husband, the hero Flint, has told me a great many things about you. He says that my father is not the first person you have murdered. He says that in order to become chieftess you drowned your older sister, who by all rights should have ascended to the chieftainship after your mother. He also claims that when your mother, Chieftess Yellow Cypress, disagreed with you about a decision to go to war, you shoved her over a cliff. Did you kill your own mother?"

Her face flushed. What was Flint doing? Trying to help her or get her killed?

"I don't remember killing anyone."

Strongheart added, "I have examined her, my chief, and I believe she's telling the truth. She does not remember because her reflection-soul isn't home when the killings happen; it's out wandering the forests."

Without taking his eyes from Sora, Horned Owl asked, "Can you find her lost soul and bring it to her body?"

Strongheart gestured uncertainly. "I don't know, but I would like to try."

Flint stepped forward and said, "If Strongheart Heals her, I assure you the Black Falcon Nation will be very grateful. They will shower the Loon People with wealth, my chief."

The youth's dark eyes gleamed, as though he could already see the bright fabrics, woven buffalo wool capes, and exotic Trade items. "As you know, Chieftess Sora, my people are poor and hungry. Not more than a moon ago we discovered eleven Black Falcon villagers stealing food from our gathering grounds. We captured them and have been working to come to a fair agreement that pays us for the damage they caused, but your people have been arrogant. You, yourself, were supposed to meet with my father twenty days ago to negotiate the release of the captives, but you never came. Your war party camped outside our village and an ugly man named Walking Bird came in to negotiate the release of hostages. You didn't come. You disgraced my father."

Twenty days ago? Blessed gods, she didn't remember it at all. . . .

She said, "I'm here now. I will discuss any arrangements you think are fair."

Horned Owl imperiously waved a hand. "Take her to the Captives' House. We will decide her fate tomorrow."

Strongheart took Sora's arm, said, "Of course, my chief," and led her away through the whispering crowd. Two warriors followed close behind them.

The Captive's House stood at the eastern edge of the village surrounded on three sides by the shallow marsh. Mist had begun to curl and twist through the tall reeds. As Dusk Girl spread her gray hem over the land, insects crept from their hiding places and climbed upward in a glittering haze.

They neared the house—perhaps four body lengths across—and Sora heard voices, a child crying, then a woman speaking in a soothing voice. Six guards encircled the house.

"Don't try to escape," Strongheart said when he stopped before the door. "There are many warriors posted around the village. They have orders to kill you immediately if you try to run."

Sora looked up into Strongheart's brown eyes and said, "Will you come for me at dawn tomorrow?"

Wind fluttered black hair around his troubled face. "Yes."

He untied his cape, removed it, and draped it around her shoulders. "Here, you'll need this."

Startled, she asked, "Why?"

"You are a captive of the Loon Nation, Chieftess. You are about to experience many things you have never experienced before."

AS HE PULLED ASIDE THE DOOR CURTAIN, STRONG-heart leaned close to her ear to whisper, "Remember, there are spies everywhere. Don't say anything you do not wish our chief to know."

Sora hesitated for an instant, wondering why he would warn her; then she ducked into the Captives' House, and silence fell like a stone blanket. The scents of urine and stale sweat were strong.

She looked around. Her eyes needed time to adjust, but she could see the vague outlines of people sitting around the circumference of the walls. Weren't they allowed to have a fire to cook and warm them? Two large pots sat along the wall to her right, probably for human wastes.

"Feather Dancer?" she called.

From the rear, a tall shadow rose. "Chieftess?" He

sounded surprised, as though she'd just awakened him from a sound sleep. "Blessed gods, we feared they'd killed you."

"Not yet."

The house burst into whispers, and people began to stand up.

"Chieftess Sora!" a young woman exclaimed. She pushed forward until she could see Sora clearly; then tears filled her eyes and she fell to her knees to kiss Sora's sandals. "The guards told us you were dead! They said Horned Owl had ordered you tortured and killed. None of us ever expected to see you again!"

She placed a hand on the woman's dirty hair, and it was like lighting a flame for moths. From everywhere, people rushed forward and hands reached out to touch Sora's garments, arms, feet. She touched as many as she could reach.

A din built, people weeping and asking questions:

"Chieftess, my five-winters-old son was with me when we were attacked. He was not captured. Is he here? In the village? Did they tell you about him?"

"Chieftess, there's a war party coming for us, isn't there?"

". . . my daughter survived. I saw her run away! Can you tell me if she made it back to Oak Leaf Village?"

"Chieftess—"

"I don't know, I'm sorry!" she called. "Truly, I haven't been in the Black Falcon Nation for days. Some of your relatives did make it home safely, but I have no information about specific people. Flint is here. Perhaps he knows. I'm sure he'll visit with you soon."

"Flint . . . Flint is here?" His name passed through the house like the hiss of a flame.

A middle-aged man came forward and knelt just out of her reach. He had filthy gray-streaked black hair and desperate eyes. Wrinkles incised his forehead and carved deep grooves around his mouth.

"Chieftess, please, I am Cold Spring. My wife was wounded during the fight. They took her to Strongheart to be Healed. Our guards said you were also taken there. Is my wife still in his house? Did you see her? How is she?"

Sora had seen no one else, which meant the woman had probably died. Hadn't anyone told this man about his wife's fate? Were the Loon People so cruel?

"I was not in Strongheart's house for long, Cold Spring. I woke, ate a few bites of stew, then guards came and ordered me outside. There could have been ten people there that I did not see. I'm sorry."

He sighed and quietly receded into the darkness.

As her eyes adjusted, she saw the cold fire hearth in the middle of the floor and the wood stacked beside it—and there were children, two girls and three boys. They sat together to her right, staring at her with wide eyes. One girl, who'd seen perhaps twelve winters, had her arms wrapped tightly around her drawn-up knees. She was biting her lower lip as though to keep words locked in her mouth. A pretty child, a long black braid draped the front of her tattered red-and-blue cape.

"My soul is happy to see you alive, Chieftess," Feather Dancer said, and worked his way forward.

When he stood in front of her, she could see his heavily scarred face. The white ridges of tissue gleamed in the faint light penetrating around the door curtain. He'd tied his long black hair back with a cord. Blood, old and brown, streaked his cape.

Concerned, she pointed to it. "Are you well? Were you injured?"

"Flint struck me in the head with a club to keep me from fighting Grown Bear's war party." An undercurrent of suppressed fury roughened his voice. "My souls were jarred loose for a time, but they're back now. I'm well enough."

Sora glanced down at the people kneeling around her feet. They stared up at Feather Dancer in shock and anger.

An old white-haired woman growled, "Why would Flint do that? He is my cousin's son. He would never—"

Sora interrupted, "I also have many questions for my war chief. I give each of you my oath that I will speak with you in the days to come, but right now I must hear Feather Dancer's words."

People murmured to each other as they moved back to allow her to pass. She gestured for Feather Dancer to walk with her to the rear of the house.

"I count only ten people, Feather Dancer. We heard they'd taken eleven hostages," she said and sat down. The thatched wall felt cool against her back.

Feather Dancer crouched to her left. "Cold Spring's wife was the other captive."

Every eye was upon her. She studied their gaunt faces. In addition to the five children and Cold Spring, there were three women and one young warrior who wore his injured arm in a sling. Blood darkened his shoulder bandage. They resembled mice hiding in a hole from a wolf.

"You've been outside?" she asked.

Feather Dancer nodded. "They come for us every morning just before dawn. They're clearing fields for crops. We chop the trees down and cut out the brush and palmettos."

"How long have we been here?"

"Two days."

The news flustered her. The sleeping potion must have been very strong to keep her shadow-soul away for so long. She swallowed hard. "What are their defenses like?"

"The Loon Nation is frightened, Chieftess. They have warriors behind every tree and in many of the branches to watch over the trails."

"If we all work together, is there any chance we can escape?"

He shook his head. "No. They are too many, and we are too few. They'll just shoot us down."

Sora studied his defeated expression. "What if we created a diversion that required every guard in the forest to fight off an incoming war party? We could flee while they were occupied, couldn't we?"

Feather Dancer looked up skeptically. "Do you have a secret army hiding in the forest that might create such a diversion?"

An unnatural hush fell over the house. The people seemed to be holding their breaths to hear every word she and Feather Dancer said.

"No," she answered with a tired sigh. "But I'll figure something out. If I live long enough."

"When will they decide your fate?"

"Tomorrow, I think. The new chief has called a village meeting at dawn. I should know by midday."

Feather Dancer glared at the floor for a time. "What about Strongheart? Has he agreed to Heal you?"

He'd said the word "Heal" as though it were a curse. Feather Dancer clearly did not believe she was sick, and she recalled that on the journey he'd repeatedly accused Flint of plotting her downfall.

"Strongheart told me that Wink had sent a runner to ask if he would be willing to Heal me, and he'd said yes. But he also told me that, since I'm accused of killing Blue Bow, he's uncertain if he can now keep that promise."

Unpleasant thoughts danced behind Feather Dancer's dark eyes. The white ridges of scars that crisscrossed his face twitched.

"What's wrong?" she softly asked.

"Things are beginning to make sense. Matron Wink told me we were taking you to Priest Long

Lance in the far north, but if she'd already sent a runner to Strongheart she knew we were going to be captured by Grown Bear."

Sora swallowed hard. "You think she was working with Flint to make sure we were captured?"

He seemed to be pondering that dire possibility. "Did Strongheart say when the runner arrived?"

"No."

"But he obviously arrived before we did. That means our matron must have dispatched him a day or two before we left Blackbird Town."

"Or a moment or two," Sora defended.

"Believe what you wish, Chieftess."

"If Wink wanted me captured, why did she order you to accompany Flint? She could have simply sent me off with Flint and saved the life of her very valuable war chief."

A half-smile turned his lips, but it wasn't pleasant. "Perhaps I am not as valuable as you imagine."

"What do you mean?"

Feather Dancer sat down cross-legged and looked around the dark house. As evening settled outside, starlight etched a narrow silver line around the doorway. "By now, her son, Long Fin, has already replaced you as chief of the Black Falcon Nation. Would you want a man loyal to the old chieftess to stay on as your son's war chief?"

She leaned back against the thatch wall; it rustled. "No. I wouldn't."

"It would seem that our matron found a very clever way of getting rid of both of us."

Sora pulled Strongheart's cape more tightly around her. The night breeze shoved the door curtain; a chill entered the house along with the rich green fragrance of the marsh.

"None of this makes sense," she whispered. "Long Fin was next in line anyway. It was inevitable that he would become chief after I was gone. Why would Wink wish to rush that?"

His gaze moved around the house, studying each captive's expression. "There are two reasons a person betrays a friend, Chieftess: love and wealth."

"You mean someone paid her?"

He gave her a strange look. "You don't recall the controversy over the jade?"

"Jade? What jade?"

He clenched his jaw. "Ten days before Blue Bow was lanced through the throat, his war chief, Grown Bear, came to Blackbird Town with a beautiful jade brooch. He said that he and a war party had paddled south along the coast for sixteen days, where they'd met the Scarlet Macaw People, who claimed they'd give him boatloads of jade if Grown Bear would only send a large war party to help them kill the quarry's owners."

Memories crept back, a thin tendril at a time. "Yes, I—I recall some moments of the council meeting about the jade. The elders were split. Wink voted against me. She wanted to send warriors after the jade."

"Yes. At this very moment, I suspect she's assembling a vast war party to do just that."

Sora shook her head. "I don't believe it. It's too dangerous. She's smarter than that."

Cold Spring walked across the floor and knelt before the fire pit. He pulled a stick from the woodpile and began dragging coals from beneath a thick bed of ash. They must have saved the morning coals, hoping they would flare to life when they returned from their work. He arranged kindling over the coals and blew on them. Ash puffed and swirled in the starlight like frost crystals. The man repeatedly glanced at Feather Dancer and Sora, but said nothing.

Sora scanned the house, looking for blankets, water gourds, pots of food.

"Are they feeding you?" she asked.

"They feed us thin corn gruel in the morning and give each of us one water bag to drink while we work. That's all." He tipped his chin to the fire pit. "We're only allowed ten sticks of wood per day, so if we wish to stay warm during the night, we can't light the fire until well after dark."

"No blankets? Not even for the children?"

He shook his head. "We have five capes for eleven of us. We try to sleep two people beneath each cape. Three of the children sleep beneath one cape."

Exhausted, she massaged her forehead. "Blue Bow told me the captives were being well-treated."

"For captives, we *are* being well-treated."

Ten winters ago, Feather Dancer had been captured and tortured by the barbarian Lily People. He'd lasted eight days. Finally, when his captors thought him too weak to oppose them, he'd risen up, killed his guards, and fought his way through the village to escape.

None of these captives showed torture wounds. They had food in their bellies and the capes they'd brought with them. Feather Dancer was right; they were being well-treated.

The fire crackled to life, and a soft yellow gleam filled the lodge. She fingered Strongheart's cape, understanding suddenly what he'd meant when he'd said she would need it. "Thank the gods we will have one more cape tonight."

"Yes. You might wish to ask young Pipit to share your cape. Somehow, in the night, her cape always winds up tucked around the two younger children she sleeps with. When the adults scold her and tell her she's going to make herself sick, she claims she doesn't know how it happened."

"Which one is Pipit?"

Feather Dancer turned to look at the twelve-winters-old girl she had noticed earlier. "That's Pipit—in the red-and-blue cape. Her mother and father were both killed in the fight at our gathering grounds, but she doesn't seem to realize it."

"What do you mean?"

"Every time the guards take us to a work site, Pipit tells the other children to keep watch for her parents, because they're coming to save her. Old Jawbone says her reflection-soul is loose." He gestured to the woman sitting with her white head propped on her knees. She looked too weary to move.

"Do you think," she asked quietly, "that Grown

Bear is organizing the war party to go south for the jade?"

"No, I don't. I've listened very carefully to the guards talking among themselves. Not one has mentioned longing to be chosen for the party. They seem to know nothing about this precious jade." He paused, and his teeth ground beneath his scarred jaw. "Unless, of course, he's working for himself, assembling a war party in secret, and his men are under a death sentence if they speak of it aloud."

"I don't understand."

"Nor do I. But I'm beginning to think that Grown Bear made up the story about traveling south to meet the Scarlet Macaw People. The night he died, Blue Bow told Long Fin that he knew nothing about the jade brooch."

Sora's head suddenly ached, as though a memory was struggling to rise through the cottony haze caused by the sleeping potion. "Then . . . where did Grown Bear get it?"

"All I know is that hundreds of warriors from your husband's village believe it came from the Scarlet Macaw People, and are willing to do anything to get it. They believe they are joining with two hundred warriors from this village."

Her head snapped up. "Rockfish's people promised warriors?"

"Yes, Chieftess, three hundred."

"But if Eagle Flute Village is not preparing warriors to go south after the jade, what will happen when Rockfish's warriors get here?"

Feather Dancer seemed to be able to track her thoughts across her souls. He said, "Who says they're coming here?"

"Well, isn't that the plan?"

Very softly, he replied, "I'm almost certain that Rockfish's three hundred warriors will head straight to Blackbird Town, where they will be joined by a few hundred of our warriors, and together they'll march south for the Scarlet Macaw People."

"Dear gods, do you think my husband could be working with Grown Bear—" She stopped.

Cold Spring had cocked an ear and was obviously straining to hear their words. Feather Dancer gave the man a lethal look.

Cold Spring rose and hurried back to his place along the far wall. The woman next to him murmured a question, but Cold Spring just shook his head and looked away.

"It's probably nothing," she said. "He's as eager to understand what's going on as we are."

Feather Dancer kept glowering at Cold Spring. "Where is Flint? Did you see him?"

"Yes." She sighed. "By betraying me, he's become the local hero. Horned Owl has been feasting him and offering Flint his choice of the village maidens."

Feather Dancer's face contorted into a grimace. "If I didn't want to kill him so much, I'd feel sorry for him."

"Yes. He's an Outcast now. He will never be able to return to the Black Falcon Nation. He will only have a home among our enemies, and he had better pray that our enemies don't suddenly wish to become our friends, because he will be the first prize offered as a sign of their good faith."

She'd seen it happen. When an alien people wanted to create a political alliance with the Black Falcon Nation, a traitor was often sent as a gift. He was killed, of course.

Deep inside her, she uttered a soft prayer that the Loon People never wanted to ally themselves with the Black Falcon Nation—but . . . if Feather Dancer was wrong, and the Loon Nation *was* sending warriors to join the jade war party, Wink and Horned Owl would very likely forge an alliance.

Either way, Flint must know his days are numbered.

Feather Dancer said, "You should sleep."

"I've been sleeping for days."

"You will need your strength, Chieftess. Please listen to me. Rest whenever they let you."

His worried expression told her far more than his words. Was he afraid they were going to torture her tomorrow?

"Yes, you're right." She touched his arm gratefully, rose, and walked around the fire toward Pipit.

The little girl anxiously gazed up at her.

"I am Chieftess Sora," she said as she knelt. "Would you like to share my cape tonight?"

Pipit's eyes widened. "Will you be warm enough if I do?"

"I think we'll both be warmer." Sora stretched out

on the floor and held Strongheart's cape open. Pipit crawled inside and cautiously lay down. As Sora lowered the cape to cover the girl, she said, "Sleep well, Pipit."

She was silent for a long while; then she whispered, "I can't."

"Why is that?"

Pipit licked her lips. "My mother whispers to me all night long. I don't know how she gets into the village past the guards, but she stands just outside the lodge and calls and calls my name, trying to get me to come outside."

A chill prickled Sora's spine. Had the woman's soul been so worried about Pipit that it had remained on earth and become a homeless ghost? Homeless ghosts frequently went insane and drove their loved ones' reflection-souls into the forest, where they, too, became homeless ghosts.

She hugged Pipit. "Well, try to sleep. You need your rest so that you can work tomorrow."

"Yes, I know, but I don't want my mother to think I'm being bad. If you hear her calling me, will you tell her I'm not ignoring her? I'm just asleep."

"Of course, I'll tell her."

How strange that the girl still feared being "bad." Pipit's mother must have scolded her often for not listening to her. Or was there more to it? Had Pipit ignored her mother's voice during the battle, and that's why she was captured?

"What happened to your father, Pipit?"

"Oh, he's well, thank you. He watches over me,

day and night. Sometimes I see him sneaking through the forest just beyond where we're working. He can't get too close, because of the guards, but he smiles at me."

All around the lodge, people spoke in weary tones as they crawled beneath their capes. Sora noticed that Feather Dancer shared his cape with the young wounded warrior.

Pipit craned her neck to look up at her. "Thank you for coming, Chieftess. We were frightened before you arrived. We're stronger now. We know your warriors are coming to rescue us."

The words were like thorns driven into Sora's heart. She wondered how on earth she was going to accomplish such a rescue.

She stroked Pipit's black hair. "Yes. They're coming. I promise you they are. Just stay alive, and you'll be free."

8

HIGH MATRON WINK DUCKED BENEATH THE leather door curtain and into the council chamber. As she marched toward the four log benches that framed the fire hearth, the shells sewn around the hem of her pale green dress flashed. "A pleasant evening to you, Sea Grass."

Sea Grass, matron of Oak Leaf Village, looked up. The old white-haired woman sat on the south bench, to Wink's right, holding a beautiful bundle on her lap. The fabric was exquisite, tightly woven in red, black, and blue stripes. "Did you bring it?"

"Yes." Wink held up the wooden box.

"Good. I wish to see it before I take my son home in the morning."

Sea Grass petted the fabric bundle, and tears filled her eyes. The cleaned bones of her murdered son,

War Chief Skinner, were inside, along with his eye-soul, which stayed with the body forever.

Wink sat down opposite Sea Grass and placed the wooden box on the bench between them. They gazed at each other, probably both thinking about her son. No one knew the exact details. Feather Dancer had found War Chief Skinner lying dead in the forest beside Sora. Both had been naked. Clearly Skinner had tried to kill Sora; his fingers were still wrapped around her throat, and she'd been clubbed in the head. In some still-unexplained way, Sora had apparently managed to slip poison into Skinner's cup before he attempted her murder. When he'd started to feel the poison invade his veins, he must have attacked her.

Wink expelled a breath and pulled her gaze from Sea Grass.

All around the walls, the sacred masks picked up the reflections of the firelight, and the empty eye sockets flared.

"Sea Grass, I hope you were satisfied with the way Priest Teal prepared your son for the journey to the afterlife."

"There is no one better than Teal. I know my son's reflection-soul is safely in the Land of the Dead with our Blessed Ancestors." She tucked a loose strand of white hair behind her ear and patted the bundle. "I will take his eye-soul home and place it in our charnel house so that my son can advise the Water Hickory Clan for the rest of our time on earth."

The hurt in Sea Grass's voice touched Wink. "I'm

deeply sorry this happened, Sea Grass. You must know that Shadow Rock Clan will help—"

"Your chieftess killed my son, Matron. You've *helped* far too much already."

Wink's lips pressed into a tight line, not knowing what to say to that. "Sora is sick. She has an Evil Spirit inside her. We are doing our best to find a Healer. Flint and Feather Dancer should have passed your village two days ago, and by now are well on their way northward to Priest Long Lance's country."

Sea Grass gave her a cold look. "What if he can't Heal her? Many have tried, including Teal, the best priest in the Black Falcon Nation. All failed."

"Just let me try one more time, Sea Grass. I beg you. If Long Lance can't cast out the Spirit, then find her wandering reflection-soul and make it stay in her body . . . I . . . I will carry out my responsibilities to keep our nation safe."

Sea Grass's eyes narrowed. Her voice came out a hiss: "You should have killed her long ago, Wink. If you had, my son would be alive, as would many other people."

Wink clenched her jaw to keep the hot words inside. After news of the murders and the failed Healing Circle spread across the Black Falcon world, there would be many who agreed with Sea Grass.

"You asked to see the jade brooch that Chief Blue Bow ordered War Chief Grown Bear to bring to Sora. Do you still wish to?" Wink shoved the box across the bench toward the old woman.

Sea Grass glanced at it, but didn't touch it. "First,

I would like to hear, from your lips, the story of how it came to Blackbird Town."

"Of course." Wink explained, "Grown Bear said his party paddled south along the coastline for sixteen days until they met the Scarlet Macaw People. They were idolaters, with strange ways, but he Traded with them. He brought Sora the brooch in this box to prove to her—to all of us—how valuable that Trade could be."

"Rockfish, the chieftess' husband, told me it could be very lucrative. He also said that Grown Bear had asked us to commit warriors to a war party that would attack the enemies of the Scarlet Macaw People, who own the quarry, so that we might take the jade."

"That's right. Sora thought it too dangerous. She said that Blue Bow was asking us first to ally with him, our enemy, then to send our warriors south to ally with an unknown people, to fight a foe whose numbers and strength we did not know, to gain access to a quarry that might not even exist. She thought it could be a trap."

"Rockfish told me his people had committed three hundred warriors to go after the jade."

Wink nodded. "They did. Rockfish's people promised three hundred. Blue Bow promised two hundred, which is practically every warrior in his village. That makes five hundred. Rockfish's will be here in a few days; then they'll march off to meet the Loon warriors, climb into their canoes, and head south around the gulf. At least that's the plan."

Sea Grass gave Wink a hard glare. "But we have committed no warriors to go after the jade?"

"Our council vote was three to two against it."

"Really? I heard that you voted *for* sending warriors. Was I misinformed?"

"Originally, I did vote yes, but I changed my vote."

Sea Grass's wrinkles rearranged into suspicious lines. "Why?"

"Because I decided Sora was right. It's too dangerous."

While Wink was the matron of the Shadow Rock Clan, and ruler of the Black Falcon Nation, there were three other clans: Matron Wood Fern ruled the Water Hickory Clan, Matron Black Birch headed the Bald Cypress Clan, and Wigeon was in charge of the Shoveler Clan. In addition, each clan village had a matron and a chief who answered to the clan matrons, and finally, to High Matron Wink and High Chieftess Sora.

Sea Grass straightened her hunched shoulders. "Your son is now the high chief of the Black Falcon Nation. What is his opinion about this jade?"

Wink folded her arms over her chest. She didn't like the way this discussion was going. Sea Grass was a shrewd old leader. What was she after? "My son is *temporarily* the high chief. He will, of course, step down when Sora returns."

Sea Grass's eyes turned glassy, as if she didn't believe Wink. "Before he became the chief, Long Fin was in favor of joining the war party, wasn't he?"

"Yes, but I see no reason to reconvene the council at this time. We need to keep our warriors here, in case—"

"Your son may be a 'temporary' high chief, but he still has a vote in the council, doesn't he?"

Wind whimpered around the walls of the Matron's House and rustled the thatch roof; it sounded like a thousand tiny teeth trying to gnaw their way in.

Wink said, "Are you in favor of committing warriors to the party?"

The old woman tilted her white head. "No, I support our clan matron, Wood Fern. But there are other members of my clan who believe that a few boatloads of stone would help to compensate Oak Leaf Village for the loss of our war chief."

"Are you saying that these 'other members' believe your son's life is worth the blood of hundreds of Black Falcon warriors?"

Sea Grass shifted on the bench. "Let us speak straightly, Wink. It is customary for the victim's family to claim the life of the murderer, or a member of the murderer's family. But you know as well as I that Water Hickory Clan will never get its hands on Sora, and out of respect we would not claim your life—or another member of the Shadow Rock Clan. The stone has become an attractive substitute."

Wink would not openly say it, but she wondered if that idea hadn't been planted by Rockfish. Perhaps to help save Sora. Perhaps to enrich his people, or himself.

"Canoeloads of jade will not ease your clan's grief, Sea Grass, nor will they assuage your anger."

Wink's words obviously rankled the old woman, but she fought to keep her emotions from showing on her face.

"Tell me something, Matron?" Sea Grass asked in a mild voice, as though merely inquiring. "If one of our clans decided to join the war party, would you object?"

Stunned, Wink replied, "Yes. I certainly would. If any clan disobeyed the council and entered into a private agreement that endangered our nation, it could cause civil war. I'm sure your people care far too much for their relatives to do something that foolish."

Sea Grass's lips curved into a practiced smile. "As it happens, Clan Matron Wood Fern agrees with you. She is vehemently opposed to sending warriors."

"Then why are we discussing this? Unless, of course, Oak Leaf Village plans to send warriors on its own?"

"I would never go against the wishes of our clan matron."

Wink studied her. Was she telling the truth? If Oak Leaf Village disobeyed Wood Fern and joined the war party, Wood Fern would have the right to declare the entire village Outcast. Wink would support that decision. Surely, Sea Grass would not risk that.

"Well," Sea Grass said. "Perhaps I should look at this brooch that everyone is talking about." She gestured to the painted box.

"Please."

Sea Grass pulled the box across the bench and opened the lid. The enormous brooch was magnificent. Rimmed in pure glittering gold, it was the size of two hands put together and made of a green translucent stone that resembled the depths of Mother Ocean's heart.

Sea Grass ran her fingers over it, and a sudden glint of curiosity lit her eyes. She said, "How strange."

"What do you mean?"

"Well, I could be wrong, but I'm fairly certain I've seen this before."

"Grown Bear just brought it. How could you—"

"Oh, I don't think so." Sea Grass pulled the brooch from the box and held it in her skeletal hand while she scrutinized it, obviously comparing it to her memory. "If I'm not mistaken, this belonged to High Matron Red Warbler."

"Red Warbler?"

"Yes. Sora's great-grandmother."

Wink's mouth gaped. "Are you sure?"

In a barely audible voice, Sea Grass said, "Oh, yes. She wore it once every winter for the solstice celebrations."

"I don't remember that!"

"You wouldn't. You hadn't been born yet. After Red Warbler ordered the Scarlet Macaw Traders never to set foot in the Black Falcon Nation again, she put it away."

Wink's eyes darted anxiously around the council chamber. "Why didn't she want their Traders—"

"It was a silly matter." Sea Grass waved a hand. "Red Warbler caught one of them stealing copper breastplates from a storehouse. She said that's all they did: They stole our sacred art and our stories, and wanted nothing more than to strip us bare before they conquered us. She ordered everyone in the Black Falcon Nation to cease Trading with them."

Wink inhaled a deep breath and held it while she carefully considered her next words. "It seems we have forgotten that prohibition, doesn't it?"

The lines around Sea Grass's eyes deepened. "The world has changed, Wink. Perhaps the Scarlet Macaw People have changed, too. We know their empire crumbled decades ago. I've heard they're living in a handful of scattered towns, just struggling to maintain their traditions. If there was ever a time to attack them and take what we wish, it is now."

Wink hugged herself. Sea Grass's eager tone was like a blackness eating at her insides. "But Grown Bear *did* bring the brooch to Sora. I saw it before she did."

"Perhaps, but I know for a fact that Red Warbler received many pieces of jewelry from the Scarlet Macaw Traders, as signs of their respect. After she ordered us never to Trade with them again, she put those pieces in a box, and sealed it with boiled pine pitch."

"How do you know that?"

"Sora's grandmother, High Chieftess Grackle, was a good friend to my grandmother, and I used to listen very closely whenever they spoke. Grackle told Grandmother about the box. It was to be handed down through the generations, unopened, in case the Black Falcon Nation ever needed it in an emergency."

"What sort of emergency?"

Sea Grass lifted a bony shoulder. "Who can say? But I assure you those pieces are worth enough to ransom an entire village."

"How many pieces were there, do you know?"

"Not for sure. Ten at least. Maybe twenty."

Twenty pieces of jade jewelry like this would be enough to ransom two villages.

"Thank you, Sea Grass. You've given me something to think about."

"I hope so," she said. The threat was barely hidden beneath her calm voice. "If I were the high matron of the Black Falcon Nation I would be wondering where an enemy war chief obtained such a valuable piece of Black Falcon jewelry."

Their gazes met like the clash of war clubs. Sea Grass would see many Traders on her way back to Oak Leaf Village, which meant that by tomorrow night, half the Black Falcon Nation would be wondering the same thing.

Very soon, Wink would need some answers.

"Well," Wink said, and rose to her feet. "If you have no more questions, I should be about my duties."

Sea Grass grunted as she stood up and handed the

jade brooch back to Wink. "Do you know where the sealed box is?"

"No. Sora never told me about it."

"Then perhaps you should search her belongings to find it. If Blue Bow's grieving relatives convince the Loon council to attack us, we may need such wealth to buy them off."

They stared hard into each other's eyes.

"The Loon Nation doesn't have enough warriors, let alone the wealth necessary, to carry out a sustained war against the Black Flacon people. They are a minor threat at worst."

"I'm sure that's true," she conceded with a contrite nod. "It's just that I have noted over the long winters of my life that oftentimes hatred is more important than numbers or wealth."

Before Wink could respond, Sea Grass clutched her son's bones to her chest and hobbled across the council chamber for the door. When she ducked out, the old woman spoke to her waiting guards, and footsteps whispered down the hallway.

Only the breeze that tousled the door curtain told Wink that Sea Grass and her party had ducked out the front entrance.

She massaged her aching temples.

"Dear gods," she murmured. "What's going on?"

FEATHER DANCER MOVED ALMOST SILENTLY, BUT IT
woke Sora.

Through the smokehole in the roof, she could see
Star People glistening. It had to be long before dawn.

Fabric rustled, as though Feather Dancer had
slipped from beneath the cape he shared with the
young warrior.

Then Sora heard them. Footsteps outside. Coming
toward the Captives' House.

The men stopped just beyond the door, and Flint
sternly said, "Do you remember your orders?"

"Of course we remember, you imbecile. As part
of your reward for helping us to capture her, Horned
Owl said you could take her as many times as you
wished."

"And *when* I wished. Your only duties are to protect me and bring her back if she escapes."

"We know that."

The guards obviously disliked Flint.

"Good," he said with a laugh. "I don't want you to get so snared by my prowess that you forget your responsibilities."

"Your prowess?" The guard snorted. "You are a feeble old man! I heard you couldn't even handle the five virgins Horned Owl presented you today."

"Yes, well, young Purple Blossom is a lioness. Remind me to show you my bruises. It's a wonder I had the strength to crawl away from her."

The men chuckled.

Flint threw the door curtain back, and stepped into the Captives' House. Silhouetted against the starlight, he looked tall and muscular. Long hair spilled over the front of his black cape and shimmered as he gazed around the house. His handsome face was sheathed in silver.

The people who'd awakened murmured, "Flint? *Flint!*" as though his name alone could save them.

Ignoring them, he called, "Sora?"

She propped herself up on one elbow. "What do you want?"

Flint stalked across the floor, grabbed her by the arm, and roughly jerked her to her feet. Almost simultaneously, Pipit let out a startled cry, and Feather Dancer leaped for Flint.

When their bodies collided, the entire house

erupted in a cacophony of shouts and gasps of disbelief. People scuttled back against the walls, leaving just enough room for Feather Dancer to slam Flint to the floor and get his hands around Flint's throat. As the two men rolled and thrashed, Sora shoved Pipit against the wall to protect her.

"Feather Dancer!" Sora shouted. "Not *now*! There are guards outside!"

"Just a few . . . more . . . instants, Chieftess, and I'll kill this traitorous pig!" Feather Dancer growled.

"But the guards—"

Cold Spring lurched to his feet and screamed, "Leave my cousin Flint alone! He's no traitor!"

Flint sounded like he was suffocating, but his hand groped beneath Feather Dancer's warshirt and he managed to gasp, "I'm going to . . . twist off . . . your testicles."

Feather Dancer slammed Flint's head against the floor several times.

Making hideous choking sounds, Flint apparently found what he was searching for, wrenched with all his might, and Feather Dancer roared in pain. As they rolled across the floor, scrambling for advantage, one of the guards outside called, "What's going on in there?"

Sora shouted, "Get in here now! What are you doing? Waiting for Feather Dancer to kill Flint?"

One guard, short and stout, stepped through the doorway with a war club in his hand, idly gazed at the two men locked together on the floor, and began beating Feather Dancer with his club.

Feather Dancer rolled off Flint and covered his head with his arms, which gave Flint the opportunity to stagger to his feet.

"That's enough!" Sora grabbed the guard's arm to prevent him from striking Feather Dancer again. "Stop it!"

She had used her chieftess' voice, which accepted nothing but obedience. The guard, shocked, stopped beating Feather Dancer to stare at her.

She ordered, "Follow me," and ducked through the door into the starlight, where seven men stood in a circle—probably the guards routinely stationed around the Captives' House. They studied Sora with silent glittering eyes. Flint and the guard stepped out behind her. Blood covered Flint's face. He rubbed his throat and gasped for air.

She turned to Flint. "Why did you come for me?"

His full lips twitched with a half-smile. "I'm taking you to the forest, my former wife," he said. "I don't want your screams of ecstasy to wake the entire village."

When Flint grabbed her wrist and flung her toward the starlit trail, he almost jerked her shoulder out of the socket. Stunned by the treatment, she blurted, "Flint, tell me—"

"Just walk." His fist slammed into her back, staggering her.

"That is not necessary!"

"I'll decide what is or is not necessary. For as long as you are alive, you are my slave, Sora. Remember that."

"I am the chieftess of the Black Falcon Nation, and when my army—"

"No," he said with a laugh. "You are nothing. Long Fin took your place days ago."

"I don't believe it. Wink would never—"

Flint snatched a handful of her flying hair and twisted her head around so he could glare into her face. The two guards behind him just watched. "Let me tell you something, Sora. I've made a good bargain with Chief Horned Owl. If you live through tomorrow, he's given me permission to supervise your 'Healing.'"

"Supervise? What does that mean?"

"I convinced Horned Owl that since I know you better than anyone alive, I am the only person who can judge if you've been Healed or not."

If he says I'm not, they'll kill me.

She struggled against his powerful grip, and he almost twisted her neck off. She couldn't help it; the sharp pain made her cry out.

Feather Dancer, yelled, *"Chieftess?"*

His cry was quickly followed by the meaty thumps of war clubs striking flesh.

Flint whispered, *"Remember that you and Feather Dancer live solely by my grace."*

He shoved her hard, and she careened down the trail with her arms flailing for balance. In all the winters they had known each other, even when he'd openly vowed to kill her, he'd never treated her this way.

The path wound around clumps of brush and

dense tangles of grapevines. Through the oaks, she saw a small grassy meadow gleaming in the starlight.

Flint shoved her to the middle of the meadow, then turned to the guards. "Black Turtle, I want you and Snail to go stand over there at the edge of the trees. I don't need you staring over my shoulder."

Both men sneered in disdain, spread their legs, and planted themselves. They didn't move a hair's breadth.

Flint glowered; then he swung around, grabbed Sora, and physically hurled her to the ground. She landed hard enough to knock the wind from her lungs. When she gasped and scrambled to rise, he fell upon her like a wolf and pinned her to the ground.

The guards laughed, causing the flock of birds that had been roosting in the nearby trees to squawk and burst into flight. Their dark wings blotted out the Star People as they sailed away.

Flint stretched out on top of her. His black hair fell around her like a silken midnight curtain. In agony, she gazed into his dark eyes. The sight of him looking down at her with hatred was almost too much to bear.

"Are you ready for me?" he shouted in her face, then ruthlessly kissed her. She tasted blood.

"No, Flint, please don't do this!"

The guards walked closer to watch. Grins spread across their faces when Flint ripped open the front of her dress and began fondling her breasts.

Very softly, she said, "Talk to me! Tell me why—"

He bit her nipple hard enough to make her cry out, and the guards' excited eyes widened. Their manhoods began to bulge through their breechclouts.

"It will be easier for you if you don't fight me," Flint said, and used his knee to pry her legs apart.

When he shoved himself inside and began thrusting, she lifted her fists to strike him. Laughing, he forced her arms to the ground. A hoarse cry of rage escaped her throat.

"Are you happy to be with me again, my sweet murderess?" he whispered in her ear.

"Flint, I would never—"

"Stop talking!"

Blessed gods, he really does hate me.

In less than ten heartbeats, he let out a deep-throated groan of pleasure. "Great Spirits, she holds a man like a fist! I had forgotten."

Snail glanced at Black Turtle and swallowed convulsively. "Are you going to let us have a turn?"

"No," Flint said.

"No?" The youth glowered at him.

"No."

"Why not?"

"Because your chief gave her to me, and when Feather Dancer was trying to choke the life from me, both of you stood outside and listened for far too long."

Snail said, "I'll help you in the future, I give you my oath! Let me have a turn?"

"No. First you must prove yourself. Do as I originally asked. Go stand by the trees while I take her; then I *may* let you have a turn."

Black Turtle slapped him on the shoulder. "Come on. Let's go."

Snail pointed a finger threateningly at Flint. "We'll do it, but don't forget about us."

Snail and Black Turtle trotted to the edge of the trees, and Flint whispered, "Tell me about the captives."

"What?"

"I don't have much time. I need to know how they are. Is anyone hurt?"

She blinked in confusion. "Why do you care?"

"They are my relatives, Sora. I care."

"You can't go home again, Flint. You must realize that. You are an Outcast now."

"I'm worried about them, not me."

He began to move slowly, unhurriedly, as though they had many hands of time to love each other, but not many more days to live. At any other time, she would have thought each motion exquisite. "Is anyone hurt?" he repeated, and kissed her earlobe.

"Yes, one young warrior."

"How badly?"

"He has a wounded shoulder."

"Can he fight?"

"I don't know. Maybe, but why—"

"What about the children?"

"They are frightened, but healthy. Feather Dancer says they are being well-treated for captives."

"Given his experience with torture, he should know, but things may get worse in the near future."

"What do you mean?" As her pain and humiliation began to recede her mind sharpened. Was he trying to warn her so that she might prepare the captives? Perhaps he wanted her to reassure them that he still cared about them.

Against her lips, Flint whispered, "Horned Owl is a brutal child. During the feast, he ordered his slaves to bring him a nest of baby birds. While he ate, he slowly plucked the feathers from each. As the little birds chirped in growing fear, Horned Owl's eyes gleamed like suns. Then he casually threw them into the fire to be burned alive—and he told the people at the feast that very soon they could watch the captives suffer the same fate."

"Is he a monster?"

"Yes. A monster that has just been given a great deal of power."

"Can we stop him before he hurts our people?"

Flint lifted his head, and his lips quirked into a smile. "How odd that you speak as though you are not one of the captives."

"Flint, I don't understand any of this. Why are you working with these people?"

"As you pointed out, I can't go home. Who else will work with me?"

She gripped his muscular forearms and whispered, "Let me help you! Maybe I can—"

"Sora, you amaze me." He laughed softly. "I just betrayed you and you want to help me? That's curious, don't you think? You can't even help yourself, let alone me. Now, please, I have a very important question to ask you."

"What is it?"

Flint slipped his hands beneath her hips and held her in place while he forced himself deeper. Snail and Black Turtle edged closer to watch. Snail had started to breathe hard.

Flint whispered, "Do they hate me?"

"Who?" She frowned up at him.

His dark eyes glistened. "My relatives."

The fear in his voice astounded her. "No. Didn't you hear them when you entered the Captives' House? They don't believe the stories that you betrayed me. The fools think you are as much a hero as the Loon People do. I'm sure they believe you are here to save them."

He squeezed his eyes closed for an instant, but in gratitude or pleasure, she couldn't tell. "Have they asked you any questions?"

"Many. Cold Spring wants to know what happened to his injured wife. Apparently she was taken—"

"She's dead. Her injuries were too severe. Strongheart couldn't Heal her. What else?"

She tried to remember all the questions that were thrust upon her when she'd first entered the Captives' House. "One woman, I don't know her name, said her five-winters-old son wasn't captured in the attack. She—"

"She's wrong. He was captured. The warrior who took the boy adopted him into his family. He's unhappy, but alive and well-fed." Flint began thrusting again, driving himself into her.

Sora watched the agony on his handsome face draining away, turning to rapture.

"Jawbone is worried about her daughter. She said she saw her run away from the—"

"Yes." His voice had constricted, and she could tell he was close. "She did run away. But they tracked her down and killed her."

Flint's back arched and he cried out, stilling the conversation between Black Turtle and Snail. Snail took an eager step forward, waiting to be summoned.

Flint glanced at the youth, then collapsed on top of Sora and murmured, "Tomorrow, during the trial, they may torture you, Sora. For the sake of the gods, do not try to be brave. *Be weak.* Make them pity you."

"But Flint . . ."

He roughly rolled away from her and got to his feet. "Snail?" he called. "Come over here."

"No, Flint, please. Don't let him—"

"I'm going to use every tool I have to accomplish my goals, Sora," he hissed. "Including you."

As Snail trotted up and tugged off his breechclout, he said, "My turn?"

In a nasty voice, Flint answered, "No. It is not your turn. I told you that you have to prove yourself before I let you taste her sweet flesh. The next time someone is trying to kill me, I expect you to help me. And give that message to your friends. If they help me, I'll let them take a turn, too."

SORA WALKED SHAKILY BACK TO THE VILLAGE. SHE felt like her heart had been cut out and left bleeding on the forest floor; but if it took all of her strength, they would never know it.

Behind her, Flint and Black Turtle laughed at something lewd Snail had said.

She kept her eyes on the ground. As the cool evening breeze blew through the palms, their shadows danced over the forest floor like gray silken veils. She concentrated on them to keep her mind off the fact that she longed to lie down in the grass and weep.

Through the trees, she saw Eagle Flute Village. The light of the rising moon gleamed from the faces of enemy warriors, crude thatched houses, and hungry people: things she had feared her entire life.

How was she going to get out of this?

Feather Dancer, if he was alive, would be nursing his wounded body. The other captives were old, or injured, or quivering with fear. They could not help her. In fact, they were looking to her with childlike faith, praying she would get them home safe.

She glanced over her shoulder at the three men following her. They smiled and continued to joke. There had to be a way . . . something she could do. But what?

Without the authority of her former position, she couldn't offer them corn to feed their hungry, or exotic Trade goods to buy them off. Only Wink, Long Fin, and the Council of Elders could make those decisions.

Just as Flint had said, she was nothing.

Her exhausted souls worked the problem, going round and round, coming back to the same dead end.

I am nothing. Flint is right.

She had never felt so powerless.

A palmetto partially blocked the trail. Her numb legs barely felt the brush of the sharp fronds as they scratched her shins.

Blessed gods, this *had* to be a dream. Her shadow-soul must be walking in the dark underworlds where the monsters lived. Surely she would soon wake to the smells of roasting venison and frying corncakes, the high-pitched squeals of children running in the plaza, and Rockfish's soft voice telling her it was very late, that she needed to rise and resume her duties as chieftess of the Black Falcon Nation.

As she stepped out of the forest, soft murmurs filled the air. Every eye seemed to be upon her.

Sora marched toward the guards who ringed the Captives' House, and the two men who blocked the doorway leered at her.

She stopped in front of them and said, "Get out of my way."

The bigger of the two men folded his arms, tipped his chin to something behind her, and said, "I have orders to hold you for him."

Sora turned.

Strongheart flowed through the darkness as though part of it. His cape billowed around his long legs. When he got closer, he glanced at Flint, and said, "I'm sure you won't object if I, too, take a turn with her."

Her heart went cold and dead in her chest.

Flint shifted uncertainly. "Of course not, Priest."

Strongheart took Sora by the arm and guided her away from the Captives' House. As they walked, he said, "You're shaking. Did they hurt you?"

She glanced sidelong at him. Anger had strained his voice.

"No. Given more time, they might have, but Flint was in a hurry."

He led her to his house and held aside the door curtain. "Go in. There are warm blankets by the fire. You must be cold."

Sora ducked into his house and looked around. The firelight silhouetted the baskets and pots that sat beneath the bench encircling the walls. Blankets had been laid out by the fire, as though prepared for her. She walked to them and eased down. Warmth seeped from the cloth and penetrated her damp dress.

Strongheart knelt to her right and studied her for a long time, his gaze taking in the old leaves tangled in her hair and the blood that oozed from her split lip. He was a homely man, his round face too wide, his bulging eyes too big, but he had a powerful presence.

He gestured to her mouth. "Which one did that?"

"Flint." She touched her lip and winced. "He was a little too 'eager.'"

Strongheart didn't say a word. He just rose to his feet, and walked around the fire to the pot that sat in the coals. As he picked it up by the handle, he checked another small pot that perched on the hearthstones and said, "Are you hungry?"

She shook her head. "No. I was, but . . . not now."

"A cup of tea, perhaps?"

"Yes. Thank you."

He dipped a cup into the pot hanging from the tripod at the edge of the flames and handed it to her.

"Won't your chief be angry that I'm here, rather than in the Captives' House?"

"I'll risk it."

Sora drank slowly, savoring the sweet flavors of maple sap and dried cactus fruit. "Why did you help me?"

"You needed my help, didn't you?"

She didn't answer.

He dipped up a cup of tea for himself and sank to

the floor a short distance away. After drinking and swallowing, he said, "My spies didn't inform me that you'd been taken until too late."

Clutching her cup in both hands, she rested it upon her drawn-up knees and stared at him. "I would find new spies if I were you."

His brows lifted. "Yes, that's good advice."

She took a long drink of tea and let the warmth filter through her cold muscles. A creeping sensation of helplessness vied inside her with the certain knowledge that she *would* figure a way out of this. She always had. No matter what boulders life had rolled into her path, she had always found a way around them. When her father died and her mother blamed her, she had sent her reflection-soul flying with the Cloud People, where no one could find it. After her sister drowned, she had fought ferocious waves to get to shore and then wandered alone in the freezing forest until she'd gotten close enough to home that her people had found her. When Flint divorced her . . .

Her belly twisted as though a stiletto were being slowly turned in her intestines.

"Are you all right?" Strongheart asked in concern.

She squeezed her eyes closed. "No. But I will be. I just need some time."

Strongheart didn't speak for a time; then he said, "Do you know why he hurt you?"

"We hurt each other for fourteen winters. Nothing has changed."

She let out a long breath, opened her eyes, and found Strongheart watching her intently.

"You are the accused murderer of Chief Blue Bow. Every action Flint takes to demean you raises his status among my people."

When he divorced me I splintered like a wooden doll hit with a war club, but I mended myself. I can fix this, too. If only I had Wink to talk to, I—

"There is only one person you can rely upon now. You know that, don't you?" he softly asked.

"Who?"

He leaned forward. "Sora, a disgraced chieftess, thirty-two winters old, alone and frightened. Everyone else you think you need, you do not."

"Really, Priest?" she scoffed. "Do you know me so well?"

His expression slackened as he looked at her. "I know you are alone."

He was, of course, right; it was a strange, hollow sensation. As the daughter of the chieftess, she had rarely been alone. There had always been someone close by who would answer if she called out.

He leaned forward and tossed another branch onto the fire. Sparks flitted upward toward the smokehole in the roof. "Don't fight it. Your loneliness may help me to Heal you."

"How?"

"It is only when we are lonely that our afterlife soul can seek us. If your reflection-soul truly is lost in the forest, it may find its way home by itself."

"You mean loneliness draws the reflection-soul back to the body?"

He lifted a shoulder. "Loneliness is more like a

signal fire lit in the darkness. The reflection-soul walks toward it out of curiosity, sees its own body, and rushes home." Pausing, he rearranged his dark cape around his feet, keeping them warm, and said, "Did you want your father to die?"

The question startled her. "No, of course not. I loved him very much."

"As much as you loved your mother?"

"More. Mother was not particularly kind to me. She preferred my older sister. I was my father's pet."

On the hearthstones, the small pot began to bubble. Suds boiled up and spilled over the lip into the fire, scenting the house with the fragrance of soap. He must have been preparing his nightly bath when his spies brought him the news that Flint had taken her to the forest.

Strongheart wrapped his cape over his hand, grabbed the pot, and set it on the floor between them. "I've been told your father was a traveler."

Her father's face formed behind her eyes, as eerie and dreamlike as it had been when she'd been a small child. In most ways, he was very ordinary; he had a plain round face with a broad nose and ears that stuck out through his black hair. Ordinary in every way except his eyes. Those eyes might be looking straight at you, but he wouldn't be seeing you. He would be seeing faraway places. Even now, twenty-five winters later, she didn't need to remember the tale he'd told her of the far western ocean. All she had to do was remember his eyes. He could look that vast blueness right into your heart until you felt you were drowning. Her tongue still tasted the salt in the air.

"Your father visited the islands far to the south, I'm told."

"Yes, he—he was a great Trader before he met my mother. He traveled far and wide. It was his reputation that gave him the right to marry into my family. But I think it was a bad choice for him. Marrying a chieftess meant he had to stay in Blackbird Town and help my mother. It withered his souls. His greatest pleasure came from seeing distant horizons."

Absently, as though thinking about other things, Strongheart brushed at the suds on the pot rim. "Did he tell you stories about those places? About the islands to the south?"

"Often."

She opened her left palm and stared at her hand. The beautiful flowers of those islands scented her fingertips—though she had never seen them. Never touched them. Her father had been there long before she'd been born. "He was a very good storyteller," she said softly.

Strongheart reached into the sudsy pot and squeezed out a cloth, then rubbed it over his own arm as though testing the temperature. "I want you to tell me more, much more, but for now, I imagine you are feeling dirty."

After what she'd been through tonight, she felt filthy, but it surprised her that he was concerned about it. She finished her tea and set the cup on the floor.

"Is that for me?" She gestured to the soapy water.

"Yes. Please," he said, and held out his hand as though he wanted her to take it.

Reluctantly, she gripped his fingers. To her surprise, rather than putting the cloth in her hand, he used it to wash her arm.

Sora let herself float in the sensations.

Strongheart kept soaking the cloth, squeezing it out, and washing her body. When he reached her face, his touch became feather-light. He washed her forehead and around her eyes like a mother cleaning a frightened child. The cloth moved over her mouth and throat, then slipped lower, cleaning her chest above her dress.

Just when she thought he might slip the cloth into her dress to wash her breasts, he stopped and patiently unlaced her sandals. After he'd set them aside, he started washing her feet. The water felt almost too hot on her cold bare toes.

"Our peoples have different beliefs about illness," he said. "To understand what I must do to Heal you, you must grasp what my people believe."

The cloth moved up her calves, and she longed to lie back and fall asleep while he worked.

"The Loon Nation believes that illness comes from three sources. The first is very similar to your beliefs: illness is caused when a person's soul wanders away from the body and can't find its way home again. Second, illness may be caused when the saliva spoils. Saliva is as important to life as blood or gall. If it spoils, a person begins to live a nightmare of despair."

"What causes the saliva to spoil?"

"A ghost person sends evil dreams. You said you often dream of being lost in the forest, of running and running, but never being able to get home. It's possible that your illness comes from a ghost person, but it's also possible that a living person, a Night-goer, has chased your soul away or captured it. Perhaps even buried it—that is the third cause of illness. In that case, we must find the burial place and release your soul."

"How long can a person live when her soul has been buried?"

"Seven or eight moons, usually, but a very Powerful Night-goer can keep his victim's body alive for many winters. Please understand even in the case of witchcraft every person is responsible for the illness he contracts. So our first step is to discover what you did that allowed the Rainbow Black to invade your body."

"I did something?" she asked.

He eased her dress hem up and washed her thighs. "You must have, or you wouldn't be sick."

"I certainly can't recall what."

"That's my task. To make you recall. There are memories locked in your bones and muscles that you do not realize are there."

She opened her eyes, and his gaze seemed to peer straight through her flesh to the sinew that tied her bones together. "How do we do that?"

"First, I must cleanse you. I've started that to-night." He rinsed the cloth again and washed the inside of her right thigh with such tenderness, it left her feeling weightless. "We begin with the flesh; then we cleanse the souls that live in the body."

With a low despairing laugh, she said, "You mean if your people allow it."

"Yes, that's right."

She couldn't help it. His hands felt so soothing, she stretched out on her back on the soft blankets. As though he'd expected it, he slipped his hand beneath her dress and washed her abdomen, then gingerly touched her breasts.

"May I cleanse your entire body?"

She hesitated. He was a Healer. He'd seen a thousand bodies. And after what she'd been through, did it matter? "Yes."

He washed her breasts in calm circular motions, then drew the cloth down her belly and left it resting over what her people called a woman's "little manhood." It felt warm.

"Let me tell you our stories of how illness entered the world."

She nodded. "I'm listening."

"In the old days, the animals, the fish, the plants and trees could all talk, and they lived in perfect friendship with human beings. But as time went on, people increased so rapidly that their settlements spread all over the whole island, and the poor animals—"

"The island?" she asked curiously.

"Yes. The earth is a great flat island suspended from the sky by four ropes and floating on a huge sea of water. The sky is a vault that covers the island, and above it is another world: the upper world, where the Master of Breath lives, our Creator, along with the pure forms of every animal and plant. Beneath our island and the waters we float upon is another world: the underworld."

He washed her "little manhood" in light sure strokes, then soaked his cloth again.

"Do your Blessed Ancestors live in the underworld, as my people believe?" she asked.

"No. The ghosts of monsters and evil spirits live there. It is a strange place, though they have their towns and clans, just as we do. The seasons are exactly opposite of ours. So if it is winter here, it is summer there. The beings in the underworld wear rattlesnakes about their wrists and ankles, the same way we wear bracelets and anklets."

"And what does all this have to do with Healing me?"

She jumped when he moved the cloth between her legs and squeezed it out. As the warm water flowed over her skin, washing away the taint left by Flint, she felt as though her lost reflection-soul was walking toward her, trying to come home. Hope filled her. A long exhalation passed her lips.

"As people spread over the island in the Old Days, the animals were crowded together into smaller and smaller spaces. Out of pure carelessness or contempt, humans crushed the smaller creatures—like insects, frogs, and worms—beneath their feet. To make it worse, people created bows and arrows, knives, fishhooks and spears, axes and nets. When people began to slaughter the animals, the animals had to do something."

"What did they do?"

"Each type of animal called a meeting and determined to make war upon people by sending diseases. For example, deer created rheumatism; worms caused the itch. Yellow frogs created kidney disease. When the plants heard of this, they resolved to help people by furnishing a cure for each of the diseases created by the animals. Every plant is a cure for something. Our task is to discover which plant works for which disease." He rinsed his cloth again and said, "If you will roll onto your stomach, I'll wash your back."

She did as he'd instructed, and yielded to his soothing touch.

When he finished and dropped the cloth back into the pot, he walked across the floor to pull something from the bench.

"Your dress is wet. It will be uncomfortable to sleep in." He held out what looked like a slave's garment, a plain, coarsely woven brown dress. "I want you to put this on."

He brought it back and handed it to her.

As she pulled her soiled blue dress over her head and slipped on the clean brown garment, he never once glanced at her body. He held her gaze, as though far more concerned with what was happening behind her eyes.

He filled her cup with tea again and gave it to her.

"Thank you, but I'm very tired. You should take me back to the Captives' House now."

"Not yet." He crouched before her, still holding her gaze, and said, "What happened the night your father died? Flint said your mother was in a council meeting and you prepared dinner for your father."

Images flashed.

As I sprinkle the herbs into the stew pot, I can see myself reflected in the broth. My seven-winters-old face is small and pretty. I have happy eyes. . . .

"Yes, Mother was gone. Father had spent that morning laughing and talking with a Trader who'd just come into Blackbird Town. He was joyous. He'd Traded pounded copper sheets for buffalo jerky from the far west. When Mother found out, she shouted at him for paying too much, and my sister, Walks-among-the-Stars, made hideous faces at him, as though she, too, was disgusted by his carelessness. It broke his heart. I could tell. He looked very sad. During his youth, he'd loved the western jerky because it was seasoned with a plant called sage. He'd begged me to use the jerky to make him a stew for dinner."

"And you did."

"Yes. We didn't ordinarily prepare our own meals. The slaves did the cooking. But Father didn't want to be bothered by slaves in the house. He asked me to cook for him. It was . . . a curious request. I could see in his eyes that something was wrong. He didn't want to have 'outsiders' close that night."

"Did he tell you what was wrong?"

She shook her head. "Not really. He said that he longed very much to be a Trader again, and told me that the only thing that kept him in Blackbird Town was his love for me."

"That must have made you happy."

"Yes. It did." Sora shifted her cup from her right hand to her left and took a sip.

Strongheart watched the shift in handedness with an unnatural attentiveness. "Do you use both hands equally well?"

She glanced down at her left hand. "I—I've never noticed." She shrugged. "I wouldn't say equally well. I just don't have a firm preference, I guess."

He didn't seem to be breathing. All of his attention was focused on her hands. "As a child, did you shift hands?"

"Yes, often, though I don't see—"

"Can you give me examples?"

"Well"—she gestured uncertainly—"my mother used to think it odd that I painted with one hand and threw a lance with the other. But I also—"

"Which hand did you paint with?"

Frustrated at the nonsense questions, she sharply replied, "My left. *Why* is it important? Doesn't everyone use both hands?"

His intent expression relaxed. He shook his head mildly. "No. They don't."

"You ask the strangest questions, Priest. I wish you would tell me—"

"What did you put in your father's stew that fateful night?"

The quick change of topics caught her in midsentence with her mouth open. She closed it and grimaced at him. Did he do that on purpose? "You change subjects like I change hands, Priest. Are you trying to confuse me?"

His gaze focused on her hands again, and Sora glanced down to see what he was seeing. Anxious, she had begun tapping her cup with her right thumb while her left was mirroring the action, creating an odd staccato.

Strongheart lifted his gaze to her face again. "Please answer me. What did you put in the stew?"

She heaved an exasperated sigh. "I'm not sure. I had seen barely seven winters. I had virtually no experience cooking, but it pleased me so much that Father had asked, that I was determined I could do it."

"You used the jerky?" he encouraged.

"Yes, I crumbled the jerky into the pot, and mixed in dried fish and cornmeal. Then I . . ." Her heart constricted as though a gigantic hand had reached inside her chest and squeezed.

"You used herbs you found in your mother's bedchamber?"

She glanced up. "Did Flint tell you that?"

"Yes."

Sora's hands started to shake. She set her cup down, folded her arms tightly across her chest, and without realizing it, began to rock back and forth. "Mother kept herb pots in her bedchamber. I went down the hall and searched through the pots. I gathered a pinch of anything that smelled good. Dried blossoms, mostly. Or at least that's what I thought they were, but . . ."

When her words dwindled, Strongheart said, "One of them was poisonous?"

"I—I don't know which one. Honestly. After Father died, I could never go near Mother's herb pots again."

His young face was smooth and serene. He might have been carved of wood. Only his eyes seemed alive. They searched her face. "Where was your sister?"

Sora gestured impatiently. "I don't know. She may have been with Mother. My sister was destined to become high chieftess of the Black Falcon Nation. Perhaps Mother had asked her to sit in on the council meeting."

Strongheart didn't move.

Finally, he asked, "What happened then?"

"Father told me to go to my bedchamber and play with the cornhusk dolls he'd made for me."

"Why didn't he ask you to share the stew with him?"

Her heart twinged, and pain shot down her left arm. She rubbed it. "I don't think I was hungry. I—I don't remember, really."

Strongheart watched her rub her arm and stood up. As he turned away, he asked, "What color was your father wearing that night?"

"What?" she asked.

"What color was he wearing?"

"Blessed gods, what does that have to do with anything?"

He picked up a stick, prodded the fire, and tossed the stick into the flames. Long yellow tongues consumed it. "Don't you remember?"

"No. No, I don't remember. Why does it matter?"

In a too-soft voice, he said, "It matters."

"Why?"

He pointed to a roll of blankets lying on the bench at the rear of the house. "I want you to sleep there tonight. Think about my question. If you remember what your father was wearing, I want you to wake me and tell me. No matter when the memory comes, even in the middle of the night, you must wake me and tell me."

She shrugged nervously. "All right."

"Good."

Without another word, he knelt before the fire with his back to her and dipped himself another cup of tea.

Sora walked across the house, unrolled the blankets, and stretched out beneath them.

He was still there, staring at the flames, when sleep overcame her, and her shadow-soul slipped from her body to run backward in time down a dark hallway through a strangely quiet house that smelled like death. . . .

"CHIEFTESS?" STRONGHEART TOUCHED HER shoulder. "It's time to wake up."

Sora opened her eyes and saw pale gray light seeping around his door curtain. The delicious aromas of fried fish and bread filled the house. "Is it dawn?"

"Almost. I woke you early so you would have time to eat."

She swung her legs over the bench and found her sandals lying on the floor within reach. As she picked them up, she said, "That is an unexpected kindness. I thank you."

He dipped his head in acknowledgment. He'd obviously bathed and dressed while she slept. His short black hair gleamed as though freshly washed, and he wore a beautiful flaxen-colored shirt that hung to just below his knees. Shell bells decorated his hem, and clicked when he moved.

Sora laced her sandals tightly and got to her feet. "I would like to borrow a comb, if one is available."

"Of course. After you eat." He gestured to the woven mats that surrounded the fire.

Sora walked to the closest mat, where she sank down. The warmth of the fire penetrated her brown dress and prickled her skin. She shivered.

"My slaves prepared breakfast a short time ago. I hope you like catfish."

"I do, but even if I didn't, I would eat it and be grateful."

Strongheart handed her a cup of tea first, then crouched beside a basket. He used a wooden spoon to scoop fish and a curious bread she'd never seen before into two bowls.

She took the bowl he handed her, picked up one of the tiny bread balls, and ate it. The sweet flavors of acorn flour and palm sap sugar coated her tongue. "This is wonderful. What is it?"

"We call them acorn balls. My people collect the palm sap from the flower stems and dry it, then mix it with acorn flour, water, and salt. The balls are fried in fat. My mother used to cut dried plums into tiny pieces and add them to the dough."

"That sounds delicious," she said around a mouthful of food. "Where is your mother?"

He pulled the skin off one side of his catfish and ate it. As he chewed, he said, "My parents are dead.

They were killed by the Lily People when I'd seen nine winters."

Sora glanced over at him. He kept eating as though the pain had long since vanished, but she wondered how that could be. The death of her father and sister had left holes in her souls that never stopped hurting.

"Was your village attacked?"

He shook his head, and the light flashed from his hooked nose. "No. My parents had gone north to attend the marriage of my uncle. They were ambushed on the trail. I was at home with my grandmother. I didn't find out they'd been killed for almost a moon."

"That must have been terrible. The hoping, I mean."

He tilted his head and looked at her. The sadness in his eyes was mesmerizing. "Hoping is always terrible. And wonderful. It sustains us, doesn't it?"

She peeled back the skin of her catfish and pulled off a large chunk of meat. "I suppose so."

They ate for a time in silence, both staring into the crackling fire.

When her bowl was empty, she set it near the hearthstones and drank her tea while he finished eating.

At last, he set his bowl down, and said, "Let me find you a comb."

Outside, she heard people talking as they gathered for the village council meeting. Fear spread gleaming wings in her chest. She closed her eyes to fight it. If they decided she was not sick, they would certainly torture her before they killed her for Blue Bow's murder. She prayed she would not embarrass her people by acting cowardly. No matter what they did to her, she had to be brave. She was the chieftess of the Black Falcon Nation.

Or at least, she had been.

"I hope this is adequate," Strongheart said, and handed her a wooden comb.

"Yes. Thank you."

Setting her tea cup down, she gathered her waist-length black hair into her hand and started combing out the grass and bits of leaves. She had to tug to remove the snarls.

Strongheart dipped himself a cup of tea and sipped it while he watched her. "Did you remember?" he asked softly.

"Remember what?"

His bulging eyes caught the orange light and held it like polished amber. "Do you recall what we talked about before you went to sleep last night?"

She blinked. "Oh. Yes, of course. I never woke you because I didn't remember the color."

"Keep trying."

"If you wish, but I don't understand why it's important."

The lines at the corners of his eyes deepened. "You will."

Puzzled, she made an airy gesture with her hand. "If it's so important, why don't you explain it to me?"

"That would not help either of us."

All priests are imbeciles. I knew it.

She tugged out the last of the snarls and ran the comb all the way through her hair until it was finally smooth; then she began plaiting it into a long thick braid. While she worked, she thought about Blackbird Town. What was Wink doing this morning? Was she still worried about being attacked by the Loon Nation? Was she, as Feather Dancer had suggested, occupied pulling together the war party to journey south for the jade?

Almost too low to hear, Strongheart said, "Do you often feel guilt?"

Sora's fingers stopped. She *had* been feeling guilty. Because she should be there. Her people needed her. "How did you know I was feeling guilty?"

He propped his tea cup on one knee, and said, "Your fear shows on your face."

"Fear? I thought you said I looked guilty."

"Guilt is fear. You can't have guilt without being afraid. Guilt is your way of punishing yourself for being afraid." He turned toward the door when the voices outside grew louder.

A high-pitched drumbeat began. Then another drum joined in; this one with a deeper, more resonant tone.

Strongheart stood up. "It's almost time. The guards will be coming. Are you ready?"

Sora let out a pent-up breath. "Yes."

"Remember," he said when she got to her feet.

"Don't defend yourself. You have nothing to defend. Our only goal is to convince the people of Eagle Flute Village that you are sick and need our help."

He pulled the door curtain aside, and a flood of pale blue light poured across the floor. People had begun to gather around Strongheart's house. They peered through the door with wide eyes, clearly trying to catch a glimpse of Sora. Four guards dressed in breechclouts and carrying spears trotted toward them.

Strongheart murmured, "Walk closely behind me. Don't speak to anyone."

She jerked a nod and clenched her fists to fight back the terror. One of the hardest things she had ever done in her life was to follow Strongheart when he stepped outside into the crowded plaza. The four guards encircled them, and hoarse whispers eddied through the crowd. The Loon villagers glared at Sora as though she were some sort of foul biting insect that needed to be crushed.

As Strongheart led the way through the crowd toward the Chief's House, people backed away and a narrow corridor opened. She couldn't bear to look into the sea of hostile eyes, so she kept her gaze focused on the wood smoke that curled lazily from the rooftops. At this time of morning, there was almost no breeze, and the smoke twined through the trees like silent gossamer serpents. Birdsong flooded the air.

Strongheart stopped ten paces from the Chief's House and said, "We must wait. Chief Horned Owl will not appear until Mother Sun does."

From the yellow halo that arched over the tree-tops, she guessed sunrise couldn't be more than a few hundred heartbeats away.

Strongheart spread his legs and bowed his head, serenely allowing the moments to pass.

The crowd edged closer to examine Sora, and she glimpsed the faces of children peeking around the adults' legs. One little boy had a toy spear in his hand that he kept playfully jabbing at her, which made his two friends squeal with laughter.

Sora had to lock her shaking knees to keep standing.

A clamor rose behind her, and she turned to see the Oak Leaf Village prisoners emerging, one by one, from the Captives' House. Feather Dancer was the last to stagger out. His face was hideously swollen, and he cradled his left arm to his chest, as though it was injured. Every captive stared at her, and their eyes went wide with hope and fear. Then the guards marched all of them, except Feather Dancer, away into the forest to work. Four men encircled Feather Dancer and ordered him to walk toward the Chief's House.

They're gathering the witnesses. . . .

The four guards stopped twenty paces away, and she could see that dried blood drenched Feather Dancer's left arm. After the beating he'd taken last night trying to protect her, he must be in misery, but he lifted his chin and gave her a stoic look, silently telling her not to worry about him.

A hush fell over the crowd when the first glimmers of Mother Sun's face filtered through the branches.

While most people turned eastward, Sora stared at the door to the Chief's House. The curtain swayed. Murmurs and the sound of footsteps could be heard inside.

Just before Mother Sun blazed to life over the treetops, and a dark filigree of shadows crept across the village, Strongheart lifted his head and announced, "My Chief, our Mother has awakened and brings life to the world."

Horned Owl threw his door curtain back with theatrical flair and stepped out into the newborn light. The crowd gasped, and many people fell to their knees. His massive bear headdress was stunning. Carved from wood, it had been exquisitely painted. The snout gleamed with red and white designs, and the huge black eyes looked alive. Long leather fringes hung from the headdress, covering Horned Owl's face and most of his chest. As though pleased with his people's response, Horned Owl puffed out his young chest and paraded back and forth, growling like a bear.

Strongheart watched without expression, but a distasteful tic started at the corner of his mouth.

Sora squinted. The sight struck her as so bizarre she was speechless.

When the new chief stopped growling and lifted the fringes on the headdress to gaze out at his people, a broad smile lit his face. "I *knew* you'd love this!" he called, and spun around. "I had my wood carvers work through the night to create it!"

Claps and hoots of approval rang out. Only the elders seemed dismayed. They watched the spectacle with a mixture of disbelief and disdain.

Horned Owl gleefully clawed at people, and growled again before convulsing with laughter. Many of the young men in the crowd joined him, clawing and growling loudly.

"My chief," Strongheart said and bowed. "It is dawn. Mother Sun is watching us. We should begin the Black Drink ritual."

Horned Owl's smile turned to an annoyed frown. "I was having fun with my people, Priest. I don't appreciate your impudence."

"Forgive me; it's just that our people have a great deal to consider this morning."

Like whether or not to kill an enemy chieftess.

Horned Owl pursed his lips and draped one side of the long fringes back over a hook on the headdress so he could see Strongheart clearly. "Oh, very well, let's sit down." He slumped to the ground like an offended child.

Strongheart gestured for Sora to sit near Horned Owl; then he knelt opposite her. From everywhere in the crowd, tribal elders came forward and created a circle behind them. Yet another circle of children and adults coalesced behind the elders. Finally, the guards took up their positions along the perimeter of the gathering. She could see Snail and Black Turtle in the rear to her left, guarding Feather Dancer. They were keeping him far away, probably for safety reasons. Despite his injuries, they must realize that if he jumped one of the elders, they would never be able to pull him off before he snapped the woman's brittle neck.

Horned Owl clapped his hands, and two slaves emerged from his doorway carrying large conch shells filled with steaming liquid. The men walked in slow measured steps, as they reverently Sang *"Ya-ho-la,"* over and over. The first conch shell was delivered to the chief, who lifted it to his lips and drank. After Horned Owl had finished drinking, the other servant delivered a conch shell to Strongheart; then five more slaves ducked out of the Chief's House carrying cups that they gave to each elder, as well as one to Sora.

When everyone had a cup, a glowing pipe and bearskin pouch stuffed with tobacco were laid at Horned Owl's feet.

"I pray my father's soul is watching over us today," Horned Owl said as he lifted the carved stone pipe for all to see, then touched it to his lips, and blew smoke, first to the east, then the other three cardinal directions.

Horned Owl passed the pipe to Strongheart, who smoked, and gave it to War Chief Grown Bear. The elders smoked next. Finally the pipe made its way through the warriors, and back to Horned Owl.

Strongheart sipped his Black Drink, and softly said, "May the Above Spirits watch over us and guide us to the right decisions. We ask these things in the names of our Ancestors."

Every person tipped his cup and drank. Sora stared down into the black brew. Steam curled from the surface and scented the air with the tangy fragrance of yaupon holly, from which sacred Black Drink was made. She knew little of the traditions of the Loon People, but among the Black Falcon Nation, yaupon was sacred. It had been the last drink to touch Black Falcon's beak before he dove straight into Mother Sun's heart, sacrificing himself to bring fire to the world so that humans might cook their food and keep warm during the winters. For that reason, light, warmth, and sacrifice were forever tied to yaupon. Black Drink cleansed selfish thoughts from the heart.

Before she sipped, she said a soft prayer, thanking Black Falcon for giving his life for human beings. The Black Drink tasted strong and bitter, just the way she preferred it; she took a long drink and clutched the conch shell in hard fists. In the next hand of time, her fate would be decided, one way or the other. They would probably kill her . . . and she knew it.

She lifted her cup and drained the bitter contents; then she squared her narrow shoulders and stared straight at the new chief of Eagle Flute Village.

Horned Owl's eyes tightened beneath her commanding gaze, as though he could suddenly feel the weight of the entire Black Falcon Nation coming down upon him. Which it would if he condemned her to death. Her people would demand it.

Unless, of course, they, too, believed she had killed Chief Blue Blow.

She had no way of knowing what was being said about her in Blackbird Town. Did they believe her to be a murderer? According to the laws of her people, and apparently those of the Loon Nation, murder was punished by retaliation. It was the duty of the male blood relatives to kill either the murderer or some other member of the killer's lineage—to make things straight. Her people would not object to her death if they believed that she had killed Blue Bow. Retaliation was the right of his people.

But there's no proof! They would never condemn me without—

Strongheart rose to his feet. His movements were so graceful the shell bells decorating the hem of his flaxen shirt barely clicked together, but the sound affected the crowd like a blast of lightning. They went ominously silent.

He extended a hand to Sora. "This woman, the former chieftess of the Black Falcon Nation, is accused of murdering our blessed chief, Blue Bow. It will be up to you today to decide if she is liable for the killing. If she is, then our chief's soul will not be able to rest until we avenge his death. If she is not liable, however, because she is sick, then we must do everything in our power to try to Heal her." He lifted his hands and held them out to the people in a pleading gesture. "I know you. You are kind and good. I have faith that, after you've heard the tales of what happened, you will make the right decision."

A low rumble of voices filled the dawn.

Horned Owl flung up an arm and called, "Let the Bears come!"

Two masked dancers emerged from inside the Chief's House, followed by Flint and War Chief Grown Bear.

The dancers, who wore enormous bear masks similar to Horned Owl's, pirouetted through the gathering shaking deer-hoof rattles and sniffing those present. They spent a good deal of time sniffing Feather Dancer, who looked like he longed to drive a lance through their hearts.

Flint stood tall and handsome, his perfectly chiseled face calm. Long black hair fell over the shoulders of his black cape like a silken wealth. He did not even grace her with a glance. He just braced his feet and folded his hands before him, as though waiting his turn to speak.

Was he afraid they'd kill her? Or afraid they wouldn't?

He'd forfeited his entire world to bring her here. She couldn't believe he'd done it just to gain the paltry wealth the Loon Nation had to offer. No, there was more to it.

In the dark place between her souls, she believed he still loved her and had brought her here for one purpose—to see if Strongheart could Heal her.

Unfortunately, the coldly logical part of her souls feared that Feather Dancer was right: Flint had betrayed her for his own gain.

But *what*?

Surely not the crude pottery, wooden seed-beads, and rancid fish oil produced by the Loon People?

Did the enormous war party that would soon be heading south for the jade have orders to deliver Flint more wealth than he'd ever imagined?

He is not above such temptations.

He'd been a low-status man before his marriage to her, the son of a common weaver. She remembered the awed expression on his face when he'd first gazed upon the extraordinary wealth she possessed. As the daughter of a chieftess, Sora had been showered with the rarest, most precious objects in the world. The second day after their Joining, Flint had knelt and sorted through the pots and baskets that lined every wall of the new house her people had built for them. He'd touched the pounded copper sheets, strings of thousands of pearls, and extraordinary fabrics as though touching the faces of the gods themselves.

It had surprised her to discover that he was, after all, exceedingly human.

When the Bear Dancers finally made their way back to Sora, they sniffed her thoroughly, tilting their enormous heads to look at her with glistening shell eyes while low growls came from their fanged muzzles. She sat perfectly still, allowing them to examine her. Since she did not know the legends that surrounded these Bear Dancers, she had no idea what their purpose was; it was better to say and do nothing, rather than risk violating some obscure Loon People rule.

One of the Bear Dancers abruptly threw his head back, revealing rows of sharp teeth, and leaped at Flint, roaring as though to tear his head off.

Surprised, Flint's eyes went wide, but to his credit, he stood his ground and let the Bear Dancer sniff every part of him.

Next, the Dancers sniffed Grown Bear, who looked irritated by their attention. They went over him in remarkable detail, far more detail than they had Sora or Flint.

When the Bears finally Danced away into the forest, Strongheart said, "The Bears can sniff out no malice or deceit among the witnesses. Let us, then, hear their tales."

Horned Owl called, "War Chief Grown Bear, come forward!"

Grown Bear walked to stand between Horned Owl and Strongheart, facing Sora. A burly man with short black hair, recently cut in mourning, his face captured her attention. One long scar slashed across his cheeks and nose, making it appear that his face had two halves. He wore a red-and-white shirt that hung to the middle of his muscular thighs. "I am here, my chief."

"Tell us what happened the night you went to Blackbird Town."

He glanced at Sora, and for one stunning moment, neither of them seemed to breathe.

Grown Bear looked away and said, "It was late. We'd been walking for two days straight. Chief Blue Bow had ordered us to march through the night in order to reach Blackbird Town as quickly as possible. All of my warriors were tired and looking forward to the sanctuary that had been promised to us by Matron Wink. Two hands of time past midnight, we were surprised to see War Chief Feather Dancer and Matron Wink's son, Long Fin, step out of the forest. Feather Dancer said that, as a gesture of good faith, Matron Wink had sent them to escort us into Blackbird Town. He told us not to be afraid when his warriors came out of the forest. He—"

"How many warriors accompanied Feather Dancer and Long Fin?" Horned Owl asked, sounding slightly bored. But, of course, he must have heard this story many times by now.

Since Sora hadn't, she listened intently.

Grown Bear replied, "I saw perhaps twenty."

Strongheart said, "Please, go on. What happened after that?"

Grown Bear clenched his fists at his sides, as though expecting trouble. "Our chief told me he wished to speak with the matron's son in private and that I was to keep my warriors twenty paces back."

Suspicious mutters eddied through the crowd.

Grown Bear continued, "I told him I thought that was unwise, that the Black Falcon Nation might be plotting to kill us all, but the chief insisted, and I did as I was told."

"Did my father walk away with Long Fin?" Horned Owl asked, and scanned the crowd, clearly trying to judge their mood.

"Yes. War Chief Feather Dancer followed three or four paces behind them."

Horned Owl waved for the guards to bring Feather Dancer forward. They dragged him up, and gripped his muscular arms tightly to prevent him from using them.

"Is that true?" Horned Owl asked. "Did you follow only a few paces behind Long Fin and my father?"

Feather Dancer's lacerated lips bled when he said, "I did."

One of the elders, a sallow-faced old woman with white hair, leaned forward. "Grown Bear, could you hear what our chief said to young Long Fin?"

"I heard a few things, Elder Littlefield, but not many. I was too far behind."

"And you, War Chief Feather Dancer, did you hear what they said?"

Feather Dancer took a deep breath and stared at the old woman for several instants before he replied, "Very little, Elder. They were trying very hard to let no one overhear their words."

Sora had known Feather Dancer for twenty-six winters. She thought he was lying . . . but why would he do that? He must think it protected her. Or perhaps it protected him.

The elders leaned their heads together and whispered for a time; then Littlefield said, "Grown Bear, tell us what you did hear."

Grown Bear waved a hand. "Toward the end of his conversation with Long Fin, Chief Blue Bow cried out as though offended, and said, 'Explain? I mean your chieftess was supposed to meet with me fourteen days ago to negotiate the release of your hostages, but I never saw her.'" Grown Bear hesitated. "Then he said something about how Chieftess Sora's war party camped outside Eagle Flute Village—as we all know it did—and she sent in a willing hostage, who told him that she promised to appear within five days, and if she didn't, Blue Bow could kill the hostage. Naturally, when the sixth day arrived—"

"We killed him!" Horned Owl shouted. "His name was Walking Bird. He was a whimpering coward."

Sora closed her eyes. Though a member of Water Hickory Clan, Walking Bird had been a good and loyal friend, dedicated to his people. . . .

I remember leaving camp with Walking Bird. He led the way. What happened after that? Where did I go?

Was she still suffering the effects of the Spirit Plant that Flint had forced her drink on the journey here?

"What else?" Littlefield demanded to know. "Could you hear anything else?"

Grown Bear shook his head. "No, their voices dropped too low again, but I later heard that this man's wife-to-be, a woman named White Fawn"— he pointed at Flint—"was murdered during those five days."

"I don't care about Flint's betrothed!" Horned Owl said. "Tell them about the lance that slit my father's throat."

The elders fixed their gazes on Grown Bear, and he drew himself up to his full height. "It was a chunkey lance, thrown from the dark forest." He rubbed his fingers over his jugular vein. "It sliced through the big vein in our chief's throat. There was no way to stop the blood. He died a short while later."

"A chunkey lance?" Littlefield turned around to the crowd. "We have all heard that Chieftess Sora is an expert chunkey player. In fact, didn't you watch her play in a chunkey game once?"

"Yes, Elder," Grown Bear responded. "Only a half-moon ago. She is very good with the lance."

Strongheart called, "So are many people in this village. Let us return to the death of our chief. Did you send your warriors into the forest to find the murderer?"

"Yes, Priest. Long Fin's warriors and our warriors immediately ran into the trees to search for the chief's attacker. I told my warriors that I wanted the killer unharmed so that I might question him."

"Because you feared the assassin had been hired by Matron Wink, isn't that correct?"

Sora's head jerked around, and she stared wide-eyed at Strongheart. Had someone told him that? Who? There were only two people here who might have had contact with Wink before Blue Bow was murdered. She and Flint. Her gaze slid back to Flint. He hadn't moved. He stood like a statue.

"Yes," Grown Bear said through a tight exhalation. "I had been worried about that all along."

Littlefield's faded old eyes narrowed. "Did you find the murderer?"

Grown Bear wet his lips. "Perhaps, Elder. We found a dead man lying a short distance away. His skull had been crushed with a club. Matron Wink told me later that the dead man was her brother's son, a young warrior named Far Eye. No one knows what he was doing in the forest. He wasn't supposed to be there."

"Where was he supposed to be?"

When Grown Bear shrugged, Littlefield swiveled around to pin Feather Dancer with her wise old eyes. "You are the war chief. Where did you assign Far Eye?"

Grudgingly, Feather Dancer said, "He was supposed to guard the Chieftess' House all night."

Littlefield's mouth puckered. "Then if he was a good warrior, he would have never left there, unless the chieftess ordered him to. Maybe she was nearby. Is it possible that she killed Blue Bow, then Far Eye?"

"To make sure there were no witnesses," Horned Owl suggested. "Yes, that sounds plausible."

Feather Dancer opened his mouth to comment, then apparently thought better of it and remained silent.

Strongheart got to his feet and quietly asked, "Isn't it just as likely that Far Eye murdered Blue Bow, and Chieftess Sora was so outraged she killed him for it?"

Murmurs rushed through the crowd, rising in volume until Littlefield slashed down with her hand to silence it. The old woman stared mercilessly at Strongheart. "If she had done that, why did she flee? The innocent do not have to run away."

"Wouldn't you be afraid that the murdered chief's warriors would let fly first, and ask who you were later?"

Littlefield folded her skeletal arms across her chest and nodded. "We need to hear more of the story. Flint? Come forward."

Flint marched to stand before the elders. He had his back to Sora, but she could see how stiffly he stood. His black cape swayed around his tall body.

Littlefield ordered, "Tell us your story. Is it true that you suspect Chieftess Sora of murdering this White Fawn who was to be your wife?"

"Yes, Elder." He paused to take a deep breath. "War Chief Skinner and I had gone out into the forest to meet the bridal procession. By the time we arrived, White Fawn was dead. Her family thought she'd been poisoned. I immediately feared the worst, that my former wife had ordered her death. It was only later, when I arrived in Blackbird Town, that I discovered Sora had been missing when White Fawn was killed."

"What do you mean, 'missing'?"

"Well"—he glanced at Sora—"she wasn't in Blackbird Town. Supposedly she'd come here to meet with Blue Bow to negotiate the release of my relatives from Oak Leaf Village, but she never came. Matron Wink told me Sora ordered Feather Dancer to camp just outside your village and told him she would be going in with only one guard, Walking Bird. Feather Dancer hadn't liked the idea, but he'd obeyed, and waited for her to return."

"When did she return?" Strongheart asked.

"Five days later. She walked into camp alone and told Feather Dancer that Walking Bird was dead. She said that a Loon warrior had tried to kill her the instant she set foot in Eagle Flute Village and Walking Bird had thrown himself in front of her to protect her."

A roar of outrage went through the crowd as people questioned each other.

"No such thing ever happened," Littlefield said.

"I know, Elder," Flint replied. "Matron Wink also told me that when Feather Dancer asked how the negotiations had gone, Sora said that Blue Bow had been obstinate. She hadn't been able to negotiate the release of the hostages. He—"

Littlefield interrupted, "Is that true, War Chief? Is that what the chieftess told you?"

Feather Dancer's gaze slid to Sora, and she nodded, telling him to tell the truth. He said, "Yes."

"Please," Grown Bear interrupted, "I wish to add something."

"Do so, War Chief."

"My scouts told me that Chieftess Sora did leave Feather Dancer's camp with Walking Bird, but before she reached our village, she walked away into the trees. As we all know, Walking Bird continued on and entered our village, but the chieftess disappeared. My scouts tried to track her, but she was too shrewd for them."

"What day was that?" Strongheart asked.

"The seventeenth day of the Moon of Green Leaves."

Strongheart turned back to Flint. "And when was this White Fawn killed?"

Flint clenched his fists. "The nineteenth day of the Moon of Green Leaves."

Littlefield whispered something to the old woman sitting next to her, then asked, "How far away from Eagle Flute Village was the bridal procession when this happened?"

"Two days, Elder." The words sounded as though they hurt Flint.

"So," Littlefield said, "the chieftess could have taken the trails north, killed White Fawn, and returned to her camp just outside our village."

"Yes," Grown Bear answered. "And with Walking Bird dead, there was no one to object to the story. She could say she was here talking with Blue Bow about the hostages."

Horned Owl leaned forward. "That's why she had to lure my father to Blackbird Town to kill him. He knew she had never entered our village. It was all a lie so that she could run north and kill this young woman!"

Blessed gods, I couldn't have done that . . . could I?

Her heart beat against her ribs like a hammer-stone. Within moments, she couldn't breathe. Her hands trembled.

It's beginning. I feel it.

Deep inside me, it wakes . . . uncoiling like a lazy serpent.

Flint gave her a strange look, as though he knew. He took a tentative step toward her.

She looked out at the crowd. Hisses slipped from mouth to mouth, and she could tell from the hateful eyes of the crowd that they wanted her dead.

Flint cried, "She's going to faint! Black Turtle! Snail! Grab her arms! Hurry!"

When Sora saw the two men lunging through the crowd to get to her, she fought to get up, but her legs wouldn't hold her.

The darkness came like a shimmering midnight blue flood, and in the depths, two enormous eyes blazed to life. . . .

CHIEFTESS SORA CRIED OUT AND TOPPLED BACK-
ward with her limbs jerking and her jaws snapping
together.

Feather Dancer lurched against the restraining
hands of his guards. "Let me go! She needs help.
Flint, help her!"

Flint was already shoving people aside to get to
the chieftess. He dropped to the ground at her side
and pulled her spasming body onto his lap. "Sora,
I'm here," he said as he stroked her hair. "I'm right
here."

Her gnashing teeth turned her spittle into foam
that dripped from her jaws like a rabid dog's. Flint
wiped at it futilely, and shouted, "I told you there
was an Evil Spirit inside her! It chases her soul
away! You have to help her. The greatest Healer in

the world lives among you! Won't you let him try to help her?"

Elder Littlefield cried, "She has the Rainbow Black! The same Spirit killed my niece!"

Strongheart moved out into the crowd, speaking softly to each person he could, gazing directly into the eyes of people too far away to speak with. Several nodded. A few shook their heads vehemently.

Horned Owl leaped to his feet, glanced down at Sora, then shouted, "This is all a trick to make you believe she's sick! There is no Evil Spirit inside her! Can't you tell this is a trick?"

The villagers scrutinized Sora, then looked back at Horned Owl, unconvinced.

"I tell you, she is *not* sick! She murdered my father!"

Strongheart boldly swung around to Grown Bear. "Matron Wink demanded that you be present at the Healing Circle held for Chieftess Sora, didn't she?"

Grown Bear swallowed hard. "Yes, Priest. She told me I had to come and bring something that had belonged to Chief Blue Bow."

"What did you take?"

"I presented her with the chief's copper breast-plate. He had planned to give it to her anyway, as a token of his respect."

"What did the other people in the Circle bring?"

Grown Bear seemed to be struggling to recall. "Several things: a copper bracelet, a shell pendant . . . White Fawn's father laid a beautifully beaded wedding headdress at the chieftess' feet. War Chief Skinner's mother brought her son's bones."

"Then," Strongheart called, "everyone in the Circle brought an item that had belonged to a person the chieftess is accused of killing."

"Yes."

A din of voices rose as the crowd began asking questions. This Black Falcon ritual was unfamiliar to them. They must find it very strange.

Above the fray, Strongheart shouted, "How did the Circle end?"

Grown Bear said, "The chieftess could remember none of the murders. Their high priest, an old man named Teal, said she didn't remember because her reflection-soul had been out wandering the forest while her shadow-soul committed the murders. Then he said that, since they hadn't been able to force her to recall what she'd done, the Healing Circle was a failure. Teal said they had to find a more Powerful priest to Heal her."

Flint clutched Sora's spasming body, and said, "The Evil Spirit drives out her reflection-soul! Matron Wink knew this. That's why she sent a runner to ask Priest Strongheart if he would try to Heal her. Isn't that true, Strongheart?"

"Yes, it's true." Strongheart nodded and lifted his hand for all to see. "It's time to cast your voices. Who votes with me that she is sick and needs our help?"

One by one people responded, "Let Strongheart

drive out the Evil Spirit!" "She is sick! Look at her!" "Let Strongheart try to Heal her!" "Sick." "I say she's sick!"

Horned Owl waited for the clamor to die down before he shouted, "Who votes with me that she is *not* sick?"

One young warrior shouted, "I do!" Another said, "I agree that it's a trick!"

Littlefield rose to her feet to stare at the warriors who had sided with Chief Horned Owl. "Are there only two people in Eagle Flute Village who agree with the chief?" A roar of voices swelled. "Cast your voice! Who else believes this is a trick?"

No one spoke.

Littlefield turned back to Horned Owl. "Our people have decided that she is sick and we should allow Priest Strongheart to try to Heal her."

Feather Dancer turned to Strongheart, expecting him to agree or perhaps give his consent.

The priest stood quietly, watching Chieftess Sora. Blood poured from the corner of her mouth where she'd bitten her lolling tongue, but Strongheart seemed to be studying her stiff arms and legs, as though the way they flailed told him something no one else understood.

"Strongheart," Littlefield called. "Do you wish to Heal this woman?"

Strongheart tore his gaze from the chieftess and nodded. "Yes, Elder. When she quiets, have her brought to my house. I think I can help her."

Then, as though in a dream, Strongheart turned

away from the elders and marched straight to Feather Dancer, softly asking, "When her father died, where was her sister?"

Feather Dancer shook his head as though he hadn't heard right. Why would Strongheart pick this moment to ask a question about something that had happened twenty-five winters earlier?

"I don't know. I had seen barely one winter pass."

"Did you ever hear anyone speak of it?"

"Yes, many times, but I don't recall hearing anyone mention her sister. They talked about her father—"

"Were you there when her sister died?" Strongheart's gaze seemed to burn.

"Yes. In fact, I remember that day very well. The entire town was in an uproar."

"What happened?"

Feather Dancer frowned. "People found Walks-among-the-Stars's body washed up on shore, and they immediately mounted a search for Sora. They found her a day later, wandering aimlessly through the forest. She'd been in the cold water for a long time. She couldn't even remember her name."

"Did Walks-among-the-Stars drown?"

Feather Dancer lifted his shoulders uncertainly. "Eventually, yes. Her skull had been crushed. Priest Teal said that, in the storm, she must have been thrown out of the canoe onto a rock."

Strongheart stood there absorbing this information while he searched Feather Dancer's face.

"I'll be in my house, preparing myself. If you remember anything else, anything at all that might be useful to me, please tell your guards you need to speak with me."

"Very well."

The shell bells on Strongheart's shirt hem made music when he strode away.

WINK BOWED TO THE ENORMOUS CARVING OF
Black Falcon that hung above the entry to the
Chieftess' House, ducked beneath the door curtain,
and strode down the torch-lit hall. She barely
glanced at the doors that led to the council chamber
and the temple where the Eternal Fire burned.

At the very rear of the house stood a small bedchamber. As a child, Sora had shared the room with
her sister, Walks-among-the-Stars.

Wink breathed in the rich fragrance of burning
cypress that filled the quiet house, hoping it would
help to soothe her raw nerves while she considered
the things Sea Grass had said last night. If the old
matron was right and the jade brooch had belonged
to Sora's great-grandmother, where had Grown Bear
gotten it? Who else knew about the sealed box of

jewelry? If Sora hadn't even told Wink about it, who would she have told?

"She might have told Flint," Wink murmured. "Or he may have seen it among her possessions. After all, they lived together for fourteen winters."

That still did not explain how the brooch had come to be in the hands of an enemy war chief.

When she stood before the door curtain to Sora's childhood bedchamber, she flexed her fingers. Sora allowed no one to enter this room. Not even her husband, Rockfish. It was more like a shrine than a bedchamber.

Though Wink had entered it a few days ago, at Priest Teal's request, to find an object that had belonged to Sora's mother for use in the Healing Circle, she still felt ill doing it again.

Wink pulled the door curtain aside and stepped into the chamber. It was dark and cold. Only the light of the hallway torches penetrated the gloom. She waited for her eyes to adjust.

The chamber measured five paces square. Pots and baskets filled each corner, and buffalohides draped the sleeping bench to her right. In the torchlight the fine black hairs shimmered.

Wink looked up. A shelf filled with cornhusk dolls adorned the wall near the doorway. Old and faded, they had been made by Sora's father. But made for Sora or Walks-among-the-Stars, she did not know.

The big black-and-red basket that stood near the sleeping bench held Sora's most precious possessions. Eight hands tall and four wide, it had been decorated with red and black zigzagging lines. Wink went to it and pulled off the lid.

A wealth of rare treasures met her gaze: brilliant feathered headdresses, copper breastplates, strings of pearls—but on the very top rested three items that really drew her attention: a shell pendant that had belonged to Walks-among-the-Stars, Yellow Cypress' copper bracelet, and a wooden box filled with copper jewelry Flint had made for Sora. A master copper-worker, Flint had created stunning pendants for his wife. Magnificent copper falcons, elaborate Birdmen, antlered snakes with human faces; they all stared up at Wink from the box.

Wink closed her eyes for a moment. This was Sora's one refuge, the place she kept everything that told her who she was. Just opening the basket was the supreme violation. . . .

"I have no choice."

Wink shoved the basket hard, and it spilled across the floor like an overturned jewel box. Bracelets rolled in every direction, while pendants cartwheeled as though alive.

"Forgive me, Sora," she said as she knelt, emptied the remaining items from the basket, and began sorting through them.

There were a dozen wooden boxes, ranging in size from barely a finger's width across to boxes four hands long. On the biggest box exquisitely carved images of birds with large curved beaks had been painted. The smaller boxes were crudely made.

Wink grabbed the exquisite box first and pried off the wooden lid. Her breath caught. It was filled with feathers. Brilliant red, blue, and green feathers, the likes of which Wink had never seen. Where had Sora gotten them? They must have come from a bird that lived far away. Had her father, the Trader who'd ventured over half the world, given them to her? Perhaps he'd gotten them from one of the mythical islands he'd claimed to have visited?

Carefully, Wink set the box aside. How strange that Sora had never had the beautiful feathers made into a headdress or used to decorate the bodice of a dress, as Wink would have done.

Perhaps they'd been too precious to think of using.

A tiny box lay canted in a pile of copper pendants. Made from cypress, it had surely been carved by a child's hand. Wink reached for it.

The lid stuck. She had to wrench it hard before it squealed and came off.

Inside, a tight coil of human hair lay beside a small deer-bone hairpin.

For several instants Wink just stared at the hairpin; then tears filled her eyes.

She touched it gently.

Sora hadn't spoken for a full moon after her father died . . . until Wink had brought her this hairpin. Wink remembered the day perfectly. A frail smile had touched Sora's lips, and she'd clutched the hairpin in her desperate little fist, whispering, "Thank you, Wink."

After that, she'd started getting better.

Wink forced the lid back on, placed it on top of the exquisite box, and reached for another. She'd just gotten the lid off when she heard footsteps coming down the hallway outside.

They stopped in front of the door curtain, and Rockfish called, "Wink?"

"I'm in here."

Rockfish drew back the curtain, but he remained standing in the doorway, as though afraid to enter his sick wife's sanctuary. He wore a dark green knee-length shirt and bright red leggings.

He made an awkward gesture. "Sea Grass passed me on her way out of town. She told me you needed to see me. Wh-what are you doing?" His gaze went over the sparkling wealth that scattered the floor.

Wink sank back and sighed. "Rockfish, do you remember seeing a wooden box sealed with pine pitch?"

"You mean something Sora had?"

"Yes. The box would have been very precious to her. I suspect she probably kept it hidden, but you are her husband, surely you must have seen—"

"No," he said with a shake of his head. "If it was precious to her, I never saw it."

Wink frowned at him. His shoulder-length gray hair stuck to his forehead in wisps, as though glued by sweat. Had he run to get here? "How can you say that?"

"Oh, Wink, you of all people know how secretive she was. She forbade me to touch anything that belonged to her. I couldn't even go through her clothing basket, let alone anything in this room. If I'd come in here and so much as gazed at that basket, she'd have ripped out my heart with her bare hands."

Wink got to her feet and tucked a lock of graying black hair behind her ear. "She was secretive, and with good reason. Like every leader, she had things to hide, so I can understand her forbidding you to *open* certain boxes. All I'm asking is if you saw an old box, very old, sealed with pine pitch?"

The nostrils of his fleshy nose flared, like a dog scenting the wind for danger. "No."

"You're certain?"

"Absolutely. I never saw an old box sealed with pine pitch."

The tone of his voice set her on edge. It was light, flippant, as though he was making an effort to get this discussion over with so he could move on to something else.

"Rockfish, you sound . . . Did Sea Grass say something else?"

He clenched his fists at his sides. "She told me to ask you about Red Warbler and the jade brooch. What was she talking about?"

The old witch.

"Let's go across the hall. We can talk while I continue my search."

Wink rose and took Rockfish by the arm, led him out into the torchlight, then crossed to the bedchamber he shared with Sora. A fire burned in the hearth in the middle of the floor. It sent curls of blue smoke up to creep across the ceiling before they escaped through the roof's smokehole. Straight ahead, above their sleeping bench, weapons hung on the wall: axes, copper-studded war clubs, lances. . . .

To the left of the bench stood Sora's clothing basket. Rockfish's comment that Sora had forbidden him to touch it had given her an idea.

She walked to the basket and, as she lifted off the lid, said, "I think Sea Grass is lying, but she said she had seen the brooch before, that it had belonged to Sora's great-grandmother, Red Warbler. She told me that Red Warbler had put it, and several other pieces of jade jewelry from the Scarlet Macaw People, in a box sealed with boiled pine pitch that was only supposed to be opened in an emergency."

Rockfish's wrinkled face slackened. "Blessed gods, are you telling me that somewhere in this village is a box filled with more jade pieces like the brooch?"

"No, I'm not. I suspect there is no box. But I can't figure out why Sea Grass would say it exists if it doesn't. How could such a lie benefit Water Hickory Clan?"

As Wink sorted through the beautiful lavender, yellow, and deep blue dresses in the basket, the silence seemed to swell.

"Wink, I"—he blinked, as though he couldn't believe he was saying it—"I may know the box you're talking about."

She straightened. "Where is it?"

Without taking his eyes from hers he pointed

across the hall, back toward Sora's childhood bed-chamber. "In there."

She strode past him, threw back the door curtain, and went into the chamber again. The strewn jewelry glittered as she draped the curtain back over the peg on the wall, allowing the hall's gleam to pour into the room. "Show me."

Tentatively, he pointed to the sleeping bench covered with buffalohides. "Under there. There's a basket. The box is inside."

Wink gave him a disbelieving look, walked to the bench, and flipped up the hides that draped almost to the floor. A cypress-stave basket had been shoved all the way to the back. Wink got down on her knees and dragged it out. As she pulled it onto her lap, she saw that the basket's lid had once been sealed with pine pitch—but the seal was broken.

"Did you open this?" she demanded to know.

"Of course not. The seal was already broken when I saw it."

Wink's eyes narrowed. The only way he could know about this basket, and what it contained, was if he'd searched this chamber very carefully.

Before she opened it, she said, "Tell me what the basket contains."

Rockfish shrugged. "A sealed wooden box, some pieces of clothing, jewelry, not much more than that."

"How many pieces of clothing?"

"I don't know," he said irritably. "Why do you ask?"

"I was just wondering how much time you had. Did you rush in here one day after Sora left for a council meeting and quickly go through her personal things? Or did you have days to pore over each item? Perhaps when she was gone to Eagle Flute Village?"

He spread his arms, as though trying to convey innocence. "Iron Hawk, Sora's favorite slave, who cleans the house, told me that Sora said she was never to touch the basket, because it contained Flint's things."

Wink tilted her head. "You mean things he forgot to take when he divorced her three winters ago and went home to his people?"

"Apparently."

"Then you came in here to . . . ?"

Rockfish clenched his jaw and ground it before answering, "Yes! I admit it. I was curious. I've been living in Flint's shadow. I wanted to know about him! I opened the basket, but there's nothing in there of any interest except the sealed box."

Wink examined him. He seemed to be telling the truth. But the fact that he'd discussed the basket with Iron Hawk raised more questions than it solved. Iron Hawk was truly a loyal servant, and she loved Sora. She would never have revealed the whereabouts of the basket unless . . . Had she caught Rockfish in here one day and told him the chieftess said never to touch that basket?

Wink tugged off the lid and looked inside. She recognized the shirt on top: a dark forest green garment decorated with circlets of conch shell. Flint had worn it the day he'd married Sora. He must not have wanted to take it with him—and she'd cherished it too much to throw it away.

She dug deeper. In the very bottom of the basket, she found a wooden hair comb, several pieces of exquisite copper jewelry, and the box.

Even in the dim light, she could tell that the box's pitch seal had been broken.

Wink turned to glare at Rockfish.

"What's wrong?" he said defensively.

She pulled out the box and tipped it so that he could see that the seal was broken.

Rockfish's mouth dropped open. "Wink, I swear I did not open that box!"

In a voice that could have frozen lava, she said, "So. Someone knew about the box. He came in here, presumably while Sora was away, opened the sealed basket, then he opened the sealed box, and did . . . what?"

She lifted the lid to look inside.

The box was empty.

But as she tipped it to the light, she saw the tiny flecks of jade and gold dust that tumbled across the bottom.

In a stunned voice, she said, "Find Chief Long Fin. Tell him to meet me in my personal chamber. *Immediately*."

WINK CLUTCHED THE EMPTY BOX IN HER HAND AND paced like a madwoman. Her chamber spread ten paces across, giving her enough space to contemplate her doom.

Oh, Sora, what were you doing? Did you take the jade jewels to Eagle Flute Village? Did you give that brooch to Grown Bear?

In front of her, a massive painting of Mother Sun adorned the white plastered wall; golden hair twisted away from her face in glowing spirals. To the left, Comet People streaked earthward with their long blue-white wings tucked behind them.

"What am I going to do?" she whispered to the gods. "If Sora took the jade . . ."

Treason was the only crime in the Black Falcon Nation punishable by death.

Voices rose at the far end of the long hallway; then she heard her son's distinctive steps. He was running.

"Mother?" Long Fin called.

"Enter, my son."

He lifted the door curtain and stepped in, breathing hard. "Rockfish said you wanted to see me immediately. What is it? Has something happened?"

A tall slender young man, he had a handsome face with large dark eyes. He looked regal today, dressed in a dark blue shirt that hung to his knees. Twists of pounded copper ringed his collar.

Wink said, "The night Blue Bow died, what happened?"

His mouth gaped as though he couldn't believe she'd summoned him in a rush to repeat a story he'd already told her. "Mother, I was engaged in a very important conversation in the plaza—"

"Blue Bow said he knew *nothing* about the jade brooch, correct? He said he had not given it to Grown Bear to bring to Sora."

"That's right. He said he'd sent War Chief Grown Bear to Sora because she had broken her promise to speak with him about the Oak Leaf Village hostages. He'd wanted to arrange another meeting, if possible."

The missing five days.

Wink tucked the box beneath her arm and began pacing again.

Long Fin frowned. "What's wrong?"

"Old Sea Grass came to me last night. She said

she wanted to see the brooch before she took her murdered son's bones home to Oak Leaf Village."

"Yes? So?"

"She told me she'd seen the brooch before."

Long Fin paused, trying to fathom the implications. "Ah," he said with a nod, "now I understand."

"Understand what?"

"Mother"—he let out a breath—"Rockfish found me in the plaza speaking with Matron Wood Fern."

"Wood Fern?" Wink stiffened. "What did she want?"

"She wants to know how an enemy war chief got his hands on a very valuable piece of jewelry that belonged to the Black Falcon Nation."

Sea Grass must have talked to Wood Fern. . . .

"Rockfish was insistent that I meet with you immediately, so I did not have a chance to ask what she meant. Perhaps you will tell me?"

Her gaze drifted to the Comet People streaking like blue fire across her wall. She felt like she was flying away with them into some great darkness. "Sea Grass said the brooch once belonged to Red Warbler."

Incredulous, he asked, "Chieftess Sora's greatgrandmother?"

"Yes. Sea Grass said Red Warbler had a box full of jade pieces like that brooch that she'd sealed with boiled pine pitch and ordered her descendants never to open, except in case of emergency."

"Then how did Grown Bear get it?"

"Someone opened the box, took the brooch, and gave it to him."

They stood in silence, looking at each other.

"Who?" he said.

"I've been asking myself that same question. The only person I can think of is Sora."

Long Fin stood unmoving for several instants, then slowly walked to her sleeping bench and sank down atop her brightly colored blankets. In the few days he'd been chief of the Black Falcon Nation, he'd aged. She could see it in his slumping shoulders. "Why would she do that?"

"She must have used them to pay off someone."

"For what service?"

The old box felt suddenly gritty in her hand, dirty. "Maybe she tried to buy the release of our hostages—though I doubt she would have seen that as an emergency. Serious, yes, but an emergency? I don't think so."

"Had you discussed the possibility of buying the hostages back?"

"Of course we had," she said impatiently. "We discussed *every* possible way to get them back without going to war. I, myself, suggested sending Blue Bow a litter overflowing with rare copper and shells."

"But the council had voted *not* to pay for the release of the hostages."

"Of course, my son," she sternly replied. "They are doddering old women. They frequently make foolish decisions. It's always been my job, and Sora's job, to find ways to keep those decisions from harming our people."

"Do you and Chieftess Sora often go against the wishes of the council?"

"No. Not often. *On occasion* it is necessary to accomplish in secrecy what cannot be accomplished in full daylight."

He massaged his temples, as though in pain. "My mother, the diplomat."

Wink thrust the box at him like a weapon. "The council voted not to pay for the release of hostages. They did not forbid us to send gifts to Eagle Flute Village."

"A technicality I'm sure the council would not appreciate."

"It doesn't matter. *We* did not decide to use the jade to buy back our hostages."

He lifted his head. "Do you think Chieftess Sora made the decision on her own to protect you, in case she was discovered?"

Wink's knees went weak. She walked over and sank down on the sleeping bench beside Long Fin. "That's exactly the sort of thing she would do—sacrifice herself to protect me."

Long Fin scrutinized the box, then held out his hand. "May I look at it?"

She handed it to him and watched as he pulled off the lid to look inside. He tipped up the box and poured the tiny flakes of jade and gold dust into his palm, where they glittered.

"Mother, all I see is a few speckles of what appear to be jade and gold. They could have come from anywhere. This may not even be jade. It could be fine flakes of green chert, for all I know. I still think it far more likely that Grown Bear traveled south for sixteen days and got the brooch from the Scarlet Macaw People. But let's assume Sea Grass was telling the truth." He shoved the flakes around with his fingertip. "Several pieces of jade jewelry like that brooch would have been worth a fortune. Two pieces, maybe three, would have been much more than necessary to buy the release of our hostages. Why would Chieftess Sora have taken them all?"

Wink smoothed the wrinkles from her sleeves while she contemplated that question. "You mean, you think she was bargaining for more than our hostages?"

"*If* they existed, and she took them, she must have been."

The possibilities left her feeling shaky. She took several slow breaths to ease her racing pulse, but the blood surging in her ears still made it difficult to think straight.

"There is one more thing you should know, Mother."

She swung around to peer at him. "What is it?"

"Matron Wood Fern asked me to reconvene the council of elders to discuss the jade."

"But . . . it would be meaningless. It's still three to two against. Unless she plans on changing her vote."

Long Fin poured the glitter back into the box and handed it to her. "Mother, I think I may have made a mistake."

"What mistake?"

"When Wood Fern first approached me, I . . . well, she said she'd heard that I had supported sending warriors after the jade, and asked if I still did."

Wink gripped the box in both hands. "What did you say?"

"I told her that I believed the jade could make the Black Falcon Nation the greatest chieftainship in the world."

Wink felt light-headed, sick to her stomach. Of course, she'd heard him say this; but that was before he'd become chief—when it didn't matter what he said. "And that's when she asked you to reconvene the council?"

"Yes."

Forcing calm into her voice, she said, "You are wise to realize that was a mistake, my son. One that we must rectify as soon as possible."

SORA WOKE NAKED AND UTTERLY EXHAUSTED. SHE was lying beneath a warm deerhide with Flint's arms around her. He had his bare body curled against her back.

Someone moved around the house, stoking the fire, tapping a horn spoon against a wooden pot. Strongheart?

She inhaled a deep breath and let it out slowly. The last thing she remembered was seeing the Midnight Fox's eyes flare to life inside her.

What had happened after that?

Obviously, and to her surprise, she was alive. If she was in Strongheart's house that probably meant the Loon villagers had voted to allow him to Heal her. But why was Flint here?

He nuzzled his cheek against her hair and whispered, "You're safe. Don't worry."

"Get away from me. I hate you," she weakly responded. "If I had the strength I'd tear out your heart."

Flint grabbed her chin and wrenched her head around to glare into her eyes. "You may hate me, but—"

"You raped me!"

"Yes, I did! But it wasn't the first time, was it? I remember when you used to beg me to surprise you in the forest. You loved it!"

"That was different. It was a game!"

"*This* was a game, too. It just wasn't played by your rules." He released her chin and more gently said, "You can hate me if you wish, but I saved your life today."

Her jaw trembled before she clenched her teeth to steady it. "I do not want you here. Leave."

"If you truly want me to go, I will. But I had no other choice, Sora. I had to find a way to make those men leave us alone so that I could talk with you in private. Raping you was the only leverage I had."

For three winters, she had longed for Flint. Sometimes the need had been so overwhelming she'd felt she would die if she couldn't hold him.

Now here he was, a dead dream born of lightning and thunder, come back to life. From a dark place in her souls she heard him whispering, *I love you. I love you so much.*

A sick rage filled her. All of her adult life, she had forgiven him. No matter how terrible the hurt, he'd coddled her and stroked her, and she'd forgiven him.

Flint said, "You don't really want me to leave, do you? You need me. You know you do."

"I've always needed you, but that doesn't mean you've always been there."

"Stop it. The role of 'abandoned wife,' doesn't suit you. You were as much to blame as I was."

For a while, she just breathed. A mixture of hatred and despair knotted her belly. The trial testimonies kept running through her souls. There were so many things she didn't understand. She needed time to think!

"Please, Sora," he said softly. "I love you so much. Forgive me." He released her hand and ran his fingers up her abdomen to her breasts, where he leisurely stroked her nipples. She tried to shove his hand away, and he took her breast in a hurtful grip and squeezed.

In a biting voice, she said, "Flint, for the sake of the gods, can you stop touching me long enough for me to ask you some questions?"

He let his hand fall. "What questions?"

"Did you really love White Fawn?"

"Yes." Pain laced his voice, and despite her anger, it made her hurt for him. "She was sweet and brave—just like you were when you'd seen fifteen winters. All I wanted was to give her the love you had rejected, to pet her and protect her, just to see her smile for me alone."

"I'm sorry she died. I didn't do it, but I'm still sorry."

He fumbled with the hides, pulling them more tightly around their bodies. "It was a . . . a frightening thing . . . when she died. Rather than hating you, I wanted you, Sora. I desperately longed to lie in your arms with my head pillowed between your breasts. We had shared so many memories, such grief, and pain. I truly believed that you were the only person in the world who could ease my hurt. And I hated myself for that."

"What made you think I'd killed her?"

For a time, he didn't speak. "We weren't sure which trail the bridal procession was going to take. The barbarian Lily People had been raiding the borders of our territory; the procession had to be careful. Skinner and I took two different trails, hoping to catch the procession and lead them to Big Cypress Spring where we would have warriors waiting to escort them into Oak Leaf Village. No matter what we found, we promised to meet up at Big Cypress Spring. Two days later, we did, but neither of us had seen the procession. Skinner told the warriors to go home, and together, he and I began searching for White Fawn's party."

"How long did it take you to find them?"

"At nightfall, we located them. Everyone in the bridal procession was weeping and tearing at their clothing. White Fawn's father said he thought he'd glimpsed a strange woman out in the trees the night his daughter died. He thought it was a Forest Spirit.

Skinner said—and I agreed—that you were the only woman who would want White Fawn dead. I knew then that I had to find someone to help you. To Heal you. Skinner suggested . . ."

The person who'd been moving in the background walked across the house, threw open the door curtain, and left. Voices rose outside. Strongheart spoke to a guard. She couldn't make out the words.

Flint squeezed her breast again, and she could feel his manhood swelling. She rolled away and turned to face him.

"What else did Skinner say?"

"Stupid things," he answered through a sharp exhalation. "He told me not to be sad, that he loved me far more than White Fawn ever could, and that he would never leave me."

Despite coming from a distinguished family and rising to the position of village war chief, Skinner had never married. She had always wondered why, and suspected that he might be a berdache. Berdaches had male bodies, but female souls. They often took on the roles of women in Black Falcon society, becoming weavers, or planters. They were sacred bridges between light and dark, male and female. The most important warriors took berdaches as 'wives,' and were considered extremely lucky to have them.

"Did you love him?" she asked.

He paused, as though deciding whether or not to tell her. "Yes, Sora, I did. During those awful winters when you and I were trying to kill each other, I used to seek him out, just to be close to him. He loved me so much. It hurt him when I married you, and I knew it. But I couldn't help myself. You were like Mother Sun to me. I truly believed that all the light and warmth in the world lived in you, and if I could have you, nothing else would matter. I could live without Skinner, and my family, even my own souls, if necessary, just to be able to touch you every day."

The pale yellow firelight flickered over his handsome face, and she could see how deeply the lines had cut around his eyes.

"Why didn't you tell me about Skinner?"

Flint gave her an anguished look. "Would you have shared me?"

"No," she answered honestly. "I wanted you all to myself."

He nodded, and a lock of long black hair fell over his bare chest. "Besides, I thought you knew. Every time I came home after being with him, you shouted at me and berated me, as though in punishment."

"I didn't know. When you were gone, my souls turned to ice. I was lonely. That's why I was unkind to you, but I didn't know."

"After I left you, I ran straight to him. He rocked me in his arms for days while I wept. For two and a half winters, we were happy together. Then I met White Fawn . . . and once again things became difficult between us."

Weariness veiled his eyes, as though the "difficulties" had been almost too much to bear.

Flint ran his hand down her arm and laced his fingers with hers, as he had every morning and night for over fourteen winters. A desperate sense of gratitude filled her. Only a short time ago, she had felt utterly alone. Now, suddenly, he was here beside her. And he was the one person who might actually be able to help her. After all, as the local hero, he could wander Eagle Flute Village freely. Perhaps, if she was very careful, she could glean information from him without asking him to spy for her.

Sora lifted herself to kiss him, a bare touch of her lips to his, but it made his eyes glow like black moons.

Against her lips, he whispered, "I want you. Do you want me? It may kindle old fires."

Almost as though it moved without her knowledge, her hand lowered to touch his rigid manhood. A small exquisite sound of pleasure escaped his throat.

Flint pushed away the deerhide, and she gazed at his muscular body. She remembered every scar and birthmark as though she had touched them only last night.

She placed a tender kiss on the white scar beneath his left breast, which he'd gotten in a knife fight as a young warrior. Luckily his enemy's knife had struck a rib and deflected the point, or he'd be dead.

Next, she kissed her way down the dark line of hair to his navel, where she pressed her mouth against three scars—smaller, barely visible lines—made by her own fingernails. She'd been young, too eager to have him inside her.

When she slid down and kissed his manhood, a shudder went through him. He said, "I had forgotten the feel of your lips."

She used her tongue, and Flint's fingers dug into the hides. After another hundred heartbeats, he said, "Take me full in your mouth, Sora."

She did it, and he put his hands on her head, and began forcing her down upon him. His breath came in short agonized gasps.

Even when he cried out and his warm seed burst into her mouth, she did not release him. For a long time, her lips continued to wring soft sounds of pleasure from his throat.

Finally, he pulled her up to look at him. Dreamlike pleasure sparkled in his eyes, softening his expression. He took her face in his hands and said, "Blessed gods, I have missed you."

She stretched out beside him, and he gathered up her long black hair and spread it across his chest like a silken blanket, then petted it.

It took her a few moments to work up the courage to ask, "Flint, did it ever occur to you that Skinner might have killed White Fawn?"

For a time he didn't move at all; then his fists clenched. "No. Why would he?"

"Out of jealousy. He'd lost you to a woman once before. Maybe he couldn't stand to let it happen again."

"He wouldn't have hurt me that way, Sora. It's impossible."

Like obsidian-sharp wings, strange emotions fluttered her belly, slicing, stabbing. Flint had easily believed Skinner when he'd suggested that Sora was the culprit who'd killed White Fawn, but he refused to even consider the possibility that Skinner had murdered her? Why had she never realized how blindly devoted Flint was to Skinner? How much he'd trusted him?

"Wasn't White Fawn murdered before the two of you met up at Big Cypress Spring? While Skinner was still out on the trail?"

"Leave it alone, Sora." His voice had turned low, threatening. "Skinner didn't kill her. You did."

"But, Flint, isn't it at least possible—"

"I said *no!*" he shouted in her face, and lunged to his feet.

As he walked over and picked up his shirt, his belly muscles tightened.

"Flint, I swear to you, Skinner tried to kill me, too. In the forest. He tried to choke me to death."

He shook his head violently. "He did that in self-defense, after you poisoned him. Wink told me all about it."

Suddenly cold, she shivered. "I don't remember giving him poison. He—"

"You'd better start remembering, my sweet murderess, or Strongheart will never be able to help you, and your best friend, Wink, will be forced to slit your throat."

He roughly jerked his shirt over his head, walked to the door, and ducked outside.

Sora sank back against the hides and stared at the swaying curtain.

I've been such a fool . . . all along.

"THERE SHE IS," WINK SAID AS SHE AND LONG FIN descended the steps that led down the face of the Matron's Mound in Blackbird Town. In the distance birds fluttered over Persimmon Lake, soaring and diving after insects. The scent of cypress fires mixed curiously with the sweet fragrance of redbud blossoms.

Wood Fern wore a buckskin cape adorned with iridescent circlets of shell. She was hard to miss, standing in the plaza propped on her walking stick and surrounded by Sea Grass and her warriors. Amid the white fuzz of hair that covered Wood Fern's age-spotted scalp, a black buzzard feather gleamed. She was known to be a great Healer. At one time, Chieftess Yellow Cypress had even hired Wood Fern to Heal her sick daughter, Sora. But

Wood Fern's specialty was arrow wounds, not casting out Evil Spirits. At the end, when all her treatments had failed, Wood Fern had flatly told Yellow Cypress that it would be kinder to kill the little girl than allow her to grow up with a malignant Spirit swelling inside her.

Yellow Cypress hadn't had the heart to do it. Or perhaps the Shadow Rock Clan had refused to condone it. Only one thing was certain: After Walks-among-the-Stars' death Yellow Cypress had worked very hard to keep her last child alive, to assure that no one else's child could ascend to the chieftainship of the Black Falcon Nation.

Slaves—dressed in plain brown robes—scurried about, carrying water pots to and from the corn and squash fields that surrounded Persimmon Lake, chopping wood for the fires with stone axes. Two large looms sat at the base of the Chief's Mound, where young women wove beautiful blankets.

As they walked toward Wood Fern and Sea Grass, Long Fin said, "What do you want me to do, Mother?"

"Just tell them your heart has changed. You do not wish to send warriors after the jade. That will settle the matter."

Long Fin's mouth pursed, as though he found the idea distasteful. "I'll do it," he said, "but you know I don't believe it. I think that brooch came from the Scarlet Macaw People, just as Grown Bear said, and we would benefit enormously from going after it."

"You can believe whatever you want; just don't tell them. Not today."

"I understand."

Sea Grass's voice dropped when she saw them coming, and both she and Wood Fern turned to look at them. The warriors parted to create a path for Wink and Long Fin.

"Greetings, Wood Fern," Wink said and smiled. "My son tells me you stopped him this morning to ask that he reconvene the council to discuss the jade."

Wood Fern tipped up her shriveled face, and her white-filmed eyes gleamed in the sunlight. "Yes. I spoke with Rockfish earlier. He tells me that in two or three days, the warriors promised by his people will march into Blackbird Town, and we will have one last chance to join them. Since our new chief supports sending warriors, I thought—"

Wink interrupted, "But in the last council meeting, you voted no. Has your heart changed?"

Wood Fern exchanged a secretive glance with Sea Grass. "It has not. I think sending warriors south into an unknown land is a fool's errand. But some of my village matrons disagree with me. They have asked me to hear the arguments again."

Long Fin stepped forward, bowed to Wood Fern, and said, "It's not necessary, Matron. After further discussing the issue with my mother, I've decided that both of you are right. We should not risk the lives of our young men and women for a few boat-loads of stone."

The deep wrinkles around Sea Grass's mouth hardened. She glared at him, then fixed her eyes on Wink. "It seems you have the ear of our new chief, Matron—which I should have suspected. I had just hoped that Chief Long Fin would prove more"—she seemed to be contemplating the right word—"independent."

Long Fin bristled and opened his mouth to respond to the insult, but Wink put a restraining hand on his arm. "Wood Fern, since Long Fin's 'no' vote would make another meeting pointless, I assume you wish to rescind your request that we reconvene the council."

Wood Fern turned to Sea Grass, as though expecting her to answer. Sea Grass glowered at Wink. She'd obviously been counting on another vote.

Why is Water Hickory Clan suddenly so obsessed with the jade? Especially when Sea Grass believes it was ours to begin with?

Or . . . is this sudden?

Even as a small child, Wink had been particularly skilled at smelling out political intrigue, and Sea Grass's expression had her nostrils quivering. Had they been planning this all along? Perhaps Wood Fern's 'no' vote in the council meeting had been designed to buy more time for Water Hickory Clan. To do what?

Assemble warriors behind my back?

Wood Fern put a skeletal hand on Sea Grass's arm and walked a few paces away. While they whispered to each other like furious bees, Wink went over every moment of last night's discussion with Sea Grass. The strands of the weave were pulling tight, but she couldn't quite make out the pattern yet.

Long Fin leaned close to her ear to ask, "You look like you want to murder someone. What are you thinking?"

"Just wondering."

The Water Hickory Clan had a bloodthirsty reputation. Only last winter, they'd voted to make war upon the Conch Shell People to gain control of their oyster beds. The winter before, they'd wanted to kill the Red Owl People to capture their buffalo-hunting territory. Sora and Wink had blocked them by convincing the other clans it was far more profitable to work out Trade agreements than to lose their own warriors in a war over lands they could occupy but never fully possess. Then, when the Oak Leaf Villagers had been taken hostage by the Loon People, Water Hickory Clan had instantly wanted to wipe Eagle Flute Village from the face of Grandmother Earth.

"Wondering about what?"

Wink took a difficult breath. "About how desperate Water Hickory Clan is to lead this nation."

"You mean you think they might . . ."

His words faded when Wood Fern turned and walked back toward them at an agonizingly slow pace, carefully propping her walking stick to brace every step.

Sea Grass remained standing twenty paces away, with a grim expression on her old face.

Wood Fern stopped in front of Wink and tilted her head in a birdlike fashion. "While I will still vote no, Sea Grass tells me that she spoke with the other clan matrons and some wish to change their votes. In deference, I think we should reconvene the council."

Wink bowed respectfully. "Then I will, of course, do as you ask. I only wish—"

Everyone turned when a man burst from the trees, shouting, *"Matron Wink! I must see the Matron! Where is she?"*

"Here!" Wink called, and walked forward with Long Fin behind her.

"Who is he? Do you know him?" Long Fin asked. He had drawn a deer-bone stiletto from his belt and held it out in front of him as though ready to protect her if the runner turned out to be dangerous.

"Yes, it's . . . it's that Trader who was here a half-moon ago, Storksbill."

Wink hurried to meet him, and the crowd followed her. Storksbill was young, twenty-two winters, but he traveled a good deal, which made him a perfect messenger. He'd twisted his black hair into a bun and pinned it on top of his head with a rabbit-bone skewer. The run had shaken strands loose, and they dangled around his face and stuck to his cheeks. "What's wrong, Storksbill?"

He knelt before her. "It's . . . Chieftess Sora. . . . She was kidnapped by the Loon People."

Gasps went up, and Sea Grass shouted, "When? How did this happen?" She shoved her way forward to study the young Trader.

Storksbill replied, "The chieftess and her party were ambushed on the south side of Jasper Lake three days ago. The Trader who passed the message to me was in Eagle Flute Village when War Chief Grown Bear arrived with the three prisoners."

Sea Grass gave Wink a suspicious look, as though she were responsible, then pushed through the crowd to get to Wood Fern. A smug half-smile turned her lips as she cupped a hand to Wood Fern's ear to whisper.

Wood Fern nodded.

Wink turned to Storksbill. "The Black Falcon Nation thanks you. Long Fin, please see that Storksbill is handsomely paid for his bravery."

He said, "Yes, Mother," but gave her a look similar to the one Sea Grass had just given her. "I'll see to his needs in a few moments."

Long Fin took Wink by the arm and walked her well away from the crowd surrounding the Trader before asking, "I saw the look Sea Grass gave you. Is this some game you're playing? Did you arrange the ambush?"

Wink gripped his hand where it rested on her arm, and squeezed it hard. "When you're done with Storksbill, come to my chamber and we'll discuss it."

As Wink paced in the firelight, the shells sewn to the hem of her pale green dress sparkled. She kept glancing at her son where he crouched before the flames with his jaw clenched. On the wall behind him, a stylized image of Black Falcon flying into Mother Sun's heart blazed in brilliant shades of red, purple, and yellow.

"And you believed him?" Long Fin asked in a dazed voice.

"Yes, I believed him. Grown Bear told Flint that once the news of Blue Bow's murder reached Eagle Flute Village, they would certainly kill every one of our hostages. It made perfect sense. I had to do something!"

"Then you *did* arrange for Sora's party to be captured?"

"No. I left that up to Flint. He told me that he had good reason to believe he could buy off Grown Bear, and all he needed was to get into Eagle Flute Village. Once there, he promised he would find a way to distract the new chief until he could release the hostages."

"Mother, I can't believe I'm hearing this. Are you telling me that you risked the life of your best friend, Chieftess Sora, for—"

"To save our people?" she shouted. "Yes, I certainly did! And I would do it again tomorrow if I thought it would work." At his stricken expression, she added more softly, "Don't look at me like that. What are three lives compared to a terrible war? There's more at stake here than you know. I'm trying to save all of us. Including Sora!"

A swallow went down his throat, as though he'd eaten a very bitter fruit. "Is that why you insisted that Feather Dancer go along? You were hoping he would be able to keep her safe?"

"Of course I was. Flint didn't want me to send Feather Dancer. He strongly objected, but I couldn't help myself. If anyone can get Sora out of the village alive, it's Feather Dancer."

Long Fin reached for a cup that rested near the hearth, keeping warm, and dipped it into the tea pot that sat in the ashes. "Would you like a cup, Mother? It may soothe your nerves."

Wink ran a hand through her graying black hair. "Yes. Thank you."

After she walked to the hearth and knelt down on

the woven mat, Long Fin handed her the cup, and dipped another for himself.

For a time, he just watched her sip her tea, then finally, he said, "Now let's speak of the other matter at hand."

"Which one?"

He drew up his knees and propped his cup on them. "Do you truly believe Sora is sick and needs to be Healed, or was she just bait to get Flint into Eagle Flute Village?"

IN THE MIDDLE OF THE NIGHT, SORA WOKE AND rolled to her back to stare up at the domed ceiling, where gray tendrils of smoke eddied. Rain pattered on the roof.

Flint was gone.

Strongheart lay curled on his sleeping bench on the opposite side of the house, his back to her. The blue color of his sleep shirt looked faintly green in the yellow firelight.

"Priest?" she said softly.

He didn't respond. She could hear the deep rhythm of his breathing.

Louder, she said, "Priest?"

Strongheart woke, lifted his head, and rolled to his side to look at her. "Did you call me?"

"Yes."

He swung his legs over the bench and sat up to rub the sleep from his eyes. "Are you all right?"

"No."

Strongheart exhaled a deep breath and walked across the house to kneel by her side. As though fearing she was ill, he drew the hides up to her chin to keep her warm and put a hand to her forehead.

"Are you fevered?"

When Sora sat up to face him, the hide fell away, revealing her naked torso. "He was wearing white."

Strongheart frowned for several moments; then, as understanding dawned, he sank to the floor and nodded. "What else do you recall from the night your father died?"

On the fabric of her souls, her father's eyes smiled at her, filled with enough love and pride to last her a lifetime. If only she hadn't . . . if he hadn't died.

"I—I made the stew and sat down to eat it with him. But he told me he wanted to eat alone. He said I should go play with the new cornhusk dolls he'd made for me."

"Did you leave?"

"Yes." Even now, the disappointment hurt. She had been looking forward to tasting the sage-flavored jerky. When she'd crumbled it into the pot, it had smelled delicious. "I went down the hallway to my room. The slaves had built a fire. I pulled down my two new dolls, sat by the fire, and played with them. A short while later, I thought I heard my father crying as he came down the hall, but the crying stopped just before he neared my bedchamber."

"Was he standing outside your door? Listening? Perhaps to see if you were asleep?"

"Maybe. I don't know. The sound frightened me. I had never heard him cry before. I sat as though frozen. I don't even think I breathed. Eventually I heard him walk past my doorway and duck into the chamber he shared with my mother. He came out a little later and walked back down the hall to the temple."

"He didn't speak to you?"

"No. He just walked away."

"And then?"

She bent forward, and long black hair fell over her shoulders, covering her breasts. "I must have fallen asleep. The next thing I remember is hearing my mother's hoarse scream. It sliced my dreams like a blade. I scrambled to my feet and ran all the way with my heart in my throat."

"What did you find?"

"My mother . . . and my sister. They were kneeling beside Father's body."

"Where was he?"

"Curled on the floor of the temple. He must have dropped the stew bowl, because it was cracked, resting by his hand. The stew had leaked out onto the floor mats."

"He was dead?"

She nodded and longed to weep all over again. Father's wide dead eyes had seemed to be staring right at her, but the love had drained away. Only fear shone. "Yes. Mother sniffed the stew and shrieked like a homeless ghost: *'Poison! There's poison in this stew! Someone poisoned my husband!'* "

Sora dropped her face into her hands and massaged her forehead.

"What did your sister do?"

"Hmm?"

Strongheart cocked his head, examining her. "Your sister. What did she do when your mother shrieked?"

Sora struggled to recall. Her mother's face, her father's clawlike hands, every detail of the chamber, were engraved in her souls. Why was her sister missing from the painting? "I don't even remember seeing her after that."

"Did she say anything to you?"

A deep ache welled inside her, and she began to sob without tears. The reaction shocked her. "This is so strange. I don't know why I'm crying."

Strongheart reached out to gently touch her cheek. "What did she say to you?"

"I—I don't recall her speaking to me at all. Maybe she ran for help when Mother screamed."

He leaned forward, and peered directly into her eyes. "I don't think so, Sora. I think your sister spoke to you. What did she say?"

"No, no. I'm sure she was gone. She must have run for help. I didn't. Mother didn't. Someone must have. Walks-among-the-Stars is the logical person."

"All right," he said with a tired nod. "Then what happened?"

Sora's shoulders heaved. The dry tears seemed to come not from her eyes, but from deep inside her chest. "Mother shouted at me, demanding to know which slave had made the stew."

From a barricaded chamber in her souls, a frightened little girl's voice mewed, *I did, Mother. I made it. Father asked me to.*

"When you told her that you had made it, what did she say?"

"I don't r-recall," Sora stammered. "A dozen people rushed into the temple, all talking at once."

"Did they question you about what happened?"

"Yes. Then I ran back to my bedchamber to go to sleep. I had the overwhelming urge to sleep."

Strongheart sat back, and the lines at the corners of his mouth tightened. For a long while, he just studied her with kindness in his eyes.

The raindrops pattering on the roof became a soft hiss, and somewhere in the distance thunder rumbled across the forests like a huge herd of buffalo.

Strongheart reached out and took her hands. As he squeezed them, he said, "Do you always remember more after the Midnight Fox attacks you?"

She looked down at his fingers, large and calloused, and a curious sensation of panic stung her veins. She drew her hands away and placed them in her lap. He didn't seem to mind.

"No, not usually."

"Why do you think the memories came to you tonight?"

Sora ran her fingers over the soft hair of the deerhide. Why had they?

"It's probably Flint's presence," she said, and beautiful memories of lying in treetops, touching each other all day long, filled her. She could hear his joyous laughter as clearly today as she had seventeen winters ago. "I don't know why. The gods know it doesn't make any sense, but I feel safe when he is close."

"Close," he said, as though not sure he understood what that meant. "You mean that intimacy makes you feel safe?"

"Yes, I think so."

Strongheart's gaze darted over her face. "Flint told me that while the two of you were married, he'd been able to keep your reflection-soul in your body for moons at a time. Is that how he did it? By loving you?"

She noticed that she was wringing her hands in her lap, and stopped. "I'm not sure my reflection-soul is loose, Priest, but Flint did make me love my body. I suppose, if my reflection-soul was wandering, he made it long to come home."

Out in the forest a night bird called, and it seemed to be a signal to the rain gods. The skies opened and released a downpour. For a time, the pounding on the thatched roof was so loud they couldn't hear each other speak. Strongheart made a helpless gesture with his hand, and sat back to watch the trickle com-

ing through his smokehole turn into a tiny stream.
When it splashed into the fire hearth, the last remaining coals sizzled and ash puffed into the air.

They both sat in amicable silence.

But Sora could tell he was thinking hard about
something. His brows had drawn together above his
hooked nose.

The rain eased a little, and Strongheart shifted to
sit cross-legged in front of her. For an instant she
didn't breathe, and it seemed virtually impossible
that the only point of contact between their two bodies was where her long hair brushed the hem of his
sleep shirt.

"Do the dangerous things slip from their hidden
chambers and walk around your souls while Flint is
loving you, or afterward, when you're lying in each
other's arms?"

She had to think about that for a time. She'd never
noticed. "They first appear while he is loving me."

"Do you look at them when they're walking
around freely?"

As the rain decreased, cold wind blew around the
door curtain and swept the house. The fragrances of
wet forest and marsh filled the air. She shivered and
pulled the deerhide up around her again.

"I don't think I look at them directly. I see them
moving at the edge of my vision. Sometimes I know
what they are. Sometimes, later in the day, I realize
that I glimpsed them earlier."

"Sora," he said in a tender voice, "the next time
you see your father moving at the edge of your vi-

sion, ask him why he needed to go back to his chamber. Did he go back to get something?"

A strange bitter smell taunted her nostrils. She blinked when she realized it wasn't coming from the house, or riding the wind . . . it was something seeping up from one of the dark rooms in her souls.

"I'll ask," she said.

"Good."

Strongheart put a hand to her hair to force her to meet his eyes. "Now, try to sleep. Tomorrow will be a busy day."

He rose and walked across the floor, where he sank down on his sleeping bench and pulled his blankets over him. His short black hair shone as he stretched out on his side.

"What happens tomorrow?"

As he adjusted his head on his arm, he answered, "We will begin the Soul-Curing ceremonies."

19

FEATHER DANCER FELT THE YOUNG WARRIOR, Adder, rise from beneath the cape they shared, then he silently made his way across the house.

Adder touched Cold Spring's shoulder and whispered, "We . . . talk."

Cold Spring nodded and followed Adder to the middle of the house, where they crouched near the fire pit, their faces gleaming in the crimson light of the dying coals.

The rest of the captives seemed to be asleep. Old Jawbone snored loudly enough to rouse her ancestors in the Land of the Dead. One of the children, probably Pipit, moaned as though her shadow-soul were being chased by monsters.

Adder cradled his wounded arm and leaned very

close to Cold Spring to whisper, "Grown Bear . . . messenger . . . Sea Grass says just . . . few . . . days."

Cold Spring shook his head, and dirty gray-streaked black hair fell over his wrinkled face. "I'm not sure the children will survive."

"Everyone knew the risks when . . . volunteered . . ." His voice became a barely audible drone.

"The children didn't volunteer," Cold Spring said. "Their parents did."

Feather Dancer fought to still his breathing so he could hear more clearly.

Adder finished, "As soon as the jade party leaves Blackbird Town, Matron . . . will dispatch warriors . . ."

"Blessed gods," Cold Spring murmured, and in the red gleam, Feather Dancer saw him squeeze his eyes closed. "I pray this works."

Adder put a hand on Cold Spring's shoulder and hissed, "It's a brilliant stroke . . . elevate our status . . ."

Cold Spring nodded weakly and stood. Before they parted, Cold Spring said something that Feather Dancer didn't catch; then the two men quietly returned to their beds.

Adder stretched out beside Feather Dancer again, and covered himself with the edge of the cape.

Feather Dancer kept his breathing deep and even, but as he worked to piece together the bits of information, his jaw clenched.

Sea Grass had obviously sent a message to Grown Bear, who communicated it to Adder, telling the captives to wait a few more days, until the party going after the jade could leave Blackbird Town and she could dispatch warriors . . . in a brilliant stroke that would elevate 'our' status. . . .

What was a Black Falcon village matron doing working with an enemy war chief?

Did she mean the 'brilliant stroke' would elevate the status of Oak Leaf Village? Or the status of Water Hickory Clan?

And what had the captives volunteered for?

The only thing he could think of was that they had volunteered to be captured.

Feather Dancer closed his eyes and watched the spidery patterns that pulsed on the backs of his eyelids. The implications were staggering. If Sea Grass had hatched a plan with Grown Bear that would elevate the status of her village or clan, and part of the plan required the capture of her villagers, she'd been plotting this for over a moon. Probably longer.

Matron Wink's words came back to him: *Just do as Flint says. He knows far more about this than I do.*

Flint was from Oak Leaf Village. He was Water Hickory Clan.

Feather Dancer had the hollow feeling that he may have been wrong. Perhaps Flint was not working with Matron Wink, after all. If Sea Grass was willing to sacrifice a dozen of her relatives, and to ally her village with an enemy war chief, the stakes were much higher. She was after more than just the downfall of one chieftess.

Slowly, dimly, he began to understand.

AFTER ALL THE OTHER MATRONS HAD BEEN SERVED tea, Wink motioned for the slaves to leave the council chamber. They filed out one by one, leaving a curiously pregnant silence in their wake.

Wink walked around the four benches, and sat on the south bench, across the fire from her son, Chief Long Fin. To Wink's right, Matron Wood Fern sat with her hands propped on the knob of her walking stick. She kept the stick in front of her as though she might need it to knock some sense into one of the other council members.

To Wink's left, Matron Black Birch of the Bald Cypress clan sat beside Matron Wigeon of the Shoveler Clan. Both old women had gray hair and shriveled faces.

Only her son looked out of place. This was his

first council meeting as chief of the Black Falcon Nation, and he kept glancing at the clan matrons as though he feared one of them might stab him in the heart at any moment. At least he had dressed well for the occasion, wearing his best cream-colored cape, painted with intricate red and yellow geometric designs. Copper bangles ringed the hem.

Wink said, "As you know, Matron Wood Fern of the Water Hickory Clan asked that I call the council together again to reconsider the matter of the jade. She suggested that one of you wished to change your vote. Who would like to speak first?"

Wigeon lifted her frail old hand. "I would," she said in a gruff voice. "I have been hearing rumors for days about things Chief Blue Bow said before he was killed. The rumors keep growing larger and more bizarre by the moment. Does anyone here know exactly what Blue Bow said?"

Long Fin nodded, and all eyes turned to him. "Yes, Matron, I do. I was speaking with him just before he died."

Wigeon's mouth pursed. "Well, what did he say?"

Long Fin took a deep breath, and replied, "He said many things, but I assume you wish to know specifically about the jade brooch?"

"Yes, of course."

Long Fin jerked a nod. "Blue Bow said he knew nothing about it. He said he had not sent it to Chieftess Sora."

A din rose as the old women all talked at once.

Above the fray, Wink called, "Who wishes to speak next?"

"I do," Wood Fern said. She tilted her head so that her white-filmed eyes caught the light. "This is just another reason *not* to send warriors after the jade. No one knows what's really going on! Sea Grass told me that she believes the jade brooch once belonged to Chieftess Red Warbler. I can't say that I recall ever seeing Red Warbler wear that brooch. Do any of you?"

Heads shook around the chamber, and the skin at the back of Wink's neck crawled. Had the old witch lied to her?

Why would she?

Wigeon said, "Sea Grass came to me, just like she did to the rest of you, to tell me that story, but I recall no such brooch. And as for a box of jade jewelry . . ." She sighed. "I never heard of such a thing."

"Nor did I," Matron Black Birch rasped in agreement. She adjusted the yellow blanket over her shoulders, and extended one bony finger, to command attention. "But let us be straight here. My memory is not as good as it once was. Perhaps Sea Grass's memory is also shaky. That leads us back to Grown Bear's original story, that he canoed south for sixteen days, where he met the Scarlet Macaw people, who gave him the brooch in exchange for his promise that he would return with warriors and help chase away the owners of the jade quarry." She lifted her chin. "What does it matter who sent the brooch?

Perhaps Grown Bear is working for himself. I don't care. I'm still in favor of sending warriors after the jade." She extended a thin arm to Wigeon. "What about you? The last time we met to discuss the brooch, you voted with Wood Fern. Since my vote has not changed, nor has Wood Fern's, I assume yours has."

Wigeon wet her wrinkled lips. "Right after Blue Bow was killed, I asked Rockfish to come to my chamber. He told me the jade could be the cornerstone of a new and greater Black Falcon Nation." She extended a gnarled fist. "Aren't any of you afraid of the Loon People, or the barbarian Lily People, or the Sandhill Crane People? Their numbers grow each winter, I think much faster than our numbers are growing. We should look to the future."

Wood Fern scowled. "Are you suggesting that someday these pusillanimous worms might overrun us?" She waved a hand. "Ridiculous. They are savages."

Wink said, "I would also mention that sending our warriors south at this moment in time would leave Blackbird Town vulnerable to attack by any of the peoples Matron Wigeon just mentioned."

"I agree," Wood Fern said.

Wink studied the expressions of the other matrons before she said, "Perhaps we should cast our voices. Let me be the first to vote no."

"I vote yes," Wigeon said, barely above a whisper.

"As do I," Black Birch called.

There was a lull, and Wink said, "Wood Fern?"

"Absolutely not." She stamped her walking stick for emphasis. "I will not have it said twenty winters from now that Water Hickory Clan sent hundreds of warriors to their deaths for nothing."

Wink turned to Long Fin. Her son shifted uncomfortably. His vote would break the tie, one way or the other. "Chief, how do you vote?"

He hesitated, and Wink longed to grab a piece of firewood and bash his brains out. "Chief?"

His throat bobbed with a difficult swallow. "I believe that Sea Grass is mistaken about the brooch. I don't think it belonged to Red Warbler. I think it came from the Scarlet Macaw People, just as Grown Bear said it did. From the moment I saw that brooch, I knew that boatloads of jade could make us the most powerful chieftainship in the world. . . ." The buzz of voices that erupted over this statement made Long Fin's expression tense. "I have spoken to Rockfish many times since that night, and he has explained to me in great detail the possible benefits to the Black Falcon Nation. Therefore, I—I vote yes."

Wink felt the blood drain from her face. By the gods, she would have him assassinated!

In a preternaturally calm voice, she said, "It is settled, then. When the war party arrives, we will join it. It is now the duty of each matron here to decide how many warriors from her clan will accompany the party. We should meet again—"

Wood Fern grunted as she braced her walking stick and got to her feet. "I don't want any rumors flying about this council session. When people ask you what I said, you tell them straightly that I believe this decision is catastrophic. If it results in the downfall of our nation, the Water Hickory Clan is not to blame." She made her way to the door, shoved aside the curtain, and left without a backward glance.

Wigeon and Black Birch steadied each other as they, too, rose and headed for the door.

That left Wink staring at Long Fin.

He squirmed for a moment, then lurched to his feet and cried, "Mother, don't look so stunned. You've known all along that I wanted us to join the war party!"

"Yes, but I thought we had an agreement that we should wait until a more fortuitous time."

He squared his shoulders. "I am the chief now. I make my own decisions."

Slowly, Wink rose to her feet. Earlier, when Sea Grass had accused him of not being 'independent,' of doing whatever Wink told him to, it must have shamed him.

"Congratulations," she said with deadly softness. "You've just cast your first bad vote. You'd better pray that none of your friends die because of it."

Wink swept out of the room and headlong down the hall.

Before Mother Sun went to sleep that night, she had to select a new war chief to replace Feather Dancer—a task she'd been dreading—and tell him that each clan would be assigning warriors to accompany the party south.

It would be an ugly day, filled with bitter accusations from those who opposed the decision, and shouts of joy from those who supported it.

Through it all, she would be thinking about one person.

The person most responsible for all of this.

Rockfish.

THE SWEET SOUND OF A FLUTE MIXED ODDLY WITH the drizzling rain and penetrated her sleep.

Sora rolled to her side and gazed around the house. The fire blazed, but she smelled no food cooking, no tea simmering. She was alone.

Lifting herself on one elbow, she used stiff fingers to comb the snarls away from her eyes. From the color of the sky through the smokehole, it must have been just before dawn. When Wind Mother batted the door curtain, iron-gray streaks of light patterned the floor.

The flute player came closer, and she could hear him Dancing in time to his melody. It became a haunting tune, sweet and high, like the cry of a dying songbird. His thumping footsteps might have been the bird's erratic heartbeat, fluttering toward an eternal stillness.

"Priest?" she called, thinking the flute player might be Strongheart.

The music stopped short.

"Strongheart?"

Out in the plaza, a sharp cry split the silence. Sora listened, taking a moment to place the rhythmic shuffling sound: bare feet moving in unison across the packed earth. She could make out the faint rattle of shell necklaces, the clacking of bracelets as the Dancers came closer. Fear tickled her belly.

Was this some prelude to an execution? Could this be part of a ritual reserved specifically for elite prisoners?

Anxiously, she glanced around the house for a weapon, but didn't see one. Didn't priests carry weapons in Loon society? A strange tradition, since so many people had reason to kill them.

Two old men stepped through the door carrying tortoiseshell rattles. Their flesh had shriveled from too many summers in the sun. Each wore a cloth about his waist, layers of necklaces on his chest, and shell bracelets that rattled loosely on his bony arms.

Neither man so much as glanced at her before going to sit on the floor mats at opposite sides of the house. Together, as though they'd done it many times, they started shaking their rattles and Singing in soft, pathetic voices:

*"Take courage woman, and you will be cured
    tomorrow.
 Take courage woman, take courage,
 And you will be cured tomorrow."*

They Sang the words over and over, eyes closed, until Sora felt as though she were being mesmerized by the monotonous drone.

Next, four old women—the village elders who had judged her the day before—ducked in and crossed to the fire.

Ignoring her, they seated themselves on the north, south, east, and west. Elder Littlefield's sparse white hair shone orange as she pulled a pipe from an otter-skin sack, filled it with tobacco, and used an ember to puff it to life. She exhaled the blue smoke, chanting under her breath as she watched it rise. The pipe passed around, and by the time it had returned to Elder Littlefield's hands, the house was filled with a thick blue-gray haze.

Elder Littlefield blew a final stream of smoke toward the roof, and gave a great shout of *"Hé!"*

The other elders echoed, *"Hé, hé!"*

Light flooded in as the door curtain was drawn back over its peg and, two by two, young women and men Danced into the house. The women were perfectly naked, except for the earrings, bracelets, and anklets Sora had heard rattling. The men wore red sashes, no more than a finger wide, around their waists. Some had painted their bodies with extraordinary designs. Others sported elaborate tattoos. Feathers had been woven into long braids and adorned with shell bells.

Sora drew the soft deerhide up to cover her own nakedness. She had heard vague stories of this ritual, tales told in low voices by Traders.

With the young women on the outside, the Dancers formed two concentric circles, surrounding Sora. In time with the old men's song, the women lifted their right legs high, then stamped their feet down with a jangling of jewelry. Then they stamped their left. After four or five short steps to the right, each young woman turned to face the man on the inside of the circle, shook her body in a way that emphasized her hips and breasts, and gave the man a challenging look.

The tension in the men couldn't be mistaken. Muscles flexed, buttocks tightened; each man clenched his fists. As Sora looked around the circle, she could see their enlarged penises beginning to stiffen.

On some cue, the women lifted their right legs high, as though to touch their knees to their breasts. The men stepped smoothly forward to take the women in their arms.

Each man swung his partner up and gently lowered her to the floor. Soft sighs rose here and there as men slid atop the women, rubbing their taut penises over smooth brown flesh. All the while, the two old men continued to sing, their voices stronger now, rising as they repeated their litany.

Sora stared in amazement at the ring of naked

bodies surrounding her. They were doing this for her? Each couple was fondling and kissing, their bodies writhing against each other. Sora's heart began to pound, and her loins stirred.

All the while, the old men Sang and the old women chanted, *"Hé, hé! Hé, hé!"*

Sora looked up when a dark form filled the doorway.

Strongheart?

No. Flint entered, his fists at his sides, a black cape hanging from his shoulders. He wore nothing beneath it but the same thin red sash the other men wore.

Their gazes locked, and he smiled when he read the desire in her eyes.

With the grace of a forest panther, he crossed to her, knelt, and laid a warm hand on her bare shoulder. His eyes narrowed when he said, "Look at them, not me."

He hardly had to tell her; she couldn't take her eyes from the entwined lovers—if that's what they were. But now everything had changed. Where they once had had eyes only for each other, now every stare was leveled at Sora and Flint. The Dancers had frozen, each man placing his right hand on the woman's shoulder, just as Flint had done.

Sora shivered in sudden embarrassment, not just from the watching eyes. Flint had tugged her blanket away, and begun kissing her neck. She tried to squirm free, but he gripped her arms to keep her there. His warm lips sucked at her skin.

The circle of watching lovers followed his every

move, the men lowering their mouths to their partner's necks and throats. The women squirmed just as she had done.

The sight of it was shocking in a way Sora had never imagined. Half of her wanted to flee in horror; the other half was desperate to see what would happen next.

"Flint, I can't do this! I have to get out—"

"Shhh!" he whispered against her skin. "Watch them, Sora. Don't take your eyes off them. You are them; they are you. We are here to free parts of your souls, to Heal them with the joining."

They are all watching me! The thought paralyzed her as Flint lowered his head to kiss her breast.

Refusing to meet the circle of eyes, Sora fixed on one particularly beautiful young woman. As their gazes met, the woman smiled, and Sora experienced an odd quickening of the soul.

The woman could have passed as a younger copy of herself. Her full breasts, narrow waist, and long legs might have been Sora's ten winters ago.

The young man who kissed her breast had Flint's same muscular body, though his face was different. His moves mimicked Flint's right down to the way he rolled her right nipple with his tongue.

She gasped and stiffened as Flint's mouth covered her breast—and saw the young man take the young woman's breast into his mouth. Sora felt as though she were staring into her own eyes. Her face, her younger face, had taken on an expression of joy.

Flint's mouth, sucking, caressing, became the

young man's. They were merging, falling together, souls rising and swaying to the Song the old men Sang . . .

Sora pulled herself back from the dizzy sensation, asking, "What is this ritual?"

Flint looked up from her breast. "It's called the *andacwander*. It's the Soul-Curing ritual Strongheart told you about last night."

"Where is he? Where's Strongheart?" Why was that suddenly so important?

"He told me he probably wouldn't be here today."

"Why not?"

"Ask him when you see him."

"But I—"

"*Watch* the Dancers," Flint insisted as he lowered his mouth to her breast again. "Strongheart told me you had to watch the Dancers."

Sora was panting as she glanced around the room. Women sighed, legs shifting, arms in slow motion as they fondled the men's heads. The beautiful young "Sora" had arched her back, forcing her breast deeper into her partner's mouth. The round globe elongated, slipping past his lips as he took as much in his mouth as he could.

Images flashed in her souls of the first time Flint had taken her breast in his mouth. The honeyed sensations, just like now . . .

She swallowed against a sudden longing, wishing she could be that young woman who was separated from her by a few paces and too many winters. If only she could go back to those free days of youth, before she had committed so many . . .

"Let yourself go, Sora," Flint whispered softly. "Watch them, and let yourself drift."

She stretched out on her back, attention focused on the beauty she called "young Sora."

She, too, stretched out, a delighted smile on her face as her muscular young man ran the flats of his hands down her lean belly the way Flint was doing.

Sora tensed as Flint's hand smoothed down her abdomen to the warmth between her legs. She watched her younger self arch with delight.

"Young Flint" spread the woman's legs and moved to kneel between them as Flint did between hers. She could almost believe the young man looked her way with Flint's eyes as he removed the red sash from his waist, and knotted it several times.

"What's he doing?" she asked.

Flint didn't answer. Instead, he tucked a finger inside her. From the slick ease of it, he'd found her already wet. When had she become so aroused?

"You'll like this, Sora. I give you my oath."

He tucked the first knot into her opening, and used his fingers to force it deeper. Slowly, as though calculating her response, he shoved in another knot, and another. With each additional knot, she felt herself filling, tingling.

. . . *A flash of memory . . . darkness . . . voices from my parents' bedchamber . . . angry shouts . . .*

After eight knots, Flint lowered his lips to her 'little manhood.' She watched the dark red cloth disappearing into young Sora, felt it inside herself, and waves of pleasure began to tighten her womb.

Someone cried out; then other cries erupted. One woman screamed in ecstasy. Sora kept her eyes on young Sora, desperate to maintain that link.

It barely registered that she and young Sora were writhing and bucking in unison. She might have been watching herself lift against her lover's lips in those hard, sure thrusts.

The slow tugging on the cloth sent stinging bolts through her pelvis. Slowly, deliciously, each knot was pulled out. Her panting gasps were mirrored in young Sora's; each whimpering cry was forced simultaneously from her throat. Their eyes were locked as the orgasm burst through their hips. Their cries came as one, the tingling waves washing up their spines, down their spread legs.

The young man rose over young Sora, and she could see a clear droplet of semen gleaming on the tip of his long, thick shaft. His scrotum had knotted tightly around his testicles.

Sora reached for Flint and ran her fingertips along the engorged veins that swelled beneath his taut skin.

She whispered, "I need you inside me, Flint."

"Yes, I know."

When he entered her, she wrapped her arms around his back, closed her eyes, and was quickly lunging against him.

"Open your eyes, Sora. Look at the Dancers."

She turned and saw dozens of other bodies entwined, slick male shafts driving deeply into warm flesh. The shadows they cast upon the walls were wild and black, like frenzied ghosts seeking to give birth to the world.

. . . I hear my father sobbing. He must have his face buried in a blanket, because the sounds are muffled. He . . .

Barely audible, she thought she heard him say, *"It's not your fault. . . ."*

The words vanished as the root of Flint's hard shaft hammered at the arch of her hips.

In desperation, she tightened her arms around him, and her nails dug into his back.

Every muscle in his body rippled when his hot seed jetted into her. A ragged cry burst from his throat, rising and falling each time he bucked.

When he finally collapsed against her, she cradled his head between her breasts, and stroked his long black hair.

To her surprise, the Dancers did not mimic her. They were staring at her, questions in their eyes as they lay intertwined with their partners.

When she glanced at young Sora, it was to see a stranger. The link was gone.

What Power does this ceremony have that it can conjure the dead and take my soul back to the past?

The old men at either end of the room began shaking their rattles, and the young men and women rose to their feet and formed the two familiar circles again.

The women lifted their right legs before stamping

their feet down. Then they followed suit with their left. They shuffled sideways for four steps. When they turned to face the men each woman suggestively shook her body and thrust her hips forward, emphasizing her charms. Their breasts and bellies gleamed with sweat; dewlike droplets sparkled on dark pubic hair. Each woman gave the man opposite her a furtive bow before they straightened. In unison they raised their right legs. Their new partners stepped forward to embrace the women. Once again they lowered their partners to the floor.

Sora asked, "How long does this go on?"

Flint nuzzled his cheek against her breast, an action mimicked by the reclining men. "Until dusk. Then it begins again at dawn."

22

WHEN THE PURPLE RAYS OF SUNSET FLOODED THE house, the two old men picked up their tortoiseshell rattles, rose, and ducked beneath the door curtain. The old women followed them out.

It took the young Dancers longer. Many of them barely had the strength to rise and drag themselves through the door. Several couples left with their arms wrapped around each other, smiling, speaking soft words.

Flint rolled off Sora and lay beside her with his arms over his head, staring at the ceiling. "Blessed gods, I thought it would never end. I'm getting old."

Sora pillowed her head on his broad chest. A warm breeze fluttered the door curtain, and the aroma of roasting duck seeped into the house. "I just realized that I'm starving."

"As am I. We haven't had anything to eat since last night."

The old women had been tending the fire all day; now, it began to die down. As Sora stared at the fire-lit shadows on the walls, a calm exhaustion filtered through her limbs. The shadows seemed to draw her. As some people were drawn to light and flames, she was drawn to shadows and darkness—a thing she had never realized until this moment. Staring at the shadows, she perceived living creatures, amorphous, moving as though their wings could not find air enough to fly. Strange iridescences tipped their wings, like stringers of lightless fire.

"In the middle of the first dance," she said softly. "I began to see and hear things."

"What things?"

"I heard shouts and sobbing. More images came with each Dance."

He smoothed her hair away from her forehead. When she tipped her face to look up at him, his dark eyes might have contained all the hope in the world. "Who was shouting?"

"My parents. I had the sense that I'd seen four or five winters."

"What were they arguing about?"

"I don't know. They screamed at each other often when I was a child. I never knew what they fought about."

He tenderly kissed the top of her head. "What about the sobbing? Was it your mother?"

"No. It was F-Father."

How strange that her voice shook when she spoke of him. She slipped an arm over Flint's chest and hugged him tightly. As she listened to his heartbeat and the steady rhythm of his breathing, things that had comforted her for most of her life, the moony pallor of early evening crept into the house. With it came the sounds of people cooking supper, laughter, and dogs playfully barking.

"Why was he crying?" Flint asked.

She closed her eyes and heard the wrenching sounds again. "I think he was sad."

"Did you know why?"

"No."

Even through the thick thatched walls, she could hear the rasping of handstones grinding seeds. The breeze smelled richly of corn and sweet sap, and of cakes being fried somewhere nearby.

"Sora," Flint said carefully, "the Spirit Plant I gave you to make you sleep should be wearing off. Can you tell me now?"

"Tell you what?"

"Where were you?"

"When? What are you talking about?"

"You camped outside Eagle Flute Village. You told Feather Dancer you were coming in with just one guard, Walking Bird. But you sent Walking Bird in alone and you vanished into the trees."

Glimpses. Faces.

They shot around behind her eyes like lightning

bolts, almost too brief to see, but they left afterimages. . . .

Warriors scouting the forest . . . a beautiful woman being carried on a litter . . . smiling . . .

"I don't remember." She shook her head violently as though to deny the images.

Flint stroked her hair. "It's all right," he said. "I was just hoping. Let me try something else."

She lifted her head to look into his black eyes. "What?"

"The council must have given you orders when you came here. What were they?"

She sank down against his shoulder. "They authorized me to come to Eagle Flute Village to negotiate with Blue Bow for the release of our hostages, but they ordered me to give away nothing. I was to tell Blue Bow straightly that the gathering grounds were ours and if he did not release our hostages and retreat from our gathering grounds, we would attack and wipe out his village."

Flint's shoulder muscles contracted. "How did my own clan matron vote?"

"Wood Fern was the most insistent of all. She hates the Loon People."

He sighed. "You knew, of course, that threats wouldn't work. They would have just made Blue Bow more recalcitrant."

"Yes, I knew that, but I had no choice."

He toyed with her long hair, wrapping it around his hand and then bringing it to his nostrils to smell the fragrance. It was such a tender loverlike gesture, it brought tears to her eyes. "How did Grown Bear get the jade brooch, Sora?"

She frowned. "He said he paddled for sixteen days—"

"Yes, I know what he said, but I'm asking you for the truth."

"What do you mean, 'the truth'?"

Flint slipped out from under her, and rolled to his side to face her. His handsome face showed signs of fatigue, but he also looked oddly serene, as though the strenuous activities of the day had leached away every other emotion. "You and I both know where the jade came from."

"We do?"

"Don't play with me. This isn't a game. You must have given that brooch to Grown Bear. I just want to know why. Were you negotiating with him for the release of our hostages?"

Totally baffled, she said, "Flint, please tell me what you're talking about."

He searched her face, and looked surprised that she really didn't seem to understand. "Sora, that brooch came from the box your mother hid behind the statue of Black Falcon in the temple."

"The box . . ." Her mouth hung open. "You mean the box that had been passed down to her by my grandmother?"

"Yes."

Stunned, she said, "Flint, are you sure?"

"Of course I'm sure. Didn't you ever look in that box?"

Sora swallowed hard. She felt as though she had something lodged in her throat and couldn't breathe. "No. It wasn't mine. It belonged to my mother."

"You didn't look in it even after you . . . her death?"

She felt so grateful he had not said, 'after you killed her,' that she honestly replied, "No, Flint. There were too many things to do. I was trying to avert a war, I had just appointed a new war chief, and my new husband was pushing me to Trade pounded copper for . . ."

She stopped, and stared at him. "How do you know the brooch came from that box?"

Flint's brows plunged down. "Because *I* am not nearly as scrupulous as you are, and apparently I'm a good deal more curious. I looked in it."

"When?"

"A few days before I left Blackbird Town. I'd found the box many winters before tucked into the niche behind the statue. I knew it had to be *the* box that Yellow Cypress spoke about. So I took it."

"You stole it?"

"Of course," he replied unabashedly. "We were competing to see who could hurt the other most. I saw no reason to let you get in the final hurt. Besides, no one would know I'd stolen it. When it was discovered missing, they would blame you."

She propped herself up on her elbow to peer at him. "But . . . you didn't steal it. Isn't that why you asked if I had given the brooch to Grown Bear?"

He put his hand on her cheek. "Yes, that's why I asked. At the end, I just couldn't do it. I left the box in my personal basket, along with other things I couldn't bear to take with me."

"But Flint, I—I . . . ," she stammered, "I never looked in your basket. I had it sealed with boiled pine pitch and put away."

His eyes narrowed. "You never looked in my basket? I was certain you would take out each item and burn it with the proper ritual glee."

"No." She smoothed her hand over the contours of his arm muscles. "I couldn't even stand to throw away the small things that had belonged to you. Every time I found one of your hairs twined in my clothing, I coiled it up and put it in a box for safekeeping."

He tilted his head, as though bewildered that she had cherished such tiny parts of him. "If you didn't do it, then someone else opened my basket and took the box."

Once again, very slowly, she asked, "Are you absolutely certain that the brooch Grown Bear brought me came from that box?"

"Yes. Unquestionably."

"Did you tell anyone you'd taken the box?"

Flint blinked, and his expression slackened. For several moments he gazed at the far wall, but she could see thoughts moving behind his eyes. A variety of emotions crossed his face: disbelief, dread, and finally . . . fear. "I told Skinner."

She couldn't speak.

Flint stared at her for another three heartbeats; then he shoved away, got to his feet, and reached for his cape. As he swung it around his shoulders, he said, "I must speak with Grown Bear."

TWO HANDS OF TIME LATER, AS NIGHT DEEPENED, Sora knelt before the fire and began feeding branches to the glowing coals. A chill wind seeped beneath the door curtain and breathed around the room. She had tried to follow Flint, but the two guards who stood outside the door wouldn't allow it.

She kept thinking about the jade brooch. Could Flint be right? Such a treasure had come from her mother's box? Yellow Cypress had first showed the box to Sora just before Sora's marriage to Flint. She'd taken Sora into the temple, reached behind the statue of Black Falcon where it hung on the wall, pulled out the box, and told her the story of how it had been passed down for generations. Sora had indeed longed to see inside, but Mother had said, *"Never touch this box. Not ever. Do you understand me? It is only to be opened in the case of a true emergency. It would be better if you just forgot it existed."*

"But why, Mother? What's in there?"

"Coiled serpents waiting to strike," she'd replied in deadly earnest. *"Open this only if our clan is disgraced and you are desperate to escape with your children's lives."*

Mother had tucked it back into the niche, and ushered Sora out of the temple.

From time to time over the next eight or ten winters, Sora had reached around the statue and touched the box to make sure it was still there, but she'd never even lifted it from its hiding place. She had feared what Mother might do if she ever discovered Sora had been handling it. After Mother's death, there were just too many more important matters to take care of.

Outside, Strongheart said, "Good evening."

One of the guards responded, "A pleasant evening to you, Priest," and Sora recognized Snail's voice. They'd changed guards. Was he on duty with his good friend, Black Turtle? Revulsion curdled her belly.

Strongheart ducked beneath the door curtain, accompanied by a slave woman carrying two steaming platters.

"You may set them near Chieftess Sora," he ordered.

The woman walked across the floor, set the platters in front of Sora, and left.

Strongheart sank down to Sora's right and gestured to the food. "I'm sure you're very hungry. The duck is excellent, and I think you'll find the corncakes and palm-berry jam tasty as well."

She reached for a succulent piece of duck and ate it. The rich dark meat melted in her mouth.

Strongheart wore his flaxen shirt with the shell bells on the hem. When he moved to sit cross-legged, facing her, the bells clicked. "Flint tells me that memories stalked you throughout the Dances."

She nodded. "Yes, I saw and heard strange things. Why didn't you attend the ritual?"

He gave her a curious look, as though she might be asking him to participate with her tomorrow. "My presence proves to be a distraction for the patient. You don't need to worry about what I might be thinking, or how to please me."

Sora reached for a corncake, dipped it into the palm-berry jam, and ate it slowly. A sweet burst of flavor coated her tongue. It was particularly delicious after a day without food.

"Would you like a cup of tea?"

"Yes, please."

Strongheart reached for the cups that always rested beneath the tea pot and dipped one full. As he handed it to her, he said, "Do you want to tell me about the things you saw and heard?"

She had to pull her attention back to grasp the cup. She'd been wondering what it would take to please him, and how many women had tried to find out. He was a priest, a young one. She doubted he'd had much experience with women; priests always seemed to be occupied mixing potions or Healing wounds.

"I heard voices. Shouting. I think I was four or five winters at the time. My parents were arguing in their bedchamber."

"What were they arguing about?"

"I couldn't tell. I just heard shouts, not words."

He dipped a cup of tea for himself and held it in his lap. Lines creased his brow. "What about the sobs?"

"Yes, I heard my—my father crying."

"As he did the night he died?"

"Yes. Except today when I heard him, his cries were more heartrending, as though everything he loved in the world had vanished. He sounded lonely."

"Flint tells me that you did not ask any of the young men to Dance with you. Why not? Did Flint pressure you to stay with him?"

Sora smiled and shook her head. "No, Priest. I wanted to stay with him. I started wanting Flint when I'd seen fourteen winters, and I've never stopped. Were it not for the fact that I am a captive in an enemy village, today would have been one of the best days of my life."

He sipped his tea and said, "Tomorrow will be different."

A tendril of fear tickled her belly. "Different? How?"

"Tonight you will dream. In the morning, I will question you about the dreams to discover the unfulfilled desires of your souls. Then I will alter the ritual to assure those desires are filled."

In a tired voice, she replied, "After today, my desires aren't of the body."

Strongheart drew up one knee and propped his cup atop it. The bells on his hem made music. "What do you mean?"

"Oh, it's just that the things I long for are things I can no longer have. I mean, I wish with all my heart that there was some Spirit Plant that could make Flint love me the way he did when we were fourteen winters. When our love was new and innocent, before we hurt each other so much."

He sighed as though he'd heard that same request too many times to count. "There are no Spirit Plants that can make love last, Sora."

"But there are love potions; I've heard priests speak of them."

"Yes, there are, but after a few days they wear off, and when they do, the two people usually despise each other."

"But why? You'd think even a little love would be better than none."

"No." He shook his head. "You see, the person who came for the love potion knows that it took a Spirit Plant to make him love her. And when the plant wears off, the man or woman usually realizes he's been deceived. I've heard it's a bitter feeling, especially when the person who came for the potion is very young."

A sad smile turned her lips. She remembered what it was like to have seen fourteen winters. She would have been willing to do anything, to try anything, even buying a Spirit potion, to make Flint love her. She thanked the gods that she hadn't had to do that. "Yes," she said, "I suppose that's true, but isn't it unfortunate that love is so . . . temporary?"

The anxious look in his brown eyes went to her heart. "Love is like a river, Chieftess. You may catch the water in your hands, or scoop it up in a pot, but the instant you do it begins to dry up. The river must be free to renew itself, every moment, or it turns to dust."

Running a finger over the rough texture of her tea cup, she smiled. "Perhaps, but I'm still sorry there is no potion that can change a person's heart forever."

When he just sipped his tea, she raised her eyes, hoping he would tell her he agreed. Instead, he smiled at her in a detached, kindly way.

She longed to ask him the question that, all day long, she had been asking herself, but wasn't certain she could actually force her mouth to form the words.

"What is it?" he said. "I can tell you wish to ask me something. Ask. I'll answer if I can."

She drew up her knees and hugged them against her chest, barricading her heart.

"I—I've been wondering . . . Do you think . . . ? Is it possible that my father killed himself?"

He nodded, as though relieved that she had arrived at that conclusion by herself. "From the moment you first told me he longed to return to being a Trader, I have been wondering that same thing. Why do you think he might have killed himself?"

A thought crossed her souls. She shoved it aside.

Gesturing awkwardly with her cup, she said, "There was something I didn't tell you yesterday. The night he died, I heard Father come out of his bedchamber, and as he passed by my door, I smelled a strange odor. It shocked me when I realized that the odor wasn't coming from your house, or being carried in on the wind."

As the coals in the hearth ate into the branches she'd added, flames licked up around the wood, and liquid amber threads shot through his short black hair. "It was a memory?"

"Yes. I'm almost certain the bitter smell was dried water hemlock."

For a time the silence was broken only by the distant groan of thunder and the echoes of children laughing.

"Do you think he went back to his bedchamber to get it? So that he could put it in the stew you'd made for him?"

Terrible hope filled her. All her life she had lived beneath the burden of believing she'd killed him. A belief spawned by her mother that cold night in the temple when she'd found Father lying dead next to the broken stew bowl. A belief her mother had perpetuated every time Sora disagreed with one of Mother's decisions. *"You killed your father. Are you going to kill me, too? Then you could have your way, couldn't you?"*

Sora gazed down into her tea cup and saw her face. Her eyes had tightened in misery. She looked like she was about to cry. "That's not very likely, is it? Why would Father take his own life? I'm probably making this up to ease my own guilt."

A fierce gust of wind shuddered the walls, and Sora shivered as though it had gone straight through to her bones. What would she do if it turned out to be true? If Father had poisoned the stew? The knowledge that she'd killed him had become such a part of her, it felt as sure as her breathing or her heartbeat.

Yet, she could imagine him doing it. He would have seen it as a strange irony, adding hemlock to the jerky. In a way, he'd killed the jerky. As the jerky, and the distant vistas it represented, had killed him, filling him with such longing that he could no longer bear it.

Strongheart rose and went to his sleeping bench. He brought back a blanket and draped it around her shoulders. "Can you let it go?"

"Let what go?"

He sat down again on the mats and heaved a sigh. "The guilt. Can you let go of something you have clutched to your heart all your life?"

She drew the worn softness of the blanket around her. Her very identity was founded upon that "fact." Who would she be if it wasn't true?

"I don't know. Honestly."

He left her alone with her thoughts for a long time before he said, "Do you think your mother really believed you killed him?"

"Oh, yes, I know she did. For several reasons. Firstly, she could never have allowed herself to believe she'd driven him to it; and secondly, every time I was bad, my mother reminded me that I'd killed my father. She said if I wasn't careful, someone would find out. Meaning, of course, that she would tell them."

His eyes narrowed, and she wondered if he, too, was thinking about what an effective method that had been of controlling her. Even at the very end, when they'd been standing on the cliff, arguing about sending warriors into the lands of the Red Owl People over what Sora considered a silly insult . . .

I glimpse her face—the last glimpse I will have of her living eyes—and see them suddenly go wide with shock just before she careens backward with her sticklike arms flailing, and topples over the precipice, slamming into old tree stumps as she rolls to the bottom of the slope.

"And your sister?" Strongheart asked with worry in his voice. "How did she punish you for killing her father?"

She brushed the cake crumbs from her hands, and he watched the motions with a curious fascination. When she looked down, she noticed that it looked as though she were washing her hands.

Washing her hands of what? Her mother?

"What are you feeling?" he asked. "Don't think about it. Just tell me."

"It's a . . . a sense of, I don't know, divine retribution, or righteous indignation. I'm not sure how to describe it."

"You were glad your mother died?"

"No, gods, no. Not glad. But I admit that I did feel relieved. She hadn't been well, and she'd been making bizarre decisions that endangered our nation."

"And when your sister died, what did you feel?"

That same sense of justice filled her, but it was swiftly followed by horror and guilt. She looked at him, and he seemed to read her expression easily.

He said, "She must have made your life miserable. She thought you'd killed her father. Did she torment you?"

An unbearable ache welled in her chest. "My sister was my only friend. I loved her very much."

"Yes, I'm sure that's true, but did she torment you?"

Like the silver-silk flashes of minnows, whispers swam up from between her souls. They were not the whispers of broad daylight, but those that nag a person in the darkness long after everyone else is asleep.

She must have tilted her head, or given him some indication that she was hearing voices, because Strongheart asked, "What's she saying to you, Sora?"

She closed her eyes. "I don't hear words."

"But you hear something. What is it?"

"Anger. No. More like hatred."

"Her tone of voice?"

Before she'd realized it, tears had leaked from the corners of her eyes and flowed soundlessly down her cheeks.

Gray mist rolls in over the water, and a great darkness rises to swallow the eastern horizon; the trees on shore vanish, replaced by huge waves that batter the canoe. Walks-among-the-Stars is shouting at me, but the roar of the wind is so loud I can't hear her. We both have oars in our hands, but we are not rowing. . . .

"Why did you go out in the canoe that day? Couldn't you see the storm moving in?"

"She asked me to go fishing with her. I wanted to go."

"Did you see the storm moving in?"

As she slowed her breathing, she heard drips falling from the thatched walls outside. She hadn't even realized it had started to rain. The voices in the plaza had ceased. People must have moved inside to eat their suppers.

"As we climbed into the canoe, I remember saying, 'Do you think we should do this? That looks like a storm is coming.' Walks-among-the-Stars told me to stop being such a baby and get into the boat."

"Were you afraid?"

"Yes. I remember being afraid."

And sinking down in that terrible blackness, the water like heavy arms dragging me under.

"Feather Dancer told me that when they found your sister's body washed up onshore, her skull had been crushed. Do you remember how that happened?"

"No, I—I . . ." She was defending herself, and she didn't understand why, or against what. She took a deep breath and held it to steady her nerves. "Are you asking if I killed her? If I crushed her skull?"

In the kindest voice she'd ever heard, he said, "Did you?"

A wave of heat flooded her body. She let the blanket fall from her shoulders and coil around her slender waist. "After we stood up in the canoe, I don't remember anything until—"

"You stood up in the canoe? During a storm?"

She realized with a start how odd that sounded.

The waves were crashing against the boat, tossing it in every direction. Why on earth would they have stood up?

Or . . . was it only she who'd stood up?

"I remember standing up. The next thing I recall is looking up through the water at Walks-among-the-Stars floating above me." Sobs constricted her throat. It was difficult to force herself to go on. "Her eyes were wide open, and she—she had blood . . . streaming from her mouth."

Strongheart reached over and tugged on her tea cup to get her to release it. He dipped it into the pot again, and handed it back. "Drink this. You'll feel better."

She lifted it to her mouth. The tea tasted warm and soothing. She concentrated on the sound of the wind groaning through the trees outside.

Strongheart said, "Do you think it's possible that, as Priest Teal surmised, your sister was thrown from the canoe onto rocks and that's how her skull was crushed?"

"I don't remember any rocks. Just. Water. Waves. Huge waves."

A fist seemed to tighten around her heart.

Strongheart leaned forward and touched her fingers where they gripped her cup. "That's enough for tonight," he said. "I want you to finish your tea, eat as much as you wish, and go to sleep. Try not to dream about what we just discussed. Think about the *andacwander*. About how, if you hadn't been here in this village, it would have been one of the best days of your life."

She jerked a nod.

Strongheart touched her arm gently, walked to his door, and ducked out into the rain.

This time, he didn't speak to the guards. He just walked away.

She listened to the sound of his steps receding and curled onto her side to watch the windblown flames. Her hunger had vanished. She was desperately tired.

When she drifted into the uneasy borderland of dreams, the air quivered with an eerie sensation of screaming, of words railed just beyond the grasp of her ears and souls.

25

FEATHER DANCER WAS LEANING HALF ASLEEP against the wall of the Captives' House when he heard the guards say, "She's not here. She's in the Priest's House."

"I know that, you fools," Flint responded. "I've been with her all day. That's why I can barely walk."

The guards laughed.

Flint continued, "I need to speak with one of the other captives."

Uneasily, the guard said, "Which one? Our orders are to let you take Chieftess Sora whenever you wish. We have no orders about the others."

"Do you have orders forbidding me to speak with someone else?"

"Well," the guard said, "no."

"Then they can't punish you for it, can they?"

Flint pulled back the curtain and stepped inside. He was wearing his black cape again. It blended with the darkness so perfectly that the only thing Feather Dancer could make out was his pale face.

When the captives saw him, they leaped to their feet and rushed to surround him, hugging him, asking him questions. "Flint, what's happening?" "Flint, when are our people coming for us?" "My cousin, please, I can't stand much more of this!"

Only Cold Spring and Adder remained sitting against the far wall to Feather Dancer's right. They'd been whispering most of the evening, but Feather Dancer hadn't been able to make out any of their words.

They watched Flint hesitantly.

And Feather Dancer found that *very* interesting.

Flint waded through the crowd and called, "Feather Dancer?"

"Here. In the back."

Flint patted the hands of several of the women who clutched at his arms, said something comforting, and made his way to Feather Dancer. He must have told the women he needed privacy, because they drifted back to their former positions and watched him with wide, curious eyes. Several whispers passed back and forth.

Flint knelt in front of Feather Dancer. He sounded exhausted as he whispered, "We must talk."

"I have nothing to say to you."

Flint cast a glance over his shoulder, made certain the others were keeping their distance, and said, "I want to know what happened the night Skinner died."

A soft laugh escaped Feather Dancer's lips. "What makes you think I know?"

"You are the war chief of Blackbird Town. You knew your chieftess was in danger. You *must* have been keeping watch on her."

Feather Dancer leaned back against the wall and surveyed Flint's grave expression. "Yes, I was."

Flint edged closer to Feather Dancer. "Tell me what you saw. I have to know. Did you follow Sora when she went to Teal's house?"

In a gruff whisper, Feather Dancer answered, "Of course I did. I sneaked in the back entrance to the charnel house and listened to her discussion with Teal."

"Then you knew that Teal had given Sora a bag of poison to put in Skinner's drink?"

"Certainly."

As though he didn't really want to hear the answer to his next question, Flint's hands clenched into fists. "Did you see her give it to him?"

Feather Dancer scrutinized the man's tortured face, and shook his head. "You don't really want me to answer that, do you? You would much rather believe that Chieftess Sora killed your lover, than . . ." He let the words dry up.

Flint searched Feather Dancer's eyes. After what

seemed an eternity, he whispered, "You were watching them, weren't you? You were in the forest watching?"

"I am war chief. I owe it to my matron and my nation to keep our chieftess safe. Of course I was. It was not an easy thing, either, let me tell you. I waited until I was sure he wasn't choking her as a way to enhance her pleasure before I moved. As it was, I was almost too late."

"You're certain, *absolutely certain,* that Skinner was trying to kill her?"

Feather Dancer leaned forward until his nose was less than a hand's breadth from Flint's. "When I came out of the forest, the first thing he did was grab his war club and strike her in the head. She was already unconscious. He didn't strike her because he thought she was dangerous. He was trying to make sure she was dead before I got there."

Flint squeezed his eyes closed as though in pain. "Then it was you who gave him the poison?"

"I had to knock him senseless first. He was a fierce fighter. But, yes, after I clubbed him into submission, I poured it down his throat and forced him to swallow it. The difficult part was rearranging the bodies. I had to make it look like he'd been choking her when he'd died from the poison. After I finished, I went back to the village. It wasn't long before Teal grew concerned and came to wake me. He told me to go find the chieftess. I took *your kinsman,* Far Eye, with me and let him find the bodies." Holding Flint's gaze, he added, "I would have killed you, too, if I'd known you were in Blackbird Town."

Flint blindly stared at the floor, as though contemplating how much easier his life would be if Feather Dancer *had* killed him that night.

"Now"—Feather Dancer pulled back and let out a breath—"tell me why you came here to ask me about Skinner."

Flint slid over to the wall and sat beside Feather Dancer like a friend of many battles. In a faint voice, he said, "I need your help."

"My help?" Feather Dancer scoffed. "What makes you think I'd help you?"

Flint turned, and true horror glinted in his eyes. "Because I think we've both been betrayed."

That got Feather Dancer's attention. He glanced around the house, judging the expressions of the other captives. Cold Spring and Adder had gone utterly silent, obviously trying hard to listen to them.

Just above a whisper, Feather Dancer said, "Matron Wink?"

Flint shook his head. "No. At least, I don't think so."

"Then who?"

"I went to talk with Grown Bear tonight, to ask him about the jade brooch. All he said was, 'You're a member of Water Hickory Clan. Don't they tell you anything?' "

Feather Dancer went rigid. "What did he mean?"

"I—I'm not sure," Flint stammered, and ran a

hand through his hair. Then, in exasperation, he said, "Gods, why are they doing this to me?"

Feather Dancer scowled, leaned toward him, and hissed, "Why do you think everything is about *you*?"

26

A GENTLE HAND REACHED OUT OF THE DARKNESS and touched her cheek.

Sora blinked and rolled to her back, still mostly asleep, though she heard a baby crying somewhere in the village. The coals in the fire hearth had faded to a pale crimson that flared when the night wind gusted around the door curtain. The fragrances of fire-warmed blankets and rain filled the air.

Just above a whisper, Strongheart asked, "What were you dreaming?"

She looked up at him, but saw only a tall, dark silhouette, rimmed in gray. It took her a moment to remember that bright world of exotic flowery scents and warm sunlight.

"We were camped on a beach on the far southern islands my father used to tell me about. You were bathing me, as you did the first night I spent in this village. I was dreaming of the feel of your hands. For a short while, they made the terror go away."

He smoothed his fingers over her hair, and said, "I understand. Go back to sleep."

WINK WANDERED AROUND HER PERSONAL CHAMBER, picking things up, examining them, and putting them down. Rockfish stood stiffly near the doorway, waiting for her to explain why she'd summoned him to her chamber at this time of night. He wore a faded blue shirt, and his gray hair shone.

Wink picked up a ceremonial chunkey stone that had been made for her in the north at Yellow Star Mounds. As she examined the superb workmanship, she said, "The matrons came to me tonight to tell me how many warriors they would be committing to the jade party."

As though annoyed, Rockfish said, "Yes, I was sure they would. What did they say?"

Wink coldly replied, "Shadow Rock Clan will commit one hundred. Shoveler clan will commit one hundred and seventy-five. Bald Cypress will commit two hundred. And Water Hickory Clan . . ." She left the sentence hanging for effect. "Will commit ten."

"Ten! You're not serious?" He appeared genuinely upset.

But, of course, he may well have known this fact before she did. He could have prepared himself to react this way.

"Yes, I was just as stunned as you are. Do you have any idea why Wood Fern is being so parsimonious?"

"Me? Why would I know?"

"Well, it just seems to me that you've been particularly talkative of late, especially with Water Hickory Clan."

His cheeks reddened. "Wink"—he spread his arms in a gesture of innocence—"I've been very straightforward with everyone. I truly believe the jade will be good for our nation. Why would it surprise you that I've been urging the clans to support the war party?"

"Because your wife opposed it, that's why. And as the husband of the chieftess, you have no say in any political matters relating to this nation. You are not—I repeat—*not* a member of our Council of Elders. Pressuring the clan matrons to vote against your wife's wishes might, by some, be considered treasonable."

He let his hands fall to his sides. "Wink, please, I regret anything I've done to offend you. Tell me what I may do to make amends."

Her face must have gotten what Sora called the *"I'm going to kill you if you don't do as I say"* look, because he cocked his head as though silently dreading what she might demand from him.

"If you truly mean that, there are some things you could do that might help *prove* your loyalty."

Warily, he said, "Of course I meant it."

Wink smiled, and the lines at the corners of her eyes crinkled. "Good. Tomorrow morning the three hundred warriors your people have committed to the war party should arrive. They will join with four hundred and eighty-five warriors from our nation and, by tomorrow night, will be headed eastward toward Eagle Flute Village to join with two hundred warriors there. Is that your understanding of the plan?"

Wink rested the chunkey stone near the hearth.

Rockfish watched her, grudgingly folded his arms across his chest, and said, "Would you like me to arrange another 'understanding' of the plan?"

"Yes," she said softly, "I would. And just to make certain we understand each other . . ." She clapped her hands, and a tall warrior ducked into the chamber. He had oddly luminescent, inhuman eyes. "I want to introduce you to Lean Elk, my best assassin."

Lean Elk silently pulled his deer-bone stiletto from his belt sheath.

Rockfish glanced at the man, then looked back at her. "Wink, I . . . I don't understand."

She said, "Do you think I'm foolish enough to believe Wood Fern only committed ten warriors because that's all she wanted to commit? Did you think I wouldn't start asking questions?"

He frowned. "Why else would she only commit ten warriors?"

Blessed gods, he really doesn't know. I can see it in his eyes.

Wink felt light-headed as the implications sank in. "Rockfish, her warriors have been on the trail for a full day."

"What warriors?" He looked truly stunned. "Wink, I don't know what you're talking about."

She studied his confused expression. "You really don't, do you? I thank the gods."

Wink walked away from him. When she passed Lean Elk, she said, "Follow me."

At dawn, when Sora heard the flute, she rolled to her side and stared at the door. A breeze tousled the curtain, revealing glimpses of the misty plaza and the naked Dancers who approached in single file, following behind the elders.

The two old men entered first, just as they had yesterday, and went to sit on opposite sides of the house with their tortoise shell rattles in their hands. Next, the four old women came in, but they did not sit by the fire. They sat together on the floor near the doorway. The wind that had entered with them carried the scents of wood smoke and marsh.

Was she sitting in their ritual places? Was that why the old women had been forced to sit by the door?

Sora rose, wrapped her blanket around her shoulders, and walked to the bench on the far side of the house.

As the Dancers filed in, their shell jewelry winked and glimmered in the firelight.

Flint entered next and stiffly stood on the opposite side of the door from the old women. This morning he wore a black knee-length shirt. He had his jaw clenched, as though he didn't like this very much, but she also noticed the puffiness beneath his eyes. Had he been up all night?

The Dancers formed two concentric circles and began the ritual. . . .

But it was different. The women stepped to the left, while the men stepped to the right. The two circles rotated in opposite directions. No one Sang. The women, who formed the inner circle, kept their backs to the men. The only sound was the rhythmic pounding of their bare feet on the floor.

She was about to call out to Flint when Strongheart ducked through the door. He wore his buckskin cape with the yellow starbursts, but she could see that he wore nothing beneath it. His magnificent tattoos gleamed. Her gaze clung to the bands of interconnected human eyes, red and black, that ringed his muscular legs from groin to ankles. They seemed to blink in the firelight. His short black hair was wet and framed his round face, making his large sad eyes seem to bulge even more. A fine mist covered the arch of his hooked nose. His gaze went directly to Sora and never left.

The circles broke for Strongheart as he walked

across the house and extended a hand to her. "Come and sit with me by the fire."

Sora clutched her blanket to her, took his hand, and let him lead her to the mats, where he gestured for her to sit down inside the circle.

For a time, he didn't speak. He walked around the fire, pulled branches from the woodpile, and added them to the coals until the flames leapt and crackled.

When he came back and sat beside her, the old men began shaking their rattles in time with the Dancers' feet and Singing, *"Euhaha, ho, ho. Euhaha, ho, ho."* Each time the men reached the end of the verse, the old women shouted, *"Hé!"*

Strongheart reached out to touch her hand where it clutched her blanket closed. "Don't be afraid," he said.

"I'm not afraid."

She let him pull the blanket from her shoulders and spread it out on the floor beside her. Despite the flames, the damp wind that fluttered the door curtain ate into her skin. She rubbed her arms to keep warm.

Strongheart untied his cape, removed it, and placed it beside the hearthstones; then he gestured to the blanket. "Join me."

Sora swallowed hard as they stretched out facing each other. She looked at his lean, naked body, and fear blended with desire to create an odd brew in her belly.

She glanced at the doorway and found Flint watching her with bright, intense eyes. She could tell he longed to talk to her.

"Where is your shadow-soul walking, Sora?" Strongheart asked as he lightly placed a hand on her arm.

"I—I think . . . paths I've walked with Flint."

He tenderly squeezed her arm. "Tell me when the paths become new."

"New?"

He bent to brush his lips against her throat. They felt cool and soft. "You'll know when to tell me."

After a few choruses, the Dancers joined the part of the old men's chant that went *"Euhaha, ho,"* and a strange hypnotic tension filled the house.

Strongheart smoothed his hand down her arm to the tips of her fingers.

When she shivered, he said, "Are you cold?"

"No, not really. It's just that I . . ." She glanced back at Flint. He'd clenched his fists at his sides. He needed to talk with her *badly*.

Strongheart murmured, "Keep looking at him, Sora."

"Why?"

"I want you to see him."

"But . . . I want to look at you."

"For now, look at Flint."

Her eyes tightened as she looked back. Flint couldn't hear what Strongheart was saying, so he seemed to take her unwavering gaze as some sort of silent request—and shook his head. His meaning was clear, *I can't.* Had he been forbidden to leave his place beside the door?

She held Flint's gaze, and his desperation, accompanied by the constant chant of *"Euhaha ho, ho, ho,"* followed by the louder *"Hé,"* gave the ritual a vaguely unreal sense—as though she were living a phantom dream that would vanish at any moment.

Strongheart's touch was so light, she almost didn't feel it. "Can you roll onto your back and relax for me?"

She inhaled a deep breath and let it out slowly. "I'll try."

"Good."

She rolled over and stared up at the soot-coated ceiling. For one hundred heartbeats, he trailed just his fingertips over her skin, never lingering anywhere for long, circling her nipples, following out the lines of her ribs, then her hip bones, drawing downward as though outlining her right leg bones, toes, moving to her left leg, and rising. When his fingers moved between her legs, she shuddered, but his fingertips only lightly glided over her opening and 'little manhood' before they proceeded up her belly.

It felt so soothing, she longed to close her eyes, but when she tried, Strongheart whispered, "Please, look at Flint."

She turned her head to do as he'd instructed, but when Strongheart moved to straddle her, it became increasingly difficult not to watch him. Strongheart's groin rested against hers, and she found herself desperately longing that he would touch her as a lover would.

He lifted his hands to warm them before the flames; then he placed his fingertips on her forehead and smoothed them around her hairline. The tension in her shoulders eased. He lightly traced the bones of her cheeks, and brought his fingers down around her jaw to the point of her chin. Then his hands dropped to her breasts, and he caressed them with exquisite patience.

Flint's eyes narrowed. He obviously didn't like the way Strongheart was touching her.

She remembered the first time Flint had looked at her that way. She'd just become a woman a few moons before. Her mother had been giving feasts for her, inviting prominent young men from surrounding villages to meet her. As the son of a village matron, Skinner had been invited. Flint had not, but he'd accompanied his best friend on the journey. There had been one stunning moment when Skinner had smiled at her, and Sora had smiled back. . . .

"You're trembling," Strongheart whispered. "Where is your shadow-soul walking?"

She blinked and breathlessly looked up at him. "I was remembering the first time I saw Flint jealous. A man smiled at me, and Flint gave me a killing look. I couldn't understand why. I'd just met him. . . ."

Skinner turns to smile at Flint, as though pleased I'm paying attention to him . . . but his smile vanishes in a heartbeat when he sees Flint's expression. . . .

"Blessed gods," she said, stunned. "He wasn't jealous for me. He was jealous *of* me. I was stepping between him and Skinner. I . . ."

As her voice began to rise, Strongheart bent and kissed her. It seemed to be an attempt to cut short her words, but when his lips touched hers, a tingle ran through her body. His lips were like warm velvet.

Against her mouth, he whispered, "Just look. Don't judge. Try to see him as he is."

She gave Strongheart a baffled look. She had loved Flint for her entire adult life—who better than she could 'see him' as he was? But as understanding sank into her thick skull, she knew Strongheart was right. She might have loved Flint, but she'd never really known him. If she had, she—well, she would have known about Skinner.

How strange that in eighteen winters, no one had told her. Surely others must have known. People always knew. Perhaps no one had been brave enough to tell her.

I would have ordered the messenger's death. I might even have killed him with my bare hands.

Without warning, tears welled in her eyes. The one great truth that could have changed everything, especially in the last winters when she and Flint had hated each other so much, had been withheld from her. And it was her own fault.

She slipped her arms around Strongheart's back and pulled him down on top of her. He lay unmoving, his tall body like a shield against the world. Her desire intensified until it was almost painful.

She hugged him hard. "I never expected . . . this."

"What?"

"You."

He lifted his head and stared at her from less than a hand's breadth away. The sadness in his eyes seemed deeper, more profound. "The gods are under no obligation to give us what we expect."

"No, but sometimes they do."

"Yes." He smiled. "And generally we regret it. Please. Look at Flint."

She turned her head. For a moment, she couldn't see him through the rotating circles of Dancers. Each time a man and a woman stood face-to-face, their fingers trailed down each other's cheeks in slow leisurely strokes; then they stepped to the next partner, and their hands moved down his or her chest. With the third partner, the man tucked his fingers inside the woman while she grasped his erect manhood, and they kissed. Then it began all over again with the next person. As the Dancers shifted, she glimpsed Flint, and what she saw made her tremble. He stood with his feet braced, his shoulders squared, ready for a fight. His chin was thrust out as he glared at Strongheart. The longer she looked at Flint, the more puzzled she felt. He hadn't wanted her for three winters. But, now, when she wanted someone else . . .

He can't let me go any more than I can let him go.

But for the first time, she wanted to let him go.

She looked up at Strongheart like a hurt bewildered child, and tears rolled slowly down her cheeks.

Strongheart said nothing but took her gently in his arms, and laid his cheek against hers. It felt so good to be held by him. Softly he asked, "Is she talking to you?"

"No, no, it's—this is not my—my—" She stammered to a stop. *I can't even say "my sister."*

He waited, stroking her hair. Against her ear, he said, "I have no blame in my heart, Sora."

As though at a signal, the Dancers' feet pounded the floor more firmly, and the old men's voices rose to a hoarse cadence.

The old women shouted *"Hé!"*

Strongheart lifted his head and touched her cheek. "Do you want me?"

Her gaze shot back to Flint, and he motioned to her as though he was desperate to talk with her. Her muscles stiffened. Had he spoken with Grown Bear? Blessed gods, had he discovered what was going on? All of the tension that had drained away at Strongheart's touch returned. Her belly knotted.

Strongheart said, "What is it?"

"I—I want Flint."

He pressed his lips to her hair. "Are you afraid of me?"

She hesitated. She wasn't sure how to answer that. The feel of his arms around her stirred powerful emotions, but fear wasn't one of them.

He looked down, and for a long time, their eyes held.

"Yes," she answered at last.

"Why?"

"Because part of me wants to unfeel the things I'm feeling for you."

She was half expecting him to ask her what the other part wanted—which is what Flint would have done—but he didn't.

Without a word, he rose, gave her a forlorn smile, and put on his cape. As he walked to the door, Flint watched him with his jaw clamped tight. Then Strongheart spoke to him, and Flint's face slackened.

Flint said, "Yes, I understand."

Strongheart ducked beneath the curtain and walked out into the mist.

A hollow ache expanded in her chest. *Why didn't I tell him how much I wanted him?*

Flint shouldered between the dancers and hurried toward Sora. As he knelt, he said, "Strongheart said you wanted me."

She sat up, pulled him close, and whispered, "Tell me what Grown Bear said."

He glanced at the Dancers. "This is hardly the best place to talk."

"Lie down. With all the other sounds, no one will hear us if we're quiet."

They stretched out together, and Flint pulled the blanket over them. As he rolled on top of her, the dark wealth of his hair fell around her, shielding their faces like a curtain.

Flint whispered, "Last night, I spoke with both Grown Bear and Feather Dancer. I think we're in trouble."

"TROUBLE?" SORA ASKED.

"Yes. Feather Dancer heard two of the captives talking. As soon as the jade party leaves Blackbird Town, Matron Wood Fern will dispatch warriors in a brilliant stroke that will elevate the status of Water Hickory Clan."

Her heart thundered. She had feared all along that she was only a minor player in this charade, that Water Hickory Clan had grander desires than just her downfall.

"Is Wood Fern plotting to bring about the fall of Shadow Rock Clan?"

Flint kissed her hair and eyelids, taking his time, moving across her temples to her cheek, and finally to her ear, where he breathed, "Maybe. All I know for certain is that one of my clan members must have stolen the jade to give it to Grown Bear."

"How do you know that?"

"When I asked Grown Bear where he'd gotten it, he said, 'You are Water Hickory Clan. Don't they tell you anything?' "

Flint covered her mouth with his, and his tongue touched hers. "Another thing," he pulled away to whisper, "my relatives here apparently volunteered to be captured."

"*What?* Did they tell you that?"

"No. Feather Dancer overheard two of my kinsmen talking."

Sora tried not to show her alarm, but as she passionately kissed him back, possible scenarios raced across her souls. Wood Fern had worked very hard after the capture of the Oak Leaf villagers to talk the other Black Falcon clans into going to war to wipe out Eagle Flute Village. She'd said a war would solve two problems in one fell swoop: They could release the hostages, and the Loon People would no longer be around to lay claim to the gathering grounds. But the capture hadn't forced the nation into war. Wood Fern was a shrewd old woman; she must have planned for that possibility. . . .

"Dear gods," Sora whispered, "that's how they did it."

"Did what?"

"That's how they got Blue Bow to Blackbird Town so he could be murdered. The hostages were a tool to lure him out into the open."

Flint stared into her eyes. "You mean—"

"I mean they gave him a lever with which to bargain for the gathering grounds. 'I'll release the hostages, if you agree to let us have the gathering grounds.'"

"Of course. Without that leverage, he'd have never left the safety of Eagle Flute Village." Flint leaned his forehead against hers and whispered, "I pray the gods forgive me for being so blind."

"What do you mean?"

"After Blue Bow's murder, Grown Bear assured me that if Water Hickory Clan didn't act quickly, the new chief, Horned Owl, would kill our hostages. For a small fee, he said he might be convinced to intercede on the hostages' behalf."

"You paid."

"I paid."

"That was wise. The hostages are still alive."

Flint shook his head, as though deeply disappointed in her. "Sora, don't you understand? That's how Wood Fern got *you* to Eagle Flute Village."

Blessed Black Falcon . . .

A terrifying admiration filled her.

"She used the hostages as tools to get rid of her two greatest opponents: Blue Bow and me. Neat and clean. Very well done."

He lifted his head and gave her a quizzical look, as though amazed she could appreciate the details of a plot designed to murder her and destroy her clan. "Don't be too envious; I suspect your murder is just step two."

"Yes, you're right. We still haven't figured out how she plans to elevate Water Hickory Clan."

Flint flipped back the blanket so that the Dancers could see what he was doing and lowered his hand to stroke Sora's 'little manhood.' All around the room, men did the same with their partners. When Flint tucked two fingers inside Sora, moans of pleasure filled the air.

Flint whispered, "Did my cousin, Far Eye, guard your house often?"

"Yes. Do you think he stole the jade?"

"Probably. Once Skinner had told him where the box was hidden, it would have been a simple matter."

Every time he said "Skinner," a deep ache laced his voice.

She stroked his hair, and he looked up. "I'm sure he was under orders from his clan matron, Flint. He had no choice."

A faint tremble moved his head. "He must have told Wood Fern that I would be a problem. They had to get me out of the way, occupy me, because if I ever figured out what they were doing I would warn you."

That's why Skinner had to kill White Fawn. He knew it would break Flint's heart. Grief clouds the mind and makes people far more malleable. . . .

"Would you have warned me?"

"After fourteen winters of marriage, I'm the *only* one who's earned the right to kill you, Sora."

Shadow Rock Clan is caught up in a maelstrom. I have to get out of here before it's too late. Have they assassinated Wink yet? Surely that's step three.

Flint rolled on top of her, pulled up his shirt, and roughly shoved his manhood inside her. His thrusts were deep and swift, like those of a careless stranger, as though he knew he had to carry out the ritual act but there was no emotion in it, no love. He was just trying to get it over with.

She suddenly longed to be lying in Strongheart's arms. The need was so powerful it was like a blow to the belly. She had never wanted any man but Flint. Until now.

Panic tingled to life and burned through her veins. Wink was in danger. The entire Black Falcon world teetered on the edge of civil war, and she was falling in love with a man from the enemy nation.

Frantic and confused, she . . .

The edges of her vision grayed. For a moment she didn't understand what was happening. Then the twitching began in her fingers and rapidly spread. Within a few heartbeats her whole body jerked spastically.

Flint gripped her head in his hands and looked down, but his eyes were not his own. They were the bright burning sun-eyes of the Midnight Fox. His mouth was moving, and she could just hear him shouting, *"Sora, Sora, Sora . . ."*

THE DRIZZLE BEGAN AT NIGHTFALL, AND PEOPLE picked up their looms and supper platters and trotted for their houses. Even the sparkflies who'd filled the trees like nets of fallen stars crept beneath the leaves and bark to hide until it was over.

Snail glanced up at the clouds and morosely leaned his shoulder against the door frame of the Priest's House. The birds clinging to the stems of the marsh had fluffed out their feathers in defense. "I hate standing guard in the rain," he said to Black Turtle, who'd just flipped up the hood of his woven hanging moss cape. "No matter what I wear, I always get soaked. Rain runs down my collar when I bend over and up my sleeves when I lift my war club." He shook his head. "It's a misery."

"Stop complaining," Black Turtle replied. "At

least you're not lying on the sleeping bench in there with your tongue lolling from your mouth."

Snail nodded heartily. The last time they'd peeked through the door to check on the "patient," she'd looked more like a poisoned animal than a human being.

"You know, that Evil Spirit inside her is very Powerful. One minute she's a gorgeous seductress, the next she's foaming at the mouth like a mad dog."

Black Turtle chuckled and glanced at him from beneath his hood. "Now would be the time to take her. Her soul is out wandering the forest. She'll never know you did it. I'll stand guard if you want."

Snail scanned Black Turtle's face. He'd been dreaming of little else since the first night he'd watched Flint rape her. "Are you serious?"

"Of course I'm serious. Strongheart has gone to speak with Chief Horned Owl. Flint is in the Captives' House. Who will know?" Black Turtle's smile widened. "Providing, of course, that once you're finished, you'll return the favor and let me have a go at her."

"You know I will," he answered. "But I—I wonder what will happen to us if we get caught. I—"

"Stop worrying. I'll warn you long before anyone gets near the house."

Snail nervously wet his lips. He drew back the door curtain and peered through the slit. The chieftess had thrown off her blankets and lay naked on the sleeping bench, her legs spread, her damp skin gleaming in the firelight. A lustrous wealth of black hair had tumbled over the side of the bench and rested on the floor. "All right," he said. "I'm going in."

"Good. Be quick. I want my turn."

Snail nodded and ducked beneath the curtain.

When the moaning and muffled half-screams of ecstasy stopped, Black Turtle surveyed the village and leaned close to the door curtain to say, "Snail? Are you finished?"

The drizzle had begun to die down, and he was afraid people would once again fill the plaza before he had his turn.

"Snail? Stop lying there panting! Come out."

No one replied for several uneasy heartbeats; then from right on the other side of the curtain a soft female voice whispered, "I'm wet and ready for you, Black Turtle. Come inside. . . ."

GROWN BEAR SMILED AS HE EXAMINED ANOTHER piece of the jade jewelry: a magnificently carved bird pendant. His people had nothing like this. In the far north, where he planned to go, it would be worth enough to set him up as chief of his own village. He stuffed it into his belt pouch. He'd been packing off and on for over a moon, but he still felt as though he was forgetting something important. He fingered his chin as he looked around his house.

Painted shields, skulls, and weapons covered the walls. He couldn't take them all. He had to decide which ones he wanted most.

He walked around the fire pit and studied a black shield decorated with two entwined serpents, one red, the other white. It was a beautiful thing. He'd taken it off the body of a dead Black Falcon warrior two winters ago. The skirmish at the edge of the disputed gathering grounds had been short. He'd killed one man; the others had gotten away.

Grown Bear pulled the shield off the wall and carried it across the room to place it beside his bulging pack with the other weapons he'd selected. As he lowered it, someone stepped beneath the door curtain behind him. From many winters of training, he grabbed a war club from the wall, spun around, and fell into a crouch, ready to bash out his assailant's brains.

The fire's low flames showed a hooded figure standing in the doorway.

He watched for a few moments, his fists gripping his club; when he realized it was a woman, he strode across the room, grabbed her by the wrist, and flung her face-first across the floor.

Her woven-moss hood fell back, and a torrent of raven hair tumbled over her face. More interesting, he could tell that beneath the cape, she wore nothing. A full bare breast gleamed.

"Who sent you?" he said, annoyed. "I didn't ask for a woman."

She lifted a slender hand, combed the hair out of her face, and looked up at him.

Grown Bear's breath caught in his throat. "Chieftess Sora! What are you doing here? I heard you were lying half dead in Strongheart's house."

"No. I've been awake for quite a while. Awake and thinking about you."

She curled her legs around and braced one hand on the floor, making no effort to cover her nakedness as she sat up. The posture was sensual. Through the open cape, he could see both of her breasts shining in the firelight, and her legs were spread just enough that he had a clear view of the dark opening between them. It looked moist. Ready for a man. The ends of her long hair spread around her hips and flowed across the floor behind her. The lustrous waves caught the light and flashed it back like polished slate mirrors. Blessed Spirits, she had the most exquisite body he had ever seen. He had to force his gaze away, and even then, his manhood seemed to keep looking.

She tilted her head and smiled at him. "You're going away soon. I had hoped we might talk before you left."

"Yes, I'm going south with the jade party—"

"I don't think so."

She pointed at his overstuffed pack and the pile of belongings that surrounded it. "Warriors travel light, so they can run if necessary. You're not going on a war walk. You're moving away. Permanently."

"You think you're clever, do you? Sniffing out what I'm up to?"

She leaned forward, placed both hands in front of her, and arched her back, like a cat stretching in the sunlight. When she tipped her beautiful face to look up at him, he felt his loins stir. She had strange, powerful eyes, as black as bottomless wells. A man could get lost in those eyes.

"Oh, I know what you're up to," she said softly. "Flint told me all about it."

"Did he? Only yesterday he pretended to know nothing about how I got the jade."

Grown Bear walked across the room, pulled a gorgeous carved war lance off the wall, and placed it beside the black shield. From the corner of his eye, he saw her rise with the leggy grace of a young deer.

"Where will you go, Grown Bear?"

He patted his belt pouch. "Anywhere I wish, Chieftess. Water Hickory Clan has seen to that."

She gazed up at him with wide dark eyes that seemed to know his very souls, and his manhood went rigid. She was a chieftess, a forbidden woman, and she had clearly come here with one intention: to seduce him.

"You don't really trust Wood Fern, do you?" she asked.

Grown Bear chuckled. "Of course not. Do you think I'm a fool? I have no doubts but that when this is over she will try to hunt me down. Gods, what an old hag." He shook his head. "I'm glad she's not my clan matron."

Like a slender, beautiful Forest Spirit, she stepped closer to him. "Yes, I've just figured out what a shrewd, dangerous woman she is. That's why she always opposed sending warriors after the jade. She knew it was a ruse. When everything was said and done, she would be a hero."

Grown Bear laughed. "So you did figure it out. I'm proud of you."

"Yes, me, too."

She edged toward him, as though trying not to

frighten him. He looked her over carefully. She couldn't possibly be hiding a weapon on that voluptuous naked body, could she? His gaze dropped to the triangle of shining black hair between her legs. That would, of course, be the first place he searched.

Against his better judgment, he allowed her to slip her arms around his neck and press her body against his. She rubbed up against him like a cat seeking to be petted. An odd feral gleam lit her eyes.

In a swift violent move, he grabbed her around the waist, holding her still with one muscular arm while he thrust his free hand inside her.

He found only smooth, tight warmth. She moaned softly and began moving against his hand, trying to shove it deeper.

"Oh, is that what you like?" he said, and forced his fingers into her hard enough to make most women cry out in pain.

She, however, reached down, took his hand in both of hers, and tried to force it even deeper. The expression of ecstasy on her magnificent face as she moved against his fingers was almost too much to bear.

He grabbed her and carried her to his sleeping bench, where he laid her down and climbed on top of her. As he jerked up his shirt, his manhood thrust out like a thick war lance.

"Have you ever had anything like this, woman?"

She looked down, grasped his shaft, and squeezed. "Blessed gods, hurry. I want you inside me."

He pried her apart with his fingers and forced his way inside. He'd heard that fool Flint say that she held a man like a fist, but he'd never in his wildest dreams imagined this! At first it felt like a hand gripping him, pulling and pushing; then it began to feel more like a greedy mouth, sucking as though to draw the very life from him.

She whispered in his ear, "When will they be here?"

"Don't try to . . . ," he gasped. "I'm not going to . . ."

He tried to hold back, to make it last longer, but too quickly he found himself lunging against her.

He almost didn't hear her say, "Tomorrow?"

He shook his head and laughed at her, and she seemed to realize he meant *sooner*. "Oh, Hallowed Ancestors, I have never . . . felt . . . anything . . ."

"I'm about to make it better," she hissed deliciously into his ear, rolled him to his back, and straddled him. Her breasts dragged across his chest as she moaned and moved against him. He gripped her right breast to suck it, and she tightened even more, milking him in sure powerful strokes. Her muscles held him captive, as though he were trapped inside her; he wasn't sure he could have withdrawn if he'd wanted to. She kept moving, moaning, and he slammed himself against her, trying to wring the last pleasure from her body. He roared when his seed jetted into her.

The metallic *tink* of a copper-studded war ax being lifted from the wall penetrated his awareness, but he . . .

FEATHER DANCER STRAIGHTENED WHEN HE HEARD swift steps coming toward the Captives' House. The guards outside whispered as the steps approached.

Strongheart said, "Is Flint in there?"

Flint, who sat beside Feather Dancer, gave him an askance look and got to his feet, preparing to go to the door.

"Yes, Priest," the guard answered.

Before Flint had made it halfway across the floor, Strongheart threw aside the curtain and ducked into the room.

"What's the matter?" Flint said as he rushed to meet him. "Is it Sora? What—"

"Where is she?" Strongheart demanded to know.

Flint blinked and took a step backward. "What are you talking about? She's in your house, under guard."

Strongheart grabbed Flint by the arm and hauled him toward the door, whispering, "No, she's not. Both of the guards are dead, butchered like animals, and Grown Bear has a war ax buried in his skull!"

Even from the rear of the house, Feather Dancer could see Flint's lips part in a silent cry before Strongheart dragged him through the door and out into the night.

Feather Dancer rose and walked to the door, listening through the curtain to the guards, who'd obviously heard the priest's words.

"Stonefly," one man hissed. "Go and see if he's telling the truth about Grown Bear."

Steps pounded away.

The man then turned and said, "Snow Cricket, come over here."

When the man ran up, he said, "Go to the Priest's House and check on Snail and Black Turtle. Come back immediately."

More steps pounded away.

Feather Dancer pulled the curtain aside enough to see out into the plaza. It was pitch black and rainy. The remaining guards gathered into a murmuring knot about twenty paces from the house. It was strange to see so many men in the village. In fact, the sight made Feather Dancer's shoulder muscles bunch. Had Grown Bear pulled them from their forest posts to guard the village? Or because he didn't want his perimeter scouts reporting . . .

From out in the drenched forest came the distinctive whoops of Black Falcon warriors and Feather Dancer's spine stiffened.

Surprised questions burst from the other captives. A few lurched to their feet.

The Eagle Flute warriors standing in the knot whirled as one to look in the direction of the cries. "What the—"

"Alarm! Shout the alarm!"

Warriors scattered like fish at a thrown rock, running in every direction to warn the village.

Feather Dancer swung around and hissed, "Get ready! We're going to try to escape!"

Pipit was the first to dash to him. The other children followed her. Then, one by one, the adults crowded around the door. Even Cold Spring and Adder got to their feet.

"Be quiet. No matter what happens, *be quiet*! I want you to follow me. But if we get separated, run into the forest and head west." He pointed in case some of the children didn't know which direction was west. "They'll never be able to track you in this darkness, and with luck, by tomorrow morning the rain will have covered your trails. Do you understand?"

Pipit's eyes were wide and frightened, but she nodded and turned to the other children. "Stay close to me. I know how to get home. Just stay close."

The warriors swept toward Eagle Flute Village like a screaming torrent.

Feather Dancer listened for an instant, trying to decipher their plan of attack. He didn't want any of the captives to run headlong into Black Falcon warriors in the darkness. No one would be able to tell friend from foe.

"All right. Follow me!"

He threw back the curtain and lunged into the rain, heading for the shallow marsh.

Like wolves freed from ancient cages, the captives flooded out the door into the night.

A few heartbeats later, the Black Falcon warriors struck Eagle Flute Village, and the screams started. . . .

WOOD FERN DREW HER DOE-HIDE CAPE OVER HER
shoulders and leaned on her walking stick. Ten paces
away, outside the front door, Wink's voice was stri-
dent, arguing with the guards posted there.

It wouldn't be long now.

She sighed and slowly made her way across the
chamber to sink down by the fire. The warmth eased
the pain in her joints. She dipped herself a cup of
dogwood berry tea, and sat back to enjoy it.

Wood Fern had taken her fourth sip when the
voices grew louder and she heard people marching
up the hall. Wink's steps pounded out authority.

"Wood Fern?"

"Come in, Matron."

Wink ducked beneath the curtain with young

Lean Elk, and Wood Fern grimly examined him. He took up his position by the door.

"I'm too late, aren't I?" Wink said.

"Oh, yes, much too late. By now, it's over."

Wink closed her eyes and seemed to be silently screaming at herself for not having realized the truth earlier. When she opened them, she asked, "Why the elaborate story about the jade quarry and the Scarlet Macaw People?"

"A diversion. I knew it would keep you busy."

"Yes," Wink nodded. "It did."

Wood Fern took another long drink of her tea and held the cup in both hands to warm her aching fingers. "Besides, I was hoping the war party would actually find the Scarlet Macaw People and be wiped out in the fighting."

"That would have really been a feather in your hair, wouldn't it? You could have blamed me."

Wood Fern smiled. "Oh, I'll get that feather anyway. By dawn people will be carrying the news up and down the trails. Everywhere, people will rejoice and say 'Look! Water Hickory alone was brave enough to wipe out the enemies of the Black Falcon Nation and free the hostages. Justice has, at last, been done.'" She lifted a crooked finger and aimed it at Wink. "And they will ask, 'Why did Water Hickory Clan have to do it alone? Where was Matron Wink when the Loon People stole our gathering grounds? Where was Matron Wink when Blue Bow took innocent villagers captive? Where was Wink when the Loon People captured Chieftess Sora? Why didn't she do something?' "

"Blessed gods, you've just started a war with the Loon People. Don't you know that?"

"You're being theatrical. I told Chieftess Sora more than a half-moon ago that we'd have to kill them to retain what was ours and rescue our hostages. The Loon People have been a thorn in our bellies for winters. It was time to put an end to it."

Wink bowed her head. She must be thinking about how simple the plan had been—give your opponent an advantage, buy off an enemy war chief, create a diversion to give you time to prepare your attack.

"Did Flint know?"

Wood Fern chuckled. "No. He's truly trying to help his former wife. He's a pathetic case, isn't he?"

Wink's shoulders sagged. She suddenly looked weary.

She started to turn away, to leave, but hesitated. "Was it Far Eye who killed Blue Bow? Or another of your warriors?"

"It was Far Eye."

"And who killed Far Eye?"

"That"—Wood Fern cocked her head—"I do not know. I assumed you'd killed him."

Wink's hand shook as she lifted it to smooth away a graying black lock that had fallen over her forehead. "No. It wasn't me." In a tormented voice, she asked, "Don't you care how many of our people are about to die?"

Wood Fern earnestly nodded. "Yes. Which is why

you would be wise to use the big war party you've assembled, and turn it instead against the Loon Nation. We must strike them fast and with overwhelming numbers if we are to win quickly. A long, drawn-out war is of no use to anyone."

Wink's face went stony. She walked away. As she passed Lean Elk, she nodded.

Just before Wink ducked through the door, she heard the assassin's stiletto strike flesh—once, twice. Wood Fern's aged body hit the floor with no more noise than a feather falling.

It seemed to take an eternity before the gasping stopped and Lean Elk stepped beneath the door curtain. He slipped his stiletto back into its sheath and looked at her, waiting for instructions.

"I want you to find War Chief Clearwing. Tell him to meet me outside as fast as he can. We have to stop this before it gets started."

"What about the chief? Should I wake him?"

She rubbed her cold arms and softly answered, "No. I'll do that."

As silent as mist, Lean Elk strode down the hallway.

Wink took her time. She felt hollow. More than anything in the world she wished Sora were here. Wood Fern hadn't instructed her warriors to kill Sora, had she? The possibility shook Wink to her bones.

"Blessed Black Falcon," she prayed, "let her be safe. Let her come home."

When she finally ducked out the front entrance, the mound top was covered with warriors. Lean Elk stood a short distance away, speaking with her new war chief, Clearwing. He was a medium-sized man with a square face and serious eyes. Down in the plaza, a crowd had begun to gather.

Clearwing broke away from Lean Elk and hurried to meet Wink. As he bowed, he said, "Lean Elk said you wished to see me?"

"Yes."

She motioned for him to follow her and headed to her own mound, where they would have the privacy to talk.

The fragrance of wet cornfields rode the wind, bathing her face. She breathed it in and looked out across Persimmon Lake. The animal bones on the roofs of the commoners' houses gleamed as though coated with liquid silver.

"Matron?" Clearwing asked in a soft voice. "People are beginning to ask questions. What should I tell them? What are we going to do?"

"I haven't decided yet."

She would not, as Wood Fern had suggested, use the war party to destroy the Loon People. But perhaps she would use it to guard Blackbird Town from the inevitable attacks that loomed on the horizon. Then she would begin the painstaking process of trying to mend the rift Water Hickory Clan had torn in the nation.

"Matron?" Clearwing said. "We're not going to war with Water Hickory Clan, are we? There is some talk—"

"Not if I can stop it," she replied. And through a long, tired exhalation, she repeated, "Not if I can stop it."

FLINT THRASHED THROUGH THE HANGING MOSS
with Strongheart close behind him.

"Are you sure you saw her?" the priest asked.

"I think so. I just caught a glimpse, but I'm almost
certain it was her."

As the flames rose from Eagle Flute Village, the
rainy forest became a wavering shadow play of amber and black. The screams had died down a hand of
time ago. Now only the whimpers of crying children
echoed.

"What of the captives?" Flint asked.

"One of the survivors said he saw them run away
with the fleeing war party. Feather Dancer was with
them."

Flint shoved aside another curtain of moss . . .
and saw her.

Sora sat on the ground, leaning against a fallen log. She wore a red war shirt that was much too big for her, and had a belt pouch snugged around her waist. Her black hair clung wetly to her shoulders.

"Sora?" he cried.

She looked up with tear-filled eyes, and her mouth opened as though with words too terrible to speak.

Flint ran to her and gathered her in his arms. "It's all right," he said. "I'm here."

Strongheart knelt at her side, and seemed to be examining her for injuries.

Sora wept, "*I did it, Flint. I—I remembered when I was . . . running. . . . I saw it. I killed my sister. We were arguing. She shouted at me that I'd killed her father, and she hated me. I hit her with my oar!*"

A sad expression came over Strongheart's face. He nodded, let out a breath, and walked away to gaze at the hideous orange halo that swelled over Eagle Flute Village.

Flint could not imagine what he must be feeling. His face showed no anger or hatred. He was watching the flames of his world fade as a man would helplessly watch a loved one die, wrenched with the knowledge that he could do nothing to stop it.

"Flint?" Sora's head trembled.

He brushed wet hair away from her beautiful face. "What is it, Sora?"

"The five days . . ."

"What about them?"

Tears ran down her cheeks.

She choked out, "I—I may have killed White Fawn. I keep seeing images. . . ."

The confession made him smile. He crushed her hard against his chest and started to rock her in trembling arms. "I know you killed her, Sora. I know. I know."

36

At dawn, Strongheart sat on a massive old oak stump, his elbows braced on his knees, looking out at the remains of Eagle Flute Village. The pale blue light outlined arrow-riddled bodies and strewn belongings. Many of his friends, cousins, aunts lay among the dead. Sparks continued to rise from the smoke-blackened chaos and blink out in the misty rain that had been falling all night.

He whispered, "I hear you."

Ghosts roamed the village. He could feel them. Every time another smoking lodge collapsed, he heard soft, pitiful voices, as if the dead continued to live in a nightmare world where the attack still raged, where the fire still roared, and they were running, running, never to escape.

He almost didn't hear the soft steps that came up the wet trail behind him.

Strongheart turned slightly to look at Flint. The man had a dazed, frightened expression on his face.

Strongheart said, "You shouldn't have left her alone."

"I didn't have any choice. She ordered me to find you." His gaze scanned the burned village. "Why did you return? This is dangerous. We must go. Now."

"Yes," he said with a tired nod, but didn't rise.

Wind whispered among the trees, whirling the smoke high into the cloudy sky. Loon villages a full day's walk away would be looking up at it. They'd probably already dispatched warriors to find out what had happened here.

Flint said, "I just . . . I can't quite believe my clan would do something like this."

Strongheart hesitated a moment, then rose to his feet. A sprinkle of raindrops glistened on the hood and shoulders of his cape. "It's not your fault. You could not stop what you did not know about."

Flint hung his head and shook it. "No, but I should have known. Water Hickory Clan has always considered itself better, wiser, than the other clans. I fear that that arrogance is about to prove fatal. In the near future, many more of my relatives are going to die."

"Perhaps Matron Wink can negotiate a truce with the Loon People. If she surrendered the disputed gathering grounds it might be a good first step—"

"Her actions would cause civil war among the

Black Falcon clans. After everything Water Hickory Clan has gone through in the past moon, everyone they've lost"—his gaze clung to the dead Black Falcon warriors who lay in the village plaza—"they would see it as the supreme betrayal. Wink is going to need all of the help she can get."

"Do you wish to go help her?" Strongheart asked in a curious voice. Flint had sounded like he longed to go to her. "Or finish Healing the woman you love? If it's the latter, we must find a safe place to work."

Strongheart had spent most of the night rocking Sora in his arms, feeling her body shudder with tears that seemed to have no end. In the darkest moments, she'd looked up at him with a yearning that tore his souls.

"You love her, don't you?" Flint demanded to know.

Strongheart noted Flint's blazing eyes and the way he'd clenched his fists at his sides, then he met that hot glare and softly said, "She needs you right now. Not me. And you need her."

Flint's words were tight with jealousy. "Yes, she does need me. I'm glad you realize it. You have to find out what's causing her illness. That's all. Do you know?"

Strongheart tilted his head. "I think a ghost person is sending evil dreams that drive away her reflection-soul. That's what the Midnight Fox is."

"Who is the ghost person?"

"Probably her sister. I suspect that after she was murdered, she did not go to the Land of the Dead."

"She remained on earth to take revenge?"

"Most likely." Again, he asked, "Will you stay and help me Heal her?"

Flint straightened. He hesitated for several instants before he said, "I left her once before. I won't do it again. Not until I know . . . for certain . . ."

"Finish that sentence."

Flint swallowed convulsively. "For many winters, I believed she could be Healed. I tried so hard, you cannot imagine. Then I was certain she couldn't be Healed. I came to the conclusion that the kindest thing I could do for her was to end her struggle. I owed it to her. And to our people. But . . ."

"You couldn't do it?"

"No." Flint turned and walked up the trail into the trees.

Strongheart had to hurry to catch up. He gave Flint a speculative glance. "That's why you left?"

Flint stopped and glared at the water that ran down the trail. Ash and bits of charcoal darkened the trickle, swirling to create oddly beautiful patterns. "I'm a coward, Priest. It's a hard thing for a man to admit, especially to himself."

Strongheart searched his tormented face. "I think it may be harder for a man to forgive himself."

"What do you mean?"

"You blame yourself for White Fawn's death, don't you? And Skinner's death?"

Flint stood rigid for several long moments, as though his world were crumbling beneath his feet, and he didn't know what to do to save himself.

Strongheart waited for an answer, but when it never came, he said, "Why weren't you there in the forest watching the night Skinner died?"

"You wouldn't understand. You don't know her well enough. If she had seen me—"

"At this moment, I'm more concerned with knowing you. Where were you?"

Flint's legs started shaking. He braced a hand against a palm trunk. Birds flitted among the fronds. Their sweet songs filled the morning. "Stop trying to Heal me, Priest. I'll do that myself. In time."

Flint strode away. Raindrops falling through the branches spun a glittering veil across the path ahead of him.

FROM EVERY PART OF THE BLACK FALCON WORLD, people had flocked in to attend the council meeting. Feather Dancer guessed the crowd at around five thousand strong. He stood before the four elders in the broad plaza of Blackbird Town, but his eyes sought out the positions of the guards, perched in the tallest trees, standing on the mound tops, covering every possible entry to the town. Matron Wink had posted Rockfish's three hundred warriors—all dressed in pale yellow war shirts—in a tight ring around the plaza to keep the crowd back. Presumably, they could not be bribed by clan members who had grudges against certain council members.

Though the Water Hickory war party that had attacked Eagle Flute Village was being kept under guard outside of town, the captives had been allowed in to testify before the elders—which they had done for most of the night, and all morning today.

To his right, Pipit sat in the front row, biting her lip. All the way back, she'd kept asking people if they'd seen her parents. Once, she'd even run off into the trees after a shadow, and Feather Dancer had been forced to leave the captives alone to go find her. When all of this was over, he planned to ask Priest Teal if he would Heal the girl.

"Were there any survivors?" Matron Wink asked.

"I did not see any survivors, Matron," Feather Dancer answered, and took a deep breath to fortify himself. The huge crowd had begun to push at the circle of warriors guarding the plaza. "We escaped just a few moments before the attack came. But the Water Hickory warriors boasted all the way home that they'd left no one alive."

"Of course they did," Matron Black Birch said, and her white head wobbled. "That's just pride. There are always survivors."

"Yes," Matron Wink agreed. "And by now, they've run to the nearest Loon village and poured out the entire story."

"With embellishments," Black Birch added.

Matron Sea Grass, who sat on a mat a few paces away with her hands bound, chuckled. Her old face resembled a shriveled winter-killed carcass. Rumor had it that Matron Wink had sent a war party to catch Sea Grass on the trail to Oak Leaf Village and to drag her back, bound and gagged, into Matron Wood Fern's bedchamber to verify her death.

No one knew who'd killed Matron Wood Fern. Her body had been discovered three days ago by slaves who'd gone in at dawn to ask what she wanted for breakfast.

But her murder had roused the nation.

Matron Wink looked up from where she'd been talking with Matron Black Birch. "Feather Dancer, is it your opinion that the war party had orders to wipe out the entire village?"

"Yes, Matron."

Black Birch turned a sharp old eye on Sea Grass, and said, "Did they have orders to completely destroy Eagle Flute Village?"

Sea Grass chuckled again, as though the fact that her life hung in the balance was a trivial concern. "They had orders to kill every man, woman, and child. They were filthy Loon People! We wanted them all dead!"

As Sea Grass's voice rose to a shout, several members of her clan, who stood just beyond the ring of guards, shouted, *"Filthy Loon People!"* and *"We want them all dead!"*

Matron Wink gestured to the guards, and they used their war clubs to shove the agitators back, but cries of outrage went up from those who sympathized.

Wink glanced at Feather Dancer, and he tilted his head uncertainly. If the crowd decided to break through the guards, they would. Three hundred warriors with clubs would be overrun in a matter of moments. She seemed to be aware of how volatile the situation was.

Matron Wink glared at Sea Grass. "It is our understanding that the Water Hickory council elected you as the new clan matron. Is that correct?"

"You know it is," Sea Grass said. "That makes it difficult for you, doesn't it? If you kill me, like you did Wood Fern"—a roar of surprise and rage swept the crowd—"you will doom our nation to civil war. Is that what you want?"

Matron Black Birch leaned forward and half shouted, "You old hag! This is what you and your clan have brought us to! We ought to slit your throat and throw your body to the alligators!"

"Wait," Matron Wink said. "If we are ready to cast our voices, let us do it clearly and for all to hear."

"I'm ready," Black Birch said, and gave Sea Grass the evil eye.

"As am I," Wigeon murmured.

Long Fin wet his lips and nodded. "I am also ready."

Wink got to her feet and held her hands up to the crowd, calling, "Silence! If you wish to hear the council's decision, listen!"

The angry roar that had been building quickly dwindled to a low hostile hum. Every eye in the crowd fastened on the Council of Elders.

Matron Wink called, "We will now vote on whether or not to cast Water Hickory Clan out of the Black Falcon Nation."

The crowd went utterly silent.

Wink said, "Matron Black Birch, do you vote to make them Outcast?"

Black Birch squared her bony old shoulders and called, "Yes, they committed treason and deserve the consequences!"

Cheers, as well as bellows of disagreement rose.

Wink gestured to Matron Wigeon, and her old eyes went huge. "Matron Wigeon, how does Bald Cypress Clan vote?"

"Bald Cypress Clan votes no. I have many relatives among the Water Hickory Clan. I will not doom them for the mistakes made by their leadership. I—"

"You senile old woman!" Sea Grass shouted. "We made no mistakes. We defended our gathering grounds from enemy thieves. We had to do it alone because the rest of you are cowards! You should be thanking us, not—"

Gasps and cheers eddied through the crowd, drowning out the rest of what Sea Grass wished to say.

"Quiet!" Matron Wink ordered in a voice that commanded obedience. "We have already voted that going against the council constituted treason. That is not at issue. We are voting on whether or not to allow Water Hickory Clan to remain as part of the Black Falcon Nation."

Long Fin seemed to be holding his breath in preparation for casting his voice.

Matron Wink turned to him and said, "Chief Long Fin, do you vote to Outcast, or not?"

Long Fin looked at his mother for several moments before he quietly said, "No. I vote with Ma-

tron Wigeon. I do not believe that Water Hickory
Clan as a whole would have approved of the attack if
they'd been given a chance to vote on the matter."

Matron Wink turned away from the council and
looked out at the crowd. It must have been like looking into the eyes of a lethal snake, because the crowd
went utterly silent, as though paralyzed and waiting
helplessly for the deadly strike to come.

Black Birch hissed, "Wink, if you let them stay
there will be no reason for clans to remain loyal!
Treason *must* be punished."

Wood Fern paid with her life.

Wink bowed her head and very softly responded,
"I know, but I cannot force myself to thrust this nation into civil war."

Sea Grass cackled like an ancient witch as Matron
Wink walked out of the circle of elders to face the
crowd and in a loud clear voice called, "The Shadow
Rock Clan votes no!"

Shouts and cheers rose like thunder, and people
began Dancing and throwing things into the air. Others ran to carry the news to those in back who hadn't
heard, and more cheers and shouts went up. It was
like a deafening wave rolling out into the forest in all
directions.

Sea Grass struggled to her feet and held her bound
hands out to her guards, ordering, "Cut me loose,
you fools. I am clan matron of the Water Hickory
Clan!"

The guards looked at Wink, who nodded, and they
sliced through the ropes that bound Sea Grass's wrists.

The old woman gave Wink a triumphant glare and walked across the plaza into a waiting throng of cheering people.

As the council rose and began talking among themselves, Feather Dancer said, "Matron? A word with you?"

Wink nodded and followed him a short distance away where they could speak privately. "What is it, Feather Dancer?"

"It gives me no pleasure to do it, but I feel it's my duty," he said through a long exhalation, "to tell you what happened in Eagle Flute Village just before the attack."

"Before the attack? What are you talking about?"

As he told her about the conversation he'd overheard between Strongheart and Flint, about the murders and Chieftess Sora's role, her mouth tightened, then trembled.

Finally, she said, "Was Sora killed in the attack? Do you know?"

"No, I don't. I know you told me to make certain the chieftess was safe, but I had to make a choice, Matron. I could have abandoned the captives and gone searching for Chieftess Sora in the middle of the battle, or done my best to get the captives out alive."

"You made the right choice," she said with forlorn resignation as she gazed out at the forest trail that led eastward toward the Loon Nation. "I'm sure if she's alive, she will come home."

SORA LEANED AGAINST THE TRUNK OF A HACK-berry tree and gazed out over the small cypress pond. As evening veiled the woods, sparkflies climbed into the branches like the last blinking remnants of a great forest fire. She watched them and listened to the frogs that serenaded the night.

They'd camped a day's walk east of Oak Leaf Village, far enough away from the main trails that no one would accidentally stumble upon them.

"Are you all right?" Strongheart's voice surprised her.

Over her shoulder, she said, "You should be a warrior instead of a priest. You have the skills for it. I didn't hear you approach."

"I think you were occupied with other thoughts."

His sandals shished in the tall grass as he followed

the trail to reach her. He didn't look at her; instead, he followed her gaze to the ducks that silently paddled across the pond in the distance. Silver rings bobbed out behind them.

The sharp green scent of the pond intensified as darkness fell.

Softly, he said, "I asked if you were all right."

Sora took a deep breath, and as she let it out, answered, "I feel broken."

He turned to look at her. A strange emptiness had grown in his eyes, as though the events of the past quarter-moon had hollowed him out like a rotted log. "You will feel that way for a time, until we've found all the pieces."

"Pieces? What pieces?"

"The pieces of your shattered reflection-soul. We've just begun, Sora. For a time, you'll feel like you're looking at yourself in a broken slate mirror."

"Do you truly believe the image will ever be whole again?"

"As we find more and more of the pieces, the picture will begin to coalesce. I think, someday, you will be whole."

For a time the reflected light of the pond shimmered in the cypress branches, silver and beautiful but for the few cloud shadows that passed over.

For days she'd been seeing faces frozen at the last moment of life—faces she had not seen in many winters. Faces, she knew now, that she had hoped never to see again.

I killed them. I loved them, and I killed them.

Tears constricted her throat.

"What is it?" he asked. "Do you need me?"

She squeezed her eyes closed. She did not want to tell him how very much she needed him, that he was the only thing that stood between her and a glittering blue torrent that spoke with the voices of knives.

She said, "Will you stay with me? Help me to find the pieces?"

He had lost so much in recent days, he must long to run for the safety of the nearest Loon village where he had relatives. What would she do if he left her now?

"Sora, please look at me."

She turned.

"I'll stay," he said softly, "but I want you to know that I'm afraid."

"Of me?" Her voice shook. "I don't blame you, I—"

"No, Sora. I'm not afraid of you. I've never feared you."

Their gazes held, and he looked at her with more tenderness than she had ever seen in a man's eyes.

He lifted a hand to comfortingly brush the hair away from her face. "The time is coming, very soon, when the Midnight Fox will seek me out. I pray that my heart is not too small to understand what he tells me."

Historical Afterword

Sigmund Freud was not the first person to discover that dreams can give us clues about illness. Many North American tribes, particularly Iroquoian and Algonquian peoples, believed that dreams were the language of the soul, and that the unfulfilled desires of the soul, as represented in dreams, could cause illness, or even death. To make certain this didn't happen, the entire community worked together to fulfill the dreams of sick people.

The *andacwander*, as those of you who read *It Sleeps in Me* know, is real.

The only detailed description of this healing ritual comes from Father Gabriel Sagard, who lived among the Huron tribe from 1623 to 1624. He was part of an apostolic ministry to the Huron and was very dedicated to the task of converting them to Christianity. In the process, he recorded his observations, his trials and tribulations, his successes and failures, and published them in 1632. His book, *Le grand voyage du pays des Hurons*, was so popular that it had to be reprinted, which it was in 1636. However, it came out under the new title of *Histoire du Canada*, and contained several elaborations on the original work.

Certainly one of the most spectacular sections of *Le grand voyage* is Chapter X, where he recounts witnessing several sexual healing rituals, particularly the *andacwander*.

Because he was not a member of the community, Sagard was forbidden to participate, or even look upon the ritual, but fortunately for us, he watched it through a chink in the walls of a longhouse.

It is especially interesting to me that Sagard only mentions dances "ordered on behalf of a sick woman." Did he simply never see the *andacwander* performed for a sick man, or were sexual healing rituals largely women's rituals? Jesuit references suggest that men were also cured in this manner (Thwaites 1896–1901, 17: 179), so it's possible that Sagard only watched ceremonies for women, which is interesting in and of itself.

In any case, the Huron worked very hard to heal the sick members of their community. Even when it went against their most basic social beliefs of propriety, they tried, by acting out the sick person's dreams, to fulfill the desires of her soul. Sagard wrote, ". . . for they prefer to suffer and be in want of anything rather than to fail a sick person at need" (Wrong, p. 118).

During the *andacwander*, the unmarried people in the village assembled in the sick person's house and had sexual intercourse while the patient watched and two shamans shook tortoiseshell rattles and sang. Sometimes, the sick person requested one of the young people to have sex with her. Based upon dreams, other types of requests were also made. Sagard describes one instance in which a sick woman asked one of the young men to urinate in her mouth. He wrote: ". . . a feature I cannot excuse nor pass over silently—one of those young men was required to make water in her mouth, and she had to swallow it, which she did with great courage, hoping to be cured by it; for she herself wished it all to be done in that manner, in order to carry out without any omission a dream she had had" (Wrong, p. 118).

The more scholarly-minded among you will be asking, "Why is a Huron ritual being used to describe a prehistoric Mississippian mound-builder culture in Florida?"

First, linguistically, Huron is closely related to Cherokee, and based upon a comparison of grave goods, chambered burial pits, earth-covered ceremonial structures, and the striking similarity of gorget styles, I think a strong argument can be made for a persistent social tradition from the Mississippian cultural patterns represented in the Pisgah phase in the Appalachian summit region to the Qualla phase of the Cherokee. Historic Cherokee Middle Towns are located within the Pisgah archaeological sphere and, as Dickens notes (1976, p. 213), there are many "carry-over traits" between the cultures.

Secondly, at the point of historic contact with European cultures, the *andacwander*, or modified versions of it, had spread from Iroquoian to Algonquian tribes (Hickerson, 1960), indicating the remarkable power the ritual possessed. I don't think it's unreasonable to assume that the origins of this particular soul-curing ritual extend into prehistoric times.

Lastly, I know of no other fictional attempt to see this sacred ritual through the eyes of the people who practiced it, and I think it's important to make that attempt.

The *andacwander*, after all, was a supreme act of generosity.

Selected Bibliography

Davis, Dave D. *Perspectives on Gulf Coast Prehistory.* Gainesville: University Press of Florida/Florida State Museum, 1984.

Dickens, Roy S., Jr. *Cherokee Prehistory: The Pisgah Phase in the Appalachian Summit Region.* Knoxville: University of Tennessee Press, 1981.

Gilliland, Marion Spjut. *The Material Culture of Key Marco, Florida.* Port Salerno: Florida Classics Library, 1989.

Hickerson, Harold. "The Feast of the Dead Among the Seventeenth-Century Algonkians of the Upper Great Lakes." *American Anthropologist* 62:81–107.

Hudson, Charles. *The Southeastern Indians.* Knoxville: University of Tennessee Press, 1989.

Kilpatrick, Jack Frederick, and Anna Gritts Kilpatrick. *Notebook of a Cherokee Shaman.* Smithsonian Contributions to Anthropology, Vol. 2, Number 6. Washington, DC: Smithsonian Institution Press, 1970.

———. *Walk in Your Soul: Love Incantations of the Oklahoma Cherokees.* Dallas: Southern Methodist University, 1965.

———. *Run Toward the Nightland: Magic of the Oklahoma Cherokees.* Dallas: Southern Methodist University, 1967.

Lewis, Barry, and Charles Stout, eds. *Mississippian Towns and Sacred Space: Searching for an Architec-*

tural Grammar. Tuscaloosa: University of Alabama Press, 1998.

McEwan, Bonnie G. *Indians of the Greater Southeast: Historical Archaeology and Ethnohistory.* Gainesville: University Press of Florida, 2000.

Milanich, Jerald T. *Archaeology of Precolumbian Florida.* Gainesville: University Press of Florida, 1994.

———. *McKeithen Weeden Island: The Culture of Northern Florida, A.D. 200–900.* New York: Academic Press, 1984.

———. *The Timucua.* Oxford: Blackwell Publishers, 1996.

———. *Florida Indians and the Invasion from Europe.* Gainesville: University Press of Florida, 1995.

Milanich, Jerald T., and Charles Hudson. *Hernando de Soto and the Indians of Florida.* Gainesville: University Press of Florida, 1993.

Neitzel, Jill E. *Great Towns and Regional Polities in the Prehistoric American Southwest and Southeast.* Albuquerque: University of New Mexico Press, 1999.

Purdy, Barbara A. *The Art and Archaeology of Florida's Wetlands.* Boca Raton: CRC Press, 1991.

Sears, William H. *Fort Center: An Archaeological Site in the Lake Okeechobee Basin.* Gainesville: University of Florida Press, 1994.

Swanton, John R. *The Indians of the Southeastern United States.* Washington, DC: Smithsonian Institution Press, 1987.

Thwaites, Reuben G. *The Jesuit Relations and Allied*

Documents, Vol. 17. Cleveland: The Burrows Brothers Co., 1896.

Trigger, Bruce G. *The Children of Aataentsic: A History of the Huron People to 1660.* Montrèal: McGill-Queen's University Press, 1987.

Walthall, John A. *Prehistoric Indians of the Southeast: Archaeology of Alabama and the Middle South.* Tuscaloosa: University of Alabama Press, 1990.

Willey, Gordon R. *Archaeology of the Florida Gulf Coast.* Gainesville: University of Florida Press, 1949.

Wrong, George M. *Sagard's Long Journey to the Huron Country.* Toronto: The Champlain Society, 1939.